Seconds From Impact

CHRISTOPHER J WILLIAMS

Cover image and design by Abir Hasan

See - https://www.fiverr.com/abirhasan911

"Battle is the most magnificent competition in which a human being can indulge. It brings out all that is best; it removes all that is base. All men are afraid in battle. The coward is the one who lets his fear overcome his sense of duty. Duty is the essence of manhood."

George S Patton

Prologue

Kunar Province, Eastern Afghanistan—March 2002

Thirty-six men sat against the webbing in the C130 Hercules as it went north along the border between Afghanistan and Pakistan. They came from the same unit, the 4th Special Forces Group, based in Fort Campbell, Kentucky. Sergeant First Class Jake Walker, call sign Luke, reclined back against the webbing on the port side of the aircraft, watching his friends and team mates. He breathed slowly, using his diaphragm to calm the nerves and anxiety that preceded battle. As he listened to the quiet conversation around the cabin, he could sense the tension and watched as some men drank water to ensure their bodies were properly hydrated. He looked at one of his friends, Andy "Spider" Francis, who was eating canned fruit from his field rations. Spider looked back and nodded. Each man had his own way to prepare and their adrenaline flowed, entering their bloodstreams as the adrenal gland did its job to prepare men for a hostile mission—to fight.

Luke closed his eyes and reflected on his first operation in Afghanistan in October 2001, some six months earlier. His unit had deployed as part of the US-led coalition to kill or capture Osama bin Laden, the head of the terrorist group al-Qaeda. Bin Laden had claimed responsibility for the destruction of the Twin Towers in New York and their combined intelligence suggested he'd fled to the high, mountainous region called Tora Bora in northern Afghanistan, supported and protected by the Taliban.

Luke recalled the failure of that mission and the reason: insufficient coalition forces on the ground. Believing the US public was unprepared at the time for high numbers of American casualties, US officials paid the Taliban and several Afghani warlords a lot of money to assist in bin Laden's capture, only to find out later that they'd aided in his escape.

The CIA knew Tora Bora well because they'd helped the mujahideen construct the elaborate system of caves deep into the mountain system in the 1980s. Twenty years on and this intelligence helped the US to direct wave after wave of B52s and drop tons of high explosive on the cave system where coalition intelligence suggested bin Laden was hiding. In December '01, after weeks of intense bombing, the weather cleared and coalition forces, including elements of the 4th Special Forces Group, flew to the top of the mountain range. By the time they arrived, however, bin Laden and his supporters, some of them sponsored by the USA, had slipped away, and the terrorist leader managed to reach the relative safety of Pakistan.

Rumor had been strong that the British Special Air Service Regiment, the SAS, had tracked bin Laden and his party that day, reporting to their commanders that he was in their sights. Those in charge told the SAS to wait while US forces came up to lead his capture. It was this delay that afforded bin Laden the time to sneak through the cordon.

Their current mission briefing had taken place yesterday evening, some eight hours ago, in their makeshift headquarters at Bagram Airbase, north of Kabul. The officer in charge of Luke's team, Captain William "Cap" Butler, gathered the team together to ensure that everyone knew what they needed to know about the mission and to go over their small role in the operation. The team consisted of Warrant Officer Ken "Buster" Durant, an eighteen year veteran and second in charge, and Master Sergeant Hal "Woody" Corder, another veteran whose service went back to the first Gulf War in the early 90s. The other team members were all sergeants, and Luke had the role of assistant operations, given his seniority and experience.

The team also included Barry "Lewis" Halliday and Spider, both engineers and demolitions specialists; Ray "Caine" Corburn and Mike "Hawkeye" Townsend, qualified medics; Andy "Panda" Griffiths and Chris "Sky" Lawson, communications; and, finally, Tony "Sensei" Evans and Vince "Shocky" Rain, the team's weapons experts, or "weps."

The twelve men comprised the Special Forces' fighting unit called an Operational Detachment Alpha (ODA) or for those in Hollywood, the A-Team. The Special Forces were also known to outsiders as the Green Berets for the distinctive forest green headdress they were awarded upon passing selection. The composition of the ODA provided for multiple redundancies, in that there were three men who could take over Cap's job as team leader and every man was trained in several disciplines: all medic trained, all competent with small arms and explosives, all capable of staying out in the field, on the ground, for weeks if necessary.

Cap had stood with his back to a map on a white board and pointed at some features of the Shahi-Kot Valley which cut between several mountain peaks in the Kunar province, about a hundred miles east of Kabul. "We will be supporting Operation Anaconda," he said, looking at each man in turn. "We have strong intelligence that al-Qaeda and Taliban forces have gathered in the Shahi-Kot Valley, here, and in the upper valley, here. This region is an old hunting ground of the Taliban, and their predecessors, the mujahideen, gave the Russians a bloody nose several times in the region during their occupation in the 80s. So remember, it is their ground. Our enemy knows it well and likes it because it has close proximity to Pakistan. The overall mission objective is to kill or capture the enemy in and around this area here, which is labeled Objective Area Remington." He pointed to an area drawn around a lower valley to the west of the high peaks.

"Tomorrow, a coalition of ground forces including troops from Afghanistan, Canada, Denmark, Germany, France, Australia, and

Norway will deploy by rotary wing aircraft and move up through the valley to kill and flush out the enemy. We expect the enemy will fight hard, but ultimately, we believe that many will choose to retreat and head across the border into Pakistan. The most likely routes are here and here, where there will be blocking forces." He pointed to several valleys leading from the mountain ranges to the east.

"Our mission is to establish a number of OPs[1] along the peaks here and here from where we can direct air support where it is needed. We'll be using conventional comms, as well as lasers to mark targets. The 4th is deploying three ODAs and we will drop into the Chumara Valley here at about 0230 hours tomorrow. As you can see, this valley is to the east of Objective Remington, and we will be climbing about 2500 feet from our drop point, aiming to get to the top of this ridge line to the north and east of this mountain called Takur Ghar. Once our OPs are established, elements of the 10th Mountain and 101st Airborne Divisions will deploy to provide a blocking force in the event the enemy comes down through the Chumara Valley on their way to Pakistan."

Luke's thoughts were interrupted as he sensed the time was near. He looked to the rear of the cabin and saw Sullivan, a huge black flight sergeant with a Bronx accent and the C130's loadmaster, rise from his seat and call out, "Ten minutes to first drop. The cabin will depressurize in five minutes." He held up his right hand, spreading his fingers, and watched the men until he was sure that all were clear of the timeframe.

The men hooked their breathing apparatus to sockets behind their seats and pulled face masks on, enabling them to breathe oxygen from the aircraft. At thirty thousand feet, they would need oxygen once the plane depressurized and during their High Altitude Low Opening (HALO)[2] descent into the valley, a low altitude opening technique used to minimize the risk of detection by the enemy. The first "stick" comprised Luke's ODA.

1   Observation Points

2   High Altitude Low Opening

Up front in the pilot's seat, Air Force Flight Lieutenant Mick Rogers checked their coordinates from the satellite navigation systems for the third time and began a slow descent to bring the plane down to the drop altitude of twenty-five thousand feet. At the same time, he throttled back the engines to achieve a cruising speed of 250 knots when the men went out the back. He spoke into his headset. "Depressurizing in thirty seconds. Five minutes to drop one. Over."

Sullivan listened to the pilot through his headset and responded, "Roger, first stick is ready to go." He signaled with his hands for Luke's ODA to move forward and then walked to the rear of the cabin, from where he operated the ramp and supervised the drops, hooking his safety gear to an anchor point on the fuselage.

Buster stood up and plugged his breathing mask into the small cylinder of oxygen attached to his webbing. The members of his team were all equipped with short range communications and he spoke into the microphone: "Gentlemen, it's time. Check each other's kit thoroughly. This is the real thing. Let's all get down there in one piece."

Luke stood up and followed Buster. His teammates also grouped together and the twelve men shuffled over to the rear of the cabin, clutching their packs to their chests to await the drop. Their battle gear included Kevlar vests, 5.56 mm M4 carbines, with some of the M4s equipped with M320 grenade launchers, and most of the team were also carrying fragmentation and smoke grenades. Sensei carried the team's 7.62 mm M60 light machine gun (usually referred to as the 60) a fearsome weapon that they would need if they contacted the enemy. Each carried a pack, perhaps fifty pounds per man, which they attached via a strap to their webbing. This arrangement enabled the pack to hit the ground first, which then eased the weight on their parachutes and the speed at which they hit the ground.

Everyone carried belt ammunition for the 60, as well as ammunition for their own M4 rifles. The exceptions to this were the communication specialists Sky and Panda, who carried the team's tactical radios. Each man also carried field rations and water, but the bulk of what they carried was to get them out of a fire fight, a situation they hoped to avoid as their mission was to use stealth and conceal themselves in vantage points where they could direct air support for the ground troops. Each man checked the man next to him, ensuring that equipment was secure and chutes were correctly positioned. The air pressure changed slowly, and once it had equalized to the outside, Sullivan pressed a switch and the rear ramp lowered down, revealing the blackness outside. Immediately, the air temperature dropped as the air within the cabin mixed with air at negative twenty degrees centigrade outside.

Luke felt his gut tensing up as the seconds ticked away and the reality of a drop into enemy-occupied territory sank in. There was always risk in any jump, particularly when in full battle order, but the imminence of battle and a potentially hot landing zone gave everyone an instant jolt of reality.

Sullivan listened to the pilot over his headset and shouted, "Thirty seconds!" Above his head, three red lights blinked. *Wait.*

Each man checked his equipment loads again. Cap, as usual, stood at the front, Buster second, Luke was third...

Sullivan held up his hand, ticked off the final five seconds and then pressed a switch. The three red lights turned to green. *Go.*

Without hesitation, the team moved forward as one, their packs and weapons held to their chests and jumped off the rear of the ramp into the blackness outside. Once out and clear, Luke dropped his pack and controlled his descent using his arms and legs. The lights in the aircraft had been dimmed, so they had some night vision and a waning moon, about forty-five degrees high, which enabled him to see his teammates as they hurtled toward the earth below. Each man's parachute included a pressure sensor to self-deploy at ten-thousand feet. The valley below was around 8,500 feet, and Luke hoped the map builders had got their contours right.

Luke saw one chute deploy, probably Buster's, and then he felt the snap as his own chute deployed. He felt the strain on his arms and shoulders and he looked upward to check that the ram, sports-type chute was full. The full canopy above was a welcome site and he reflected on how he had never had to use his reserve. He grabbed the steering toggles and watched carefully as the ground came closer.

Five minutes later, they'd gathered up their chutes and were preparing their gear for the ascent. After the chutes, including the reserve chutes, had been roughly hidden in a depression and covered by rocks, Cap gathered the team around him and thumbed on his communications mike so that he wouldn't have to shout. Following the team's SOPs[3], Panda, Sensei, and Hawkeye deployed fifty yards from the team to form a rough defensive perimeter, watching in case their insertion had been detected. Cap pointed upward and along the valley where they could clearly see the summit of Takur Ghar to the left and a long ridgeline lower and to the right. "Our destination is the ridgeline to the right of the peak." He checked their position on the GPS device in his hands before putting it into a pocket against his right thigh. "The horizontal distance to top of the valley is two miles, but the ascent is 1500 feet. The final climb will be the toughest part, from the saddle to the ridgeline. We need to get two OPs established before daylight, which gives us two hours to reach the top. Stay alert. Remember our job is to avoid the enemy, not engage him. If you spot anything, call it in.

"Buster and Spider, you two will lead. I want two staggered lines, about thirty yards apart, about ten between each man. Caine and Lewis will be second, then me and Luke. Sensei and Shocky will be next, Sky and Hawkeye and, at the rear, Woody and Panda. No chatter unless it's operational. Sky?"

"Sir."

3   Standard Operating Procedures

"Call in and give a sitrep⁴."

"Will do."

"Okay, let's move."

Slowly the two lines formed and headed up toward the saddle. Approximately three miles above them, a radio operator in the forward air control C130 took Sky's radio call and noted their position on his computer.

The route through the valley to the saddle was steep, and they concentrated on putting one foot in front of the other. Like much of Afghanistan at this altitude, vegetation could not survive and most of the landscape consisted of rocks, pebbles, shale, and a scattering of large to very large boulders.

Luke focused on his breathing. The team was fit and had been together for about eight months. Most had seen action in Somalia, Iraq, and Kosovo. Only Hawkeye and Shocky were new to battle, barely weeks from selection. With large equipment loads, the group struggled to keep a good pace up and down the inclines, and the rocky conditions and darkness slowed them to some degree. Each man's weapon incorporated a night vision scope, but the two men up front, Buster and Spider, also carried NVGs⁵ so they could better navigate the terrain. It was unusual for an ODA's warrant officer and second in charge to lead, but it was Buster's style to lead from the front, and Cap knew he was not in a position to argue with him.

After an hour, they'd progressed about one mile and the gradient became steeper. Buster called a halt while he assessed the route in front of them. The men crouched and took the opportunity to drink some water and rehydrate. After about a minute, Buster called the all clear and they continued up the incline, maintaining formation, with Luke

4   Situation Report

5   Night Vision Goggles

positioned in the line on the right side of the team.

As they crested the rise, the gradient got easier and they maintained a faster pace for a further thirty minutes. At this point, they found themselves traversing a ridge feature, which cut across and into the valley. The moonlight illuminated the saddle feature, their destination, no more than four hundred yards away. The team traveled fifty paces beyond the ridge feature, and Luke noticed a flash of light up and to their left. Each man registered the same thing as an RPG[6] screamed down toward them from a position about 150 yards away.

Before anyone could react, the RPG impacted the ground about ten yards from their left flank and there was a terrific explosion. As the men were blown off their feet by the blast and they hit the ground, small arms fire started up from positions to their front and a light machine gun marched a lethal stream of tracer-led rounds towards their position. Cap's calm voice came over the net. "Stay low and hold your fire. Any injuries?"

As the incoming fire intensified and peppered the ground around them, Luke felt a familiar calmness. They'd been contacted by the enemy and their mission would be compromised if they couldn't disengage quickly. The enemy's shooting was missing its mark, but they were very exposed and couldn't remain out in the open. He thought back along their route, stood up and ran over to Cap. As he reached him, the ground around them was peppered by small arms fire and his boss cried out. Luke lay beside him and assessed the situation. "Where you hit?"

"My left leg."

Luke clicked his throat mike. "This is Luke. There is cover behind the ridge feature fifty yards to our right and rear. Time to move, everybody."

Each man rose and ran back to the cover provided by the ridge, which featured a natural depression and a steep gradient to their front

6   Rocket Propelled Grenade

rising to a rocky ridge at the top. As Luke had correctly surmised, this provided good, solid cover from the light machine gun fire.

As the team took stock, Luke helped Cap onto his good leg and lifted him up and onto his shoulders. The combined weight of the man and his equipment was around 240 pounds, but carrying a man was a regular part of their physical training and Luke was full of adrenalin. The air hummed with small arms fire, but he walked purposefully down and over the ridge and set his boss on the ground. He looked around, counting ten, including himself. *Two down.* "Who's missing?" he asked.

Woody came up next to him and they crawled to the top of the ridge. Woody pointed to two prone figures sixty yards up the valley. "Buster's down and Shocky. It looks like they got hit when the RPG came in."

Luke could count at least ten or more small arms against them. "Mission's fucked," he said.

"Yep."

As they descended back down the slope, Hawkeye had already unstrapped his pack and examined Cap's leg wound. The others gathered around Luke and Woody.

"Panda, get onto the boys above, report the contact and see if you can get some air support," began Woody.

"Roger that."

Luke looked at Woody and continued, "Buster and Shocky are both down and Shocky has the 60. I suggest we get Sensei and Spider up there." Luke pointed to the ridge line above them. "The mission is compromised and we need to put down some suppressing fire while the others are retrieved."

Woody looked at Sensei and Spider and nodded. "Let's move."

Luke shrugged off his pack and put his M4 on the ground while Sensei and Spider moved up to the top of the ridge above them and started to take aimed shots toward the machine gun. Luke scaled the slope again, and as the fire was redirected toward his teammates, he breathed deeply and sprinted over to Buster, who was prone on the ground and about sixty yards or so from where the team had taken cover. When he got there, he quickly saw that the man was deceased as half the left side of his face was missing.

He crawled back to Shocky who moaned when he reached him. Luke found a weak pulse in his neck and saw blood coming from his shoulder and left arm. He winced as a few rounds came close and shards of rock were thrown into his face. The light machine gun was presently silent due in part to Sensei and Spider putting down effective fire. Shocky was barely conscious, a dead weight, and Luke knew he could not lift him, his pack, and the M60. He took off Shocky's pack, picked up the 60 and grabbed him by the webbing around his shoulders. As he pulled him surely and steadily back toward their cover, another RPG flew past him, well wide, impacting several hundred feet down the valley. As he crested the ridge, Sky and Hawkeye came forward and helped Luke over the last twenty yards.

Luke handed the 60 to Woody and offered his advice on who should take it. "Sensei?"

"Yes, I'll get it up to him."

"I'm sorry, but Buster's gone. The RPG got him bad, a head wound. We'll pick him up before we go."

Luke could see the pain in his friend's eyes and watched as he walked away to organize their defense. He called Lewis over. "Lewis, get as much of the belt 'munition for the 60 as you can and take it up to Sensei, okay? I want you to feed and spot for him."

"I'm on it."

Panda came over. "Luke, a bird is on its way to take us out. Air control said we are to hold our position in the interim."

Luke checked his watch: 04:30. Yet it seemed only minutes had passed since the initial contact. Behind him on the slopes above and to their left, small arms fire recommenced, and Luke figured they were up against a force of perhaps twenty on the lower slopes of the mountain. As he watched, the forward elements of the enemy came farther down the slope and shots started to impact around them now that they had a line of sight into their position of cover. He picked up his M4. It was the under-and-over version with an M320 grenade launcher. He had eight twenty-round magazines for the rifle and six high explosive (HE) projectiles for the grenade launcher, which were sitting in a purpose-built belt on his webbing. He also carried four conventional M67 fragmentation grenades in pouches.

He looked around, spotted Woody, who was now assisting Hawkeye to put a field dressing on Shocky's shoulder, and called out to him. "Woody?"

The man came over, keeping low as the shooting intensified. "Get some covering fire onto the hostiles on the slopes over there." Luke pointed behind him. "If we don't get those fuckers, we're not going to last to the extraction."

The team took what cover they could and Lewis, Panda, and Woody responded to the threat, firing single, aimed shots at the figures on the slopes above and to the left of the valley. The SOP when one was pinned down by enemy gun fire was to dig a shell scrape to try and get as much of his body covered as possible, but the strategy wouldn't work here, given the rocky nature of the landscape. Still, they all knew that being low minimized a man's profile and everyone hugged the ground as best they could.

Luke checked his M4, then turned and ran as fast as he could for the slope opposite, noting a high volume of fire being directed toward the enemy. He figured the shooters were about one hundred feet above and to his right. He commenced climbing the slope, slipping on the shale and rocks but managing to make progress.

Caine stood and called Woody over where he was tending to Cap, whose left leg was bound tightly. "'Bout all I can do. He's okay. Took a round in the calf, came out through his shin, which is a mess. He's had one syrette of morphine."

Woody crouched down and Cap managed a weak smile, even though the opiates coursed through his body. "How's it going?" he managed.

The small arms fire picked up and Woody winced as a couple of rounds came close enough to kiss him. "An extraction has been organized, boss. Things'll be okay. Just chill out while we get ready to move." He stood up and watched as Hawkeye took a round in the chest and doubled over. Woody moved quickly over to him. "You okay?"

Hawkeye sat down and saw that his body armor had saved him. "Yeah, I'll be fine."

Above them, a grenade exploded and Woody turned. He looked through his NVGs and saw Luke moving forward along the ridgeline firing aimed shots from his M4. A minute or so passed and the small arms fire ceased.

Caine came over. "Shocky's lost a lot of blood. A large piece of shrapnel has penetrated his vest, and he has a large gash in his right shoulder. He has also taken a round in his right arm. I've stabilized him and given him a shot of morphine, but he's lost a fair amount of blood and will die if we don't get him out."

"How soon?"

Caine shrugged. "Could be an hour, could be five, but he needs attention soon."

"Okay, keep an eye on him."

Luke had eliminated the immediate threat on the slopes that overlooked their position, but Woody knew they were still vulnerable as the high ground gave the enemy a huge advantage. Sky came over to him. "Woody, air control has patched me through to the French Air Force tasked to support us. I talked to one of the pilots and their jets are three minutes away."

Woody looked around. "Spider, come here, buddy. Thanks Sky. Get onto the pilots again and ask them to attack the ridge line and slopes to the west and above our green, okay?"

"Roger that," said Sky, and he retreated several yards to communicate with the pilots.

Spider came down from his position on the ridge above them. Woody checked his watch and clicked his throat mike. "Team, jets are only seconds away. Keep your heads down. Spider, tell me you have the green flares."

Spider dropped his pack and pulled out a smoke/flare canister. He put it into Woody's hand.

Sky's voice came over their earpieces, "Thirty seconds!"

Woody pulled the pin on the canister and threw it into the middle of the valley. It started spewing green smoke and had a visible green flame.

"The jets have a visual on green," said Sky.

Woody clicked his throat mike again. "Down, gentlemen."

At about a thousand yards between them and with an approach speed of over eight hundred miles an hour, three Mirage F1 jets screamed down toward the valley and everyone took to the ground. Luke was on the high side of the valley to the team's south. He saw the first jet arrive and noted its twin thirty-millimeter cannon blasting away. Two rockets detached from under its wings and shot out toward the ridge line and the side of the mountain above him. The roar of the Mirage's twin jet engines was simply deafening, and Luke felt the ground shake as it passed overhead.

Twenty seconds later and the second jet performed the same maneuver with a third following. As the jets departed upward using their afterburners, Woody's voice came into Luke's earpiece. "Luke, how you doing? Over."

Luke came into a crouch and looked at the scene above him. "I'm okay. There are still a number of hostiles above me, I think. The jets have made some impact but were not fully effective. Over."

"Roger that. We have an extraction coming in twenty. Can't do it here, though. We'll need to retreat about two fifty or so."

Luke looked up toward the saddle and saw several small fires burning—fuel, munitions, and people. He sighted along the night scope on his M4 and could see the detail of the light machine gun emplacement just below and to the right of the saddle feature, perhaps two hundred yards away. It was dug in well and he could just make out some of the enemy fighters as they peered over it. Some small arms fire peppered the area around him and he moved forward ten yards to gain some cover in a small depression. He looked over the top and saw about ten figures heading down from the upper slopes toward him. He realized they had totally underestimated the enemy's numbers.

Luke clicked his mike. "Woody, the light machine gun is still operational, and I have at least ten hostiles heading down toward me. Over."

"Roger that. Hold on and we'll get some fire on it."

Luke replaced his magazine with a full one and looked through his scope. The figures were about seventy-five yards away and shooting from the hip. *The unmistakable sound of the AK47.* He loaded a 40mm HE round into the grenade launcher and pulled out the aiming sight on the left of the rifle. He peered through the sight, aiming for the figure closest to him, pulled the trigger, and the projectile exploded from the barrel with a *thunk.* He selected the three round burst option on his M4 and watched as the projectile struck the leading figure, his body disintegrating in the explosion. He sighted on the remaining figures and fired aimed bursts, noting his team was also engaging them. Within twenty seconds, all the hostiles appeared to be eliminated.

"Cease fire," said Luke.

Below him, Woody noted the first glimmer of daylight approaching to the east. He checked his watch—0515—and walked over to Sky. "What's the situation on the extraction?"

"They are twenty out, Woody. I've given the extraction coordinates as two fifty east of our current position, back down the valley."

"Hawkeye, how are Shocky and Cap?"

Hawkeye was applying pressure to the wound on Shocky's shoulder. "Still no change with Shocky. The Cap will be fine."

Luke's voice came through Woody's earpiece. "More hostiles, Woody, and I can see several more coming down the slopes above you."

"Roger that. We need to get off this position and be moving within ten minutes. Try and hold them off, and we'll do what we can from our end."

Woody organized his men, but the light machine gun was putting down effective fire and keeping his men from engaging the enemy. He noted that the route back down to an extraction point would place them directly in the sights of the gun, and darkness would no longer protect them.

Luke's voice again: "Give me cover, Woody. Over."

"Will do."

Luke loaded another HE projectile into his M4 and changed his magazine. He stood and ran upward, firing instinctively across the valley to the figures coming down the slope above his team. His team also engaged fire and another eight figures dropped. Up ahead, Luke could see the light machine gun emplacement, about 150 yards away, but he could see no way to get to it unless he descended into the valley. "Keep that machine gun off me," said Luke into his mike. He watched as his team put some serious firepower up and toward the machine gun, which stalled for about thirty seconds until someone got it going again. He looked across to the slopes above the team and saw another six figures heading carefully downward. The range was about a 150 yards and he sighted just below the lead figure and pressed the trigger on the grenade launcher.

As the round impacted, the machine gun swung around toward him and he dropped to the ground and crawled behind the cover of a nearby rock. The gun found his range and Luke could literally feel the rounds chipping away at the boulder. He lay prone and sighted the M4 across the valley toward the slope above his team retaining cover behind the rock. He saw five figures using the M4's telescopic sight and they were well within his range. He selected single shots on the M4, aimed at the lead figure, and dropped him with one shot. A second man went down before the remaining three dropped to the ground and commenced firing in his direction. The machine gun continued to pour rounds in his direction and he thought hard about what to do.

Woody's voice came through his earpiece. "Luke, we are running out of time."

"Tell the bird to hold, Woody. I'm going to have to take that gun out."

1

Ilo, Southern Peru—June 2012

The man walked slowly up the two flights of stairs to the top floor of the motel, one of only two in the small seaport of Ilo in Peru. He checked his wristwatch—close to midnight—and he paused on the landing to get his bearings before heading left toward room two-two-one. Tariq Qadir had a weathered, tanned face, short graying hair, and sharp features punctuated with a sharp beak of a nose. If you'd been asked to guess his age, a stranger might have said anywhere from fifty to fifty-five years. Qadir was, in fact, only thirty-six. His life had been tough.

Dressed in a cream-colored, rumpled suit, Qadir looked like he'd traveled far and indeed he had—all the way from Afghanistan. He left his home in Kabul a month ago, traveling overseas by freighter into Yemen, then on a commercial flight to Brazil and finally another flight into Lima, where he stayed two nights in a rundown hotel near the waterfront. He carried a Pakistan passport, which identified him as Rahim Lashari and, when asked by Customs officials in Lima about his travel intentions, he told them he was a businessman, a carpet maker, interested in buying wool for his carpet factory.

The trip to Ilo by bus, some five hundred miles, took him another two days. It had been the longest journey of his life, and he was tired yet excited to have finally reached his destination. Qadir checked the number on the door and listened. The landing opened to the outside and he tried to look through the window, but the curtains blocked his view. He couldn't hear any sounds from inside. He gently tapped on the door.

After about thirty seconds or so, he heard movement and sounds of the door's lock being disengaged. A thin, weathered face with sharp black eyes peered out. They assessed each other, and the man inside said in Pashto: "Hello, have you traveled far?" *The right question.*

Qadir knew his coded response by heart. "Yes, but only as far as here." *The right answer.*

The man opened the door wide and beckoned him inside, closing and locking it behind him. "Please take a seat." He gestured to one of the two cheap plastic seats, which surrounded a small round table, scarred with cigarette burns and the marks of many drink glasses that had permanently stained the cheap pine wood. "A drink perhaps, after your journey?"

Qadir nodded, not really wanting alcohol, but he knew it would be rude to refuse the man's offer, and he could do with something to warm himself anyway. He placed his small suitcase on the floor next to him and sat at the table observing his host, who Qadir guessed was in his sixties. The other man busied himself in a small kitchen alcove in the corner and reappeared, offering Qadir a small glass of clear liquid. Qadir bowed his head in thanks, wished the man good health and a long life, and swallowed the liquid in one go.

"I too have traveled far, my friend," said the man. "But I am confident that I have what you want."

He walked over toward a cheap pine dresser opposite the bed and opened the top drawer, removing a Nike shoebox. Qadir's gaze went to the man's feet and he saw a pair of brand new white sports shoes with the familiar swoosh. He smiled.

The man brought the box back to the table and sat down opposite Qadir. "You have dealt with explosives before?"

"Yes, many times, but not perhaps as sophisticated as what you are about to show me."

The man opened the lid and took out a small package wrapped in cloth, which he unwrapped and placed on the table between them. Qadir could see an object roughly eight inches by four by four, although not quite box shaped. Gray duct tape, the type you can find in any store, totally wrapped the object, and Qadir noted that the top was convex and painted a shade of bright red. The side nearest to him had a large patch of 3M double-sided tape and a small electronic device, about the size of a matchbox, dominated the end nearest to him with three colored buttons.

"This looks complex, but it is not," said the man. "Knowing something about your mission, I have created a shaped charge using four ounces of military-grade high explosive. Once detonated, 90 percent of the device's energy will be emitted from this surface here, painted red, under which are hundreds of ball bearings." He tapped the device on the uppermost side. "More than enough for your purposes, I believe.

"On both sides of the device, here and here, is double sided tape." He showed him the tape on the two opposite sides of the device. "By peeling back the tape on either of these two sides, you will expose the adhesive and have no trouble placing the device in the chosen area. Once the adhesive is exposed, press hard against the area where you want the device positioned and hold it hard for about thirty seconds."

Qadir thought back to his extensive research and knew exactly where he would place the device for its intended purpose.

The man paused and turned the device so that the end with the electronic device pointed toward Qadir. "There are three switches or buttons, here, here and here. The blue one brings up the digital clock, like this." He pressed the blue button and the led display lit up, showing

0:00. "The red switch sets the time until detonation. Simply hold it down until the desired number of hours and minutes are showing; the maximum is twenty-four hours. If you go past, keep pressing and it will cycle around again. Once you have the right time displayed, press the green switch. This will arm the device and the display will go out. Don't be fooled into thinking the device is then disarmed. Once the green switch is pressed, the device cannot be disarmed and it will explode once the elapsed time has passed."

He pressed the blue button again and the LED display shut down. "It is now safe."

Qadir watched closely and the man gave him a small smile of satisfaction, a man proud of his work. The man wrapped the device again in the cloth and placed it back in the box. "The device is robust and stable, but you know what you can expect if you are caught by the police or security forces."

Qadir placed the box into his suitcase and arose from his seat. "Many thanks, my friend. My heavy heart is about to be freed, *inshallah*." The man walked to the door, cracked it open and peered outside. *All clear.*

As he passed the man on his way out, Qadir offered his hand and was surprised when the man embraced him and gave him a customary kiss on each cheek. "Allahu Akbar," he said softly. Qadir replied in kind and left the room. He did not look back.

2

US Embassy, La Paz, Bolivia

Four days after Qadir's meeting in Peru, Jake Walker waited as Jennifer Barnett, the US Embassy's security chief in Bolivia, studied the final report on her desk. Jake worked for an L.A.-based security firm, Jerico Security, which had a contract with the Department of State to provide security advice and solutions to a range of embassies in South and Central America. A former soldier, Jake had left the life in 2004 and went back to his home state of California. He rented a condo overlooking Venice Beach in L.A. and learned to surf. He ran every morning but had no plans or goals. In time, he became bored and restless and knew that he needed to get busy again. One day while he was enjoying a coffee at his local café, he met a former army buddy who was working for Jerico. The meeting was timely as he'd been contemplating going back to the war and had even contacted a friend who worked for Halliburton, one of the biggest firms providing armed support and security in Iraq and Afghanistan.

The Jerico pitch had been good, and Jake started work the following week. Initially skeptical about his new role, his experiences and skills were a good fit for looking at security issues and, to his surprise, he found that he was pretty good at it. He'd done work for a number of celebrities in Hollywood and had traveled throughout Europe and the Middle East. This was his third trip down to South America, having also provided advice to the United States embassies in Chile and

Brazil.

Several weeks ago, an intoxicated man had been found wandering the grounds of the embassy and Jennifer asked Jerico to fly in a consultant to conduct a threat risk assessment—Jake's area of expertise. His security clearance gave him full access to personnel, systems, and procedures, and he'd needed only seven days to analyze the situation and prepare the report and its recommendations. Jennifer looked up and focused her green eyes on the man opposite. She was pleased and smiled at him, giving Jake his cue.

"Broadly, Jennifer, security here is pretty good," said Jake. "The only real concerns are in your procedures at the main gate and the need to update some of the electronic monitoring devices in the grounds and the software controlling the cameras, which are old and should be replaced. I have recommended the types you should be looking to buy. Our firm can fly down here and implement the recommendations, but there are other sources that you may wish to consider."

"Thanks, Jake. I have been trying since I arrived here to update our procedures, equipment, and processes." She tapped the report and smiled again. "I think your analysis and recommendations are sound and will enable me to obtain the funding I need to get things right. When you get back to the States, why don't you draw up a proposal for the new hardware and software we will need and I'll let you know." She took off her glasses and relaxed back in her chair. "What are your plans now?"

"Well, my flight doesn't leave till tomorrow evening, so I was aiming to do a bit of sightseeing around the city."

"If you're looking for some presents to take home to your family, you should go up to Calle Sagárnaga. You'll find everything from watches to alpaca sweaters."

Jack got up from his chair. "Thanks, Jennifer. I never had time for a family, but I need a few personal items. I may end up having a look through some of the shops before I leave." At that moment, his cell rang.

"Anyway, I'll leave you to it; please excuse me." He gave her a wave and pushed the green "accept" button, stepping out into the third floor corridor and closing the door behind him. "Jake Walker."

"Jake, sorry to bother you, pal. It's Dan." *His brother.*

"That's okay, what's up?"

"It's Dad. He's had another stroke. This time, the docs don't think he's going to pull through."

Jake's mind raced. "When? How did this happen? Where is he now? Is he conscious? Is—"

"Jake, he's stable and in good hands. It happened last night at his home. A neighbor who looks in on him found him slumped over the kitchen table and then called 911. I spoke with the surgeon, who told me that the bleeding into his brain has been extensive. They put in a drain, but the prognosis is not good. He has been conscious and knows I am with him, but he hasn't spoken. He's here at the Good Samaritan."

"Shit, Dan. I knew he wasn't well, but I'm in Bolivia at the moment, working at the embassy."

"When are you scheduled to finish there?"

"My job's finished, but my flight back to L.A. isn't until tomorrow night. I'll call the airline and see what I can do."

"Okay, Jake. Let me know when you are on the way and I'll pick you up at the airport."

"Will do. Take care of him in the interim."

Jake walked to the stairwell, forgoing the elevators, and headed downstairs to the canteen where he poured himself a coffee from the self-serve station and sat down. He scrolled through the numbers in his cell and called American Airlines. He heard a recorded message and was put on hold.

His thoughts turned to his father, Henry "Harry" Walker, US Marines Colonel, retired, never remarrying after his mother's death. *I knew this was going to happen and here I am thousands of miles away.*

"American Airlines," said a pleasant voice, "this is Judy."

Jake came out of his reverie and, once his credentials were established, explained his situation. The woman paused, looking up alternatives. "Sorry, Mr. Walker, we have absolutely nothing today, but I can get you on a direct flight to Los Angeles that leaves at 10:30 tomorrow morning."

Jake took the new reservation, thanked the woman, and hung up.

At that point a person came into his view and said, "Jake, Jake Walker!"

Jake looked at the face, searching for the point of recognition. The man beamed a set of very white teeth at him and then he had it. "Well, I'll be. Mick Rogers! What the hell are you doing here? How long has it been?"

3

El Alto, La Paz, Bolivia

As Jake and Mick caught up, Emily Parker was coming to the end of her speech. She looked over the lectern at her audience, a mixture of dignitaries, parents, and teachers. "This is the third school we have helped to build in South America. The people I have met here in El Alto, and throughout my travels in Bolivia, are caring and wonderful..."

Special Agent Karen Duffy tuned out the words and focused on the task at hand. She glanced across the dais at her senior partner, Pete Murray, who was alert and focused on the people and perimeter on her opposite flank. Duffy watched everyone in her zone, looking for anything out of the ordinary, continually scanning the small crowd that had turned up for the opening of the school.

To her left and about three rows back, her eyes paused on a young man, clean shaven and wearing a suit. As he reached into an inside pocket, her hand went to her shoulder holster and she let out her breath as his hand came out, revealing a small digital camera. Her gaze returned to others in the crowd. The Secret Service provided personal protection to the young woman on the dais, the youngest daughter of the Honorable William H. Parker, the most recent former president of the United States. The detail was not strictly entitled, but Parker had served two terms of office, commencing 2001, and was still very popular, even among the Service. Providing a much larger perimeter and backing up the two Secret Service agents were approximately twenty-five men from the Bolivian president's own personal security force. Duffy forced herself to relax.

As an agent of the Secret Service for seven years, she had served on protection details with the secretary of state, the president and, now, his daughter. During her first protection role with the secretary of state, she demonstrated a cool head under pressure and her strong work ethic had been noticed. Four years ago, her boss assigned her to President Parker's protection detail and, for the last two years, with the smaller team assigned to the former president. Emily Parker was her regular client and the two became good friends, particularly during recent times when she traveled overseas to fulfill her duties as an ambassador to her father's charitable organization, the Parker Foundation.

She sensed, rather than heard, Emily's speech coming to a conclusion and scanned the crowd once more as they rose in applause. Emily picked up her papers and, as she stepped down, Duffy and Murray moved closer to her, still watchful. Emily moved toward the group of dignitaries at the front, shook a number of hands and chatted away happily with a couple of women, who Duffy believed to be involved in the Ministry of Education.

After three or so minutes, Pete Murray looked at his watch: 11:35 a.m. He spoke into his throat mike, "Karen, it's about time to go. We have to be at the airport at 1330." Duffy looked at him, nodded, and approached Emily, touching her arm gently.

"Please excuse me," said Emily to the two women.

Duffy gazed coolly at her boss. "Ma'am, sorry to bother you, but we have a plane to catch and have to get back to the embassy and out to the airport in about two hours."

At this point, the US ambassador to Bolivia, Bob Grainger, and his wife, Denise, approached them. "Emily," the ambassador beamed, "you have done a magnificent job here for us. The Parker Foundation and this new school will do wonders for relations here with the Bolivians."

"My father and I have been very glad to help, Ambassador. Bolivia remains a very poor country and we are hoping our contribution will go a long way to build a future for the children that will learn here."

Emily looked around and realized that her work was done. She also knew that her father had organized a function for the evening in Houston, a fundraiser of sorts, and that she was expected to be there. She turned to Duffy. "Thanks, Karen, of course." She smiled warmly at Bob Grainger. "Ambassador, I am sorry, but we have a plane to catch."

Ten minutes later, flanked by four motorcycles and the Bolivian president's security detail in vehicles front and rear, Emily and the two agents were safely ensconced in one of the embassy's armored Chevrolet Suburbans and heading back to the embassy. The ambassador and his wife followed in a second Suburban.

Emily welcomed the silence in the vehicle and looked out the window without really seeing. She was tired—tired of being in focus, tired of being in the public eye. Being born into a famous and wealthy family had its advantages, but being the daughter of a former president would not have been her first choice as it interfered with what she wanted to do and where she wanted to be. As the younger of two daughters, her parents closeted her from the real world. She could hardly remember ever spending a day alone. Even at college, Secret Service agents followed her everywhere. It seemed to her that her father had been born a politician. As such, constantly followed and photographed by the press and commented upon in the media, she had never experienced a normal childhood. Now in her current role for her father's charity, she remained in the public eye. By contrast, her sister, Belinda, had studied law at Stanford and was now working as an associate with a top law firm in Houston. Emily had been good at math at school and wanted to pursue a career in finance, but her father had steered her toward politics and she had relented. She found academic life at Princeton okay and had excelled in her studies, but she remained unsure just what a political science degree was going to lead to.

This was her first year since finishing college and she was still living at home, taking an allowance from her dad as he groomed her for a life in politics. She felt trapped. Working for the foundation had its high points, but she wanted to be doing something else. She detested politics and felt her integrity—her goodness—slipping away. In ten hours or so, she would be back with her father and preparing for another boring fundraiser, shaking hands, making small talk, and having to smile and be nice to everyone. If only she could have a few days to see the sights of Bolivia and a chance to enjoy herself, to forget about Houston, her father, and the foundation.

Duffy was also deep in thought. She'd listened to the Secret Service's rhetoric about equal opportunity, but she knew that the reality for the young female agents coming through the ranks was far different. Sure, equality within the Service improved as the older guys retired, but the protective detail side of the Service remained a "boy's club," making it difficult for women to rise through the ranks. For Duffy and her female colleagues, proving that you were equal was not enough. Throughout her career, she'd needed to excel at everything and her need to demonstrate the right stuff drove her. It had her running five miles every morning and she spent more time on the range than her colleagues, firing clip after clip with her pistol until her arms ached. Despite all her efforts, at times she still felt like the token female.

In five hours or so, they would be back in Houston and the Service owed her a five-day break. She usually relished her time off but not this time. Nine days ago, she'd wondered if she was in love for the first time. That had since changed. Being away so often, she rarely had time for relationships, or so she told herself. Nearly all her friends were in the Service and Duffy was well aware that she projected a hard, hands-off image to men, and to women, for that matter. Nonetheless, she attended a retirement party six weeks ago to honor and celebrate the career of a thirty-year veteran, Harry Patterson. It was a typical affair, full of Service men and women talking shop, although a few brought their partners. And, of course, everyone was drinking booze like you would at an end of the world party. Boy, could the Service drink! She'd been topping up her bourbon in the kitchen when she met Sam, Harry's son.

Sam built houses for a living. He was fit too, and funny and very handsome. Duffy dropped her guard, assisted by several shots of Jack Daniels. Two years older than she, Sam had a thriving business, his own apartment, and he loved to travel. The hours passed quickly that night and, when it ended, she agreed to go on a dinner date the following week.

On the second date, to her surprise, she took Sam to her bed— her first lover since agent school. For the next four weeks, they talked or met every day and she made every effort to see him when not at work. It was definitely the most serious relationship Duffy had ever experienced, leaving her literally breathless in his company and totally unprepared for her feelings. Ten days ago, they were sitting in her apartment sharing a bottle of wine after some wonderful sex, Duffy telling Sam about her coming trip to Bolivia and the five-day break from her work. They made a plan to fly to Vegas, even looking online for any shows they might want to see.

The following day, Duffy needed to go into Houston to participate in some corporate training. At morning tea, she found herself talking to Dana Roberts, a longtime friend from agent school. Dana knew of her relationship with Sam and suggested to Duffy that he might be a player as she'd seen him with another woman in a city bar on the previous Saturday. Sam was well known around the singles circuit, Dana told her.

Duffy called Sam immediately and he didn't deny it. Duffy never cried, but she remembered well the tears welling up in her eyes and her thumping heart as she said good bye to him. Sam made her feel so good, so happy. She didn't know what she could do to occupy herself over the next five days.

4

La Paz, Bolivia, a day earlier

Qadir got out of his rental car in *Avenue 20 de Octubre*, a popular restaurant strip five minutes from the city center of La Paz. He'd arrived in the capital the day before, having driven from the border town of Desguardero. Now 8:30 p.m., the sun was just setting on the horizon, the sky magnificent and glorious. Qadir did not notice. As he stood beside the car, he automatically scanned the street looking for anything out of the ordinary. His trip from Peru took two days, with the border crossing occurring overnight by horseback with help from a guide who'd been waiting for him as promised. The trip over the border had been long; he couldn't remember when he'd last sat on a horse. Tired and sore, his spirits rose when he found the rental car waiting for him, its key in a magnetic box above the driver's side front tire. He'd only driven a hundred miles to La Paz, but Bolivia did not have the best roads; the entire journey had taken time and tired him beyond measure.

He locked the car, crossed the street and entered the restaurant, which was about three-quarters full. When greeted by a waiter, he whispered into his ear and was promptly escorted out the back and into a small office at the rear of the kitchen area. Inside sat a man, about fifty years old, dressed in traditional Afghan *perahan tunban*, but with a Western suit jacket, which Qadir guessed to be made from silk. He smoked a rather sweet smelling but pungent tobacco and rose to greet Qadir. In Pashto, his host said, "Wonderful. It was getting late, and I was beginning to think something had happened to you." He gestured for him to take the other seat in the small room. "Sit, sit. You must be hungry." He went to the door and called out, "Some food, quickly, and some wine."

He closed the door and sat opposite Qadir, who said, "Thank you, some food would be perfect, but I can't accept your offer of wine, as I have work to do tonight."

The man waved his thanks away. "Of course, but you must eat."

Thirty minutes later, Qadir was finishing a plate of meat and rice, mopping up the last remnants with some flat bread. He paused and picked up a glass of water and drank deeply. "Thank you, my friend. That was very much needed. Now that I am refreshed, what can you tell me?"

5

El Alto Airport, La Paz, Bolivia, earlier that day

At 2:50 a.m. on the same morning that Emily was due to open the school, Sanchez Romero walked the perimeter of a hangar at the northern edge of El Alto Airport in La Paz, the hangar that contained Bill Parker's Gulfstream jet. Twenty-eight year old, Sanchez had worked for the same security firm for five years. Jobs were hard to find throughout Bolivia and he was grateful for what he had, and for the wife and two daughters with whom God had blessed him. *Why, then, had he agreed to be part of what was about to happen?*

About one week earlier, as he unlocked his ten-year-old Corolla at the end of a shift, a stranger approached him out of the dark. He immediately thought of attack and braced himself, but the stranger held up his hands and said clearly to him, in excellent Spanish, "Please, Mr. Romero, I wish you no harm. I just want to talk."

Cautiously, Sanchez bid the man into the passenger seat and asked the man what he wanted. The man explained that times were hard, that if one could earn a little extra money, a man could afford a better car, a holiday. How long ago since he had taken his family on a holiday? A long time, agreed Sanchez. Wouldn't it feel good to buy a better car, afford some better things for his family?

Just before Sanchez lost his patience with the man, he pulled an envelope from his jacket pocket and passed it to him. "Look inside. That is what thirty thousand Boliviano looks like. About what you earn in a year, no?"

The sight of the money made Sanchez instantly suspicious but also excited at the same time. "What do you want in return?" he asked, as he looked at all the crisp new bank notes.

"A simple request, nothing really. I just want you to make sure you are on a particular midnight to dawn shift at a particular hangar in a week's time. The hangar is one of your normal places of duty, so a swap of shifts will not be noticed."

Sanchez looked at the man. He was smartly dressed, his hair well barbered and he wore a well-cut gray suit. *European*, he thought. He also smelled strongly of cologne and coffee. He looked into the envelope again and thought of what the money could do. The shift that the man wanted him to take was not a popular one and he believed he would have no trouble in swapping shifts for the night in question. "Is that all you want? Why?"

"That is my business," the man replied. "Good money for you, a simple job."

Sanchez thought for about two minutes. How would he explain the additional money? Perhaps, he could introduce the money in small amounts? Maybe explain some luck at gambling, even though he rarely gambled? There were many things he wanted in life and he weighed up the opportunity against the risks. He put the envelope in his pocket. "How do I contact you?"

"There will be no need for us to contact each other. I will be watching to ensure you keep your side of the bargain. If you do this, you will never see me again."

On the day following the meeting with the man, Sanchez checked the roster and caught up with a colleague whom he knew to be working on the night in question. There'd been no problem in convincing the man that he needed a day off to help his family with an issue. So a swap of shifts was formalized and the roster changed. Sanchez started to spend some of the money, just a bit, careful to include his wife, buying her some perfume he knew that she liked. And the perfume brought its own reward…He forgot about the man.

Two days before the shift in question, Sanchez noticed an envelope under the wiper blade as he commenced driving home after work. He took the envelope and sat back in the car. Inside he found several, high resolution, full color photos of him looking into the envelope full of money and another of him putting it into his jacket pocket. He looked further into the envelope and found a message, printed on plain paper:

> MR SANCHEZ. IN TWO DAYS TIME, YOU ARE TO UNLOCK THE NORTHERN DOOR TO THE HANGER AND BETWEEN 3:30 A.M. AND 4:00 A.M. YOU ARE TO KEEP YOUR COLLEAGUE FULLY ENGAGED.
>
> WE KNOW WHERE YOU LIVE. YOU HAVE A BEAUTIFUL FAMILY. IF YOU DO THIS SIMPLE TASK, THERE WILL BE NO NEED TO SHOW THESE PHOTOGRAPHS TO YOUR EMPLOYER.

Sanchez turned white when he read the message and it took several minutes before he could compose himself and drive home. His wife noticed the difference in him, but he explained it away as tiredness.

◊

At 3:00 a.m., Sanchez went to the rear door and unlocked it using a key from the keychain on his belt. He opened it and tested that it could be opened from outside. There were two guards on this particular duty, normal when certain planes or cargoes needed additional security. He didn't know whom the plane belonged to and he didn't care. Their routine included a half-hourly tour of the perimeter, while the other guard stayed inside the hangar and walked around the inside.

At 3:25 a.m., his colleague, Carlos, returned from a walk around the outside of the hangar. "It is a very quiet night, Carlos," said Sanchez. "What say we go into the office and have a game of chess?"

Carlos loved his chess but was surprised because every time he had asked Sanchez for a game, he'd been put off. He looked quizzically at him. "You don't like chess."

"I never said that," replied Sanchez. "I'm just not very good. I need someone to learn from."

"Well, why didn't you say so? Come. We'll set the board up and I'll show you some of the opening moves."

6

El Alto Airport, La Paz, Bolivia

While Sanchez and his colleague set the board up for their chess game, outside and well away from the perimeter of the airport, Qadir sat in his rental car. He recalled his conversation earlier in the evening with the restaurant owner. A Pakistani restaurant no less, but owned by an Afghani, like himself.

"The plane is a Gulfstream G200," his host said. "A fairly new model. It will be the only one in the hangar and the baggage compartment will be unlocked and open. There will be two guards on duty from a local, private security firm. Between 3:30 and 4:00 a.m., both guards will be otherwise engaged and you will have that half hour window in which to work. The rear door to the hangar faces the perimeter of the airport and is about a hundred and fifty meters from the fence. This door will be unguarded and unlocked. How you get past the fence and across to the hangar is your business."

"When is the plane due to depart?" Qadir asked.

"There is no set departure time. What I do know, however, is that the woman is due to open the school at 11:00 tomorrow morning and she is on the guest list for a fundraising function in Houston tomorrow night. I figure around 2:00 p.m. is a likely departure time as the flight time to Houston is around four hours."

In the car, Qadir picked up the package and slowly took off the cloth wrapping. He turned the interior light on and, recalling the bomb maker's advice, pressed the blue button once to bring up the LED display—00:00, as he expected. Assuming he armed the device now, he counted forward and figured about twelve and half hours. By then, the plane would still be airborne.

Eight painful years to get here, recalled Qadir. He could taste his revenge. What did they say in the West? A dish best served cold.

◊

Born into a wealthy Afghan family, Qadir's father had owned several hotels in Kabul. When the Russians invaded Afghanistan in December of 1979, his father had chosen to collaborate with the Russians during their occupation. It was either that or lose everything. In 1988 as the defeated Russians contemplated their failure, his father feared reprisals from his fellow countrymen and decided to leave everything and move overseas. Although he was only 12 years old, Qadir could not contemplate life in another country and, when told of the danger to the family from the departing Russians and of his father's plans to move to Brazil, he grabbed some clothes and left the family home in the middle of the night, not knowing what lay ahead. Qadir had not seen his parents or his younger sister since.

Qadir's real name was Tariq Assan. But even at that young age, he was smart enough to know that he needed a new one, that the family surname would bring him trouble. Within a few days of leaving Kabul, he took on a new surname, Qadir, a name he had seen on a tombstone in a cemetery. No one questioned his orphan status given the large number of people who'd perished during a decade of bloody conflict. He headed into the remote north of Afghanistan and, a year after he had given up his family, he was a full-fledged member of the mujahideen and rejoiced with them when the Russians finally pulled out of Afghanistan, their tails between their legs.

Chaos and anarchy replaced the relative order of the Russians as

39

a large number of different groups sought and competed over the right to rule. Eventually one group, which had its foundations in the refugee camps on the Pakistan border, became more powerful than all others: the Taliban, which, roughly translated, means students or seekers of knowledge.

In 1997, disaffected by war and conflict, Qadir joined the Taliban and, as an experienced warrior, he found his calling and became a member of a brotherhood that believed totally in the strict enforcement of Sharia, the Western name for Islamic religious law.

In 2000, Qadir sat within a group of Taliban leaders and listened to an address by Osama bin Laden. By then, he was married to a wonderful, loving woman, his Sayeda, and blessed with a beautiful daughter called Talia, yet his beloved country was nonetheless still a mess as the Taliban had been unable to introduce the social and economic reforms needed to bring Afghanistan into the modern world. Bin Laden's speech inspired the still young Qadir. His views offered a more targeted, fundamentalist Islam and promised a future Qadir wanted to be part of, a future that promised a jihad, or holy war, to weaken the West and to spread the power and influence of Islam. That night, he thought long and hard about his options.

Following the September 2001 bombings in New York, the world turned on Afghanistan, and the Taliban in particular. As his country was invaded by the Coalition of the Willing and led by the Americans, Qadir left his family in Kabul and followed a number of his fellow Taliban into the mountains, where he gained notoriety with the Taliban and al-Qaeda forces alike as a wise leader and fearless warrior. Eventually, he gained acceptance with the al-Qaeda forces, and he left his Taliban past behind forever.

Two months into the conflict, the apartment block that housed his wife and daughter was completely destroyed during an aerial bombing raid on Kabul. Struck by a bunker buster bomb and guided to its target by laser, the building disintegrated completely. Over a hundred

Afghan civilians died and, as the media caught up with the story, Washington was forced to publicly address the issue. Qadir could still remember watching President Parker make an address on television. "War is a terrible business and it is inevitable, given the evil forces we are up against, that there will be civilian casualties," he said. "We had credible intelligence about a specific, high profile target in that building and we make no apology for our decision and the unfortunate collateral civilian damage."

Collateral damage! Qadir wept for his family and vowed revenge. At the time, Qadir formed part of the security detail that protected bin Laden while he hid in the intricate tunnel complex in the Tora Bora mountain range in Afghanistan. As the US-led coalition closed in on their redoubt, the irony was never lost on them that the tunnel system had been financed by the CIA in the early 1980s when the common enemy had been the Russians.

By December 2001, bin Laden and his followers, including Qadir, fled Tora Bora as it became clear that the mountainous region was going to be overrun by the US and its allies. Once clear, they took refuge in a safe house in Jalalabad for several weeks and later traveled to the remote province of Kunar in northeast Afghanistan where they lived rough.

As the years passed, Qadir rose in rank and influence, eventually leading the team of men that provided bin Laden with protection as he traveled around the region. Qadir forgot the exact moment, but gradually it became clear to bin Laden's followers that he was a figurehead and no more than that. Isolation and other factors finally caught up with him and, in due course, bin Laden no longer made a contribution operationally.

In 2007, bin Laden's second in command, the Egyptian-born Ayman al-Zawahiri, took the decision to send bin Laden to a safe house in Abbottabad, Pakistan. From there, bin Laden occasionally provided video recordings for the media, but he effectively no longer commanded the organization he created. Shortly after, Qadir traveled back to Afghanistan to lead the planning and coordination of insurgent activities in the east of the country.

Despite his involvement in the ongoing fight against the US and its allies, Qadir never lost sight of what Parker was up to. So when bin Laden was assassinated by the Americans in May 2011, he moved back to Kabul, where he coordinated some of the al-Qaeda's activities in the south of Afghanistan. Three months previous, he traveled to see the newly elected al-Qaeda leader, al-Zawahiri, and asked his permission to plan and implement an attack on the Parker family. Al-Zawahiri asked him what he was planning and Qadir told him of Parker's daughter's flights to and from Bolivia and his belief that he could succeed in getting a bomb aboard the former president's private jet. Al-Zawahiri gave the mission his blessing and personally oversaw the manufacture and delivery of the bomb that Qadir now had in his possession.

◊

Qadir looked down at the device in his lap. He checked the time on his watch and saw it was 3:37 a.m. *Time to move.* He made some calculations and pressed the red button until the clock showed 12:53, so that it would activate at 4:30 p.m., almost thirteen hours hence, as sure as he could be that the aircraft would be flying at that time. He paused, pushed the green button, and watched as the LED display went out, just as the bomb maker said it would. He re-wrapped the device carefully, switched off the light, and exited the car. Five minutes later, he lay adjacent to the fence. Lighting was fairly nonexistent around the perimeter and he lifted the poorly maintained chain link fence with ease and stood inside the airport proper. He scanned the area for movement and, seeing none, walked purposefully toward the hanger where he knew the plane to be.

He turned the door handle slowly. It made no sound and he quickly walked inside, closed it behind him, and waited a few seconds for his eyes and ears to adjust. The hangar was roughly two hundred feet wide, and the Gulfstream sat in the middle, sleek and powerful. From the night lights around the perimeter, he could see that the area was clear and moved silently toward the jet. He crouched underneath the fuselage and poked his head into the baggage compartment. Dark and empty, he could just see the forward bulkhead. He climbed inside. Once airborne, he knew that the fully pressurized and heated compartment could be accessed from inside the plane and, from his own personal inspection within a similar aircraft, he knew just the spot where he could conceal the device from view.

He reached the forward bulkhead and removed the cloth that had protected the device. He couldn't see clearly, but he peeled off the film covering the double sided tape on one side, reached around the spar closest to the forward bulkhead and pressed the device onto it, making sure it was firmly attached and out of sight from someone loading baggage.

He made his way to the exit hatch and slowly lowered himself to the ground. Thinking on what he had just achieved, he suddenly remembered the bomb maker's advice to point the red, convex side of the device toward the cabin. He realized that he could not be certain and would have to recheck his placement and possibly change its orientation. He was about to do this when he heard voices.

Whether the device exploded toward the cabin or through the fuselage, Qadir felt sure the plane would crash to the ground. He ducked down under the plane and could see two guards talking to each other near an office structure in a corner, about seventy feet or so away. With the exit door on his side of the plane, he quickly made his way to the door and outside. Ten minutes later he unlocked his car, sat inside and drove back to his hotel.

7

US Embassy, La Paz, Bolivia

Mick Rogers sized up his former friend. Jake looked to his left and noticed a younger man, with fair, short hair and a friendly face. "Jake, this is Nigel Saunders, my co pilot. Nigel, this is Jake Walker, one of the hardest, bravest soldiers I have ever served with. We met during a tour of Afghanistan in '01."

Jake pushed thoughts about his father aside and quickly sized up the two men. Both wore the same uniforms: short sleeve white shirts with epaulets, black trousers, and pilot's peaked caps. He rose from his chair, shook Mick's hand, and turned and shook his co-pilot's. "Nice to meet you, Nigel. You're in capable hands with this man. There's nothing he can't fly."

Mick sat down and motioned to Nigel to join them. Jake still looked fit, Mick thought; the years had been good to him. Just short of six foot, the man had a solid frame, sandy hair, and blue eyes that twinkled. "Of all the people, I never expected to see you here. It's been what, four, five years?"

"Closer to ten, Mick. Last time we saw each other was just before I jumped from twenty-five thousand feet over Shahi-Kot or somewhere near there. I've been out of the life since '03." Although Mick's hair was starting to gray around the ears, he was tanned, and only the small paunch over his belt suggested he was not as fit as he used to be. "Looks like life has been good to you."

"Too good," said Mick, patting his stomach. He turned to Nigel. "Jake was a sergeant in the Special Forces and I flew on several missions with him, first in Afghanistan and later in Iraq. Not once did I think Jake would fail to come back from a mission. He was invincible. I remember one of the missions, Nigel. Operation Anaconda, one of the early ones. It was where—"

Jake cut him off before he could start talking about getting the Congressional Medal of Honor. "It was not what we expected, Mick. And it's history now."

Trying to lighten the mood, Nigel asked, "How did you find his sense of humor, Jake?"

"How can I put it? The worst goddamn jokes you have ever heard." Jake laughed.

"You know him well, then." Nigel laughed, too.

"What was that one about the frog who wanted a burger and a side order of ketchup?" asked Jake.

"Hey, you two, that's enough. Anyway, buddy, what brings you here today?" asked Mick.

Jake's smile faded and he looked at Mick. "It's a long story, Mick. I had a couple of bad moments in Iraq back in '03. One experience in particular hit me hard. Some of my people were killed in bad firefight in Baghdad, and I knew it was time to go. Perhaps I hadn't really planned things, but when I got back to L.A., my hometown, or what passes for one these days, I was at a loss. Like many veterans, particularly Special Forces, I considered signing on with one of the civilian firms but realized I would simply be back in the Middle East. The pay on offer was four times what I was making as a soldier, but I simply wasn't ready to step back into that sort of conflict. Not sure I ever will be.

"Just as my money was running out, I caught up with a guy named Steve Baldwin, a former grunt I'd served with. We shared a coffee and he told me about Jerico, an L.A.-based security firm that specializes in undertaking threat assessments, protection detail, and installing systems for high profile clients."

"I've heard of them," said Mick.

"Anyway, two weeks later I was wearing a suit, this one in fact, and was learning the ropes of security consulting. Been with them over five years now. Didn't realize my military background was perfect experience to assess security risks and develop strategies to mitigate them. I write up the reports—been a steep learning curve, that one—and include options for clients to upgrade their existing systems and procedures to address threats. Another team then comes in and implements new systems and so on."

"And that's why you're here in La Paz?" asked Nigel.

"Yeah, Jerico has a contract with the State Department for all the embassies in South and Central America, and I'm here providing some advice on the status of the embassy's security systems and procedures—they've had a couple of breaches. Anyway, I've been here for almost a week and am heading back to L.A. tomorrow."

"Well, I thought you would be the last person to leave the military," said Mick. "I always saw you ending your days as a grizzled old grunt in his fifties yelling at boots in basic. That said, I'm really pleased you found a good gig, one that suits your talents by the sound of things."

"What about you, Mick? Doesn't look like you're on vacation."

Mick leaned onto the table. "Here's the short version," he said, taking a glance at Nigel before looking upward. "I was back on leave from the Middle East, enjoying the sun in Miami. This would've been mid-2008 or thereabouts. I was on my second drink at the pool, the Sands, I think it was, reading *Plane and Pilot...*"

"As you do," said Nigel, smiling.

Mick smiled back. "There was an advertisement in the magazine from a local charter firm seeking pilots to fly private jets commercially. I checked them out and got a pay offer I couldn't refuse. I'd been in the Air Force by then for thirteen years." He looked at Jake, who returned his look. "Well, like you, I'd had a few close shaves and wasn't looking forward to going back into the zone. Within two months, I'd taken my discharge and was in training again, getting a rating for Gulfstreams. Spent over a year with the firm and then got a real break. You'll never guess whose plane we are flying today." He looked at Nigel.

Jake looked at the two men. "Okay, CIA, FBI, Charlie Sheen, Tiger Woods—who is it?"

"Tiger would've been a good gig, don't deny it. But no, I am only flying the goddamn former President Bill Parker's personal jet. I, er, we go wherever he goes. You should see some of the places we've been to—France, Canada, the Bahamas. We flew in yesterday with Parker's youngest daughter, Emily. She's been taking an active role in the Parker Foundation, Bill's personal charity. Right now, she should just about be finishing the opening of a new school that the good Bill's foundation has funded here in La Paz."

"Hey, that's what I call a good set up," acknowledged Jake.

Nigel said, "We're just waiting for Emily and her protective detail to arrive, and then we're heading out to the airport. Emily has a function to attend with her father in Houston tonight."

Jake looked at his friend. "Hey, Mick, you couldn't..." he started.

"Couldn't what?"

"No, forget it. It's good to see you."

"Hang on, buddy," said Mick. "You can't just start something and leave us hanging. You need something—ask."

Jake thought for a moment. "I've just had some bad news about my father. He's had a stroke, his second one. Doesn't look good, according to my brother. He's in L.A. in the Good Samaritan. I've managed to get a flight out tomorrow morning, but I admit I'm worried that I might not make it in time." He looked away out the window.

"Shit, Jake, that's awful news. I'm sorry. I take it you were hoping we might have some room?" He looked at Nigel, who shrugged. "No promises, pal. There are spare seats, but it's not my call. When Emily arrives, I'll talk to her and see what happens, okay? Why don't you get over to your hotel and get your things. I'll see you when you get back."

8

US Embassy, La Paz

At the gate of the embassy, the Bolivian police escorts peeled away, and the two Suburbans rolled through the checkpoint without delay. They stopped outside the embassy's main entrance and Emily Parker and the two Secret Service agents exited the vehicle. Emily looked up at the six floors of the unspectacular building and squinted in the sun.

Bob and Denise Grainger were waiting for her and, as they came forward, Mrs. Grainger took Emily's arm. "Please pass on our best wishes to your father, Emily. He's a fine man. One of our greatest presidents."

"I will, Mrs. Grainger."

"Denise, please," said the older woman. "Bob and I have been here three years and our time is nearly up. I take it Bob has already told you how this generosity will be perceived locally."

"Don't mention it, Denise. It's been a great pleasure to come here. To see all those young, smiling children is all the thanks I need."

The two women, arm in arm, went up the steps and into the foyer, with Bob Grainger and the two agents following. "Are you able to join us for lunch, Emily? When are you planning to leave?"

Emily looked at her watch. "Sadly, Denise, I can't stay this time. I know it's been a whirlwind visit, but Dad is expecting me back in Houston tonight. He has another one of those fundraising functions and, more and more, he's been pushing me as the face of the foundation. I'd love to stay and see more of the city, I really would. I just can't this time."

"Of course." Mrs. Grainger turned to face the younger woman and took her hands in hers. "Emily, it has been great to see you again. Bob and I will be back stateside soon, three months, I think. We are both retiring. We have a small farm holding in Wisconsin and we would love to have you come and visit." The two women hugged.

Jennifer Barnett approached. "Ms. Parker, your luggage is in the vehicles. With the drivers, your pilots, your two agents, and yourself, you'll be taking both vehicles. We will also be providing three marines as a precaution, but we are not expecting any trouble."

"Thank you," said Emily. She turned to her protective detail. "Pete, could you go and find our pilots? Karen, let's wait outside."

Several minutes later, Mick and Nigel came outside with Peter Murray and Jake. "Ms. Parker," said Mick, "before we go, could I introduce you to Jake Walker? Jake, this is Emily Parker."

Emily noticed Jake for the first time. She smiled and shook his hand. "Pleased to meet you, Mr. Walker."

"Jake has a problem, ma'am," said Mick. "I knew Jake when I was in the military and just found him an hour ago in the canteen. His firm has a contract with the State Department, and he's been providing security advice to the embassy here. He tells me he needs to get back to L.A. urgently, as his father has suffered a stroke. With our plane being somewhat light on passengers, I was hoping we, I mean you, could offer him a lift." He gave her his best smile.

Emily turned to Jake and said, "I am sorry to hear that, Mr.

Walker." She turned to her two agents. "Karen, Pete, any issues for either of you?"

"I'll have to call it in, ma'am," said Murray, looking at Jake and noticing his embassy pass that identified him as a contractor. "Who do you work for, Mr. Walker?"

"Jerico Security in L.A. We have a State Department contract and I've been security cleared by Homeland," replied Jake.

"Good, okay. I need to call my boss," said Murray, pulling his cell phone out of his jacket. He moved away and the group made some small talk.

After a minute, Murray came back and looked at Emily. "George gave the okay, ma'am. Jerico is a well-respected company and, as Mr. Walker has been security cleared to undertake consulting tasks for the US government, I think we can give him a lift. Plus, Mick vouches for him and I trust his judgment."

"Right," said Emily. "Put your gear in one of the vehicles, Mr. Walker, and let's get on our way."

9

Panama-Colombian Border

Around the same time that Emily and the others were preparing to depart for the airport, Eduardo Ortiz, his younger brother Aristo, and four of his father's men made slow but steady progress through the rain forest that borders Colombia and Panama. Astride small, sturdy horses, they moved along well-defined trails; two additional horses brought up the rear, roped together, each of them burdened by two heavy crates.

Eduardo was not in a good mood. He didn't normally do these trips, and he knew it was his father's way of punishing Aristo. As he followed the man in front, he reflected on the last seven days and the circumstances that had brought him and Aristo to this task.

◊

The fault lay with Aristo. A little over a week ago, he'd skipped the family property in Medellin and took a commercial flight to Brazil to party. As there'd been two similar instances, his father, Leandro, had been furious and took his temper out on Eduardo, dispatching him to Rio de Janeiro in a private jet to fetch his brother. Leandro's long-standing lieutenant, Fabio, accompanied him.

Aristo left a trail, via his credit card, a school kid could have followed, and he was quickly located at a $700 a night suite in the Intercontinental in Rio. A well-endowed blond opened the door to the suite, and Fabio shoved some hundred dollar bills in her hand, asking her to leave. Empty bottles and overturned trays of food littered the apartment, and a large quantity of cocaine on the coffee table suggested the party had been a good one. As the girl departed, Eduardo located Aristo in bed. He was none too pleased to be woken up and got out of bed, naked, and walked into the kitchen looking for water.

Eduardo followed him. "You are breaking all the rules, little brother. You and I will take over our father's business in the near future, but we will fail if we can't both be strong. You know what failure means in our business." He moved into the living area. "This shit," he kicked over the coffee table, "is how we make our money, not by snorting it."

"Why don't you just leave me alone, Lalo," Aristo replied from the kitchen area, using the nickname he had called his brother since he was small.

Eduardo went and stood next to Aristo. Fabio stood by the door and watched as the older man laid his arm around his brother.

"I know how you are feeling. It is a dirty business we are in, but while Papa is alive, we have a duty to support him. And I," Eduardo put his hand over his heart, "have a duty to look after you." Aristo wiped his eyes. "We have to go back. You know this. Because of this, Papa wants us to make a routine trip up to Panama, and I have promised him that you and I will go."

On the plane trip back to Colombia, Eduardo reflected on the ongoing argument between Aristo and his father. It was pretty much the same argument since Aristo finished school, and it involved his unwillingness to take on responsibilities in his father's business. Like Eduardo, who was four years his senior, Aristo attended boarding school in Argentina and had spent many of his holidays in Rio de Janeiro with his mother's brother and their family. Aristo loved Rio, its vibrancy and excitement, and his school holidays made it one of his all-time favorite places to be.

Eduardo sympathized with Aristo, as he also secretly yearned for a different life. Nonetheless, he was realistic and knew an exit strategy was impossible while his father still lived. Although he'd finished school early, Eduardo was intelligent and wanted more than the life of a *narcotraficante*. Just over six feet tall and 175 pounds, he was a handsome Latino man, with dark green eyes, longish black hair and perfect teeth. His own personal dream was to be a movie actor, but he knew it would remain a dream. Because money. And cocaine.

He knew the sums, the enormous riches from the business they were in. His father's "franchise" enabled the creation and sale of approximately one hundred metric tons of Colombian *Puro* each year— 100 percent uncut cocaine. The business involved small crop holdings throughout the northwestern district of Colombia, some three hundred square miles surrounding his father's property and fortress in Medellin. A large number of farmers grew the coca plant and, through a complex but traditional process, converted the coca leaf into *pasta,* which typically contained 40-50 percent cocaine. The farmers received a small payment for the *pasta* and several bush labs operated to convert the *pasta* into pure cocaine.

At the wholesale level, the product sold in its purest form for $10,000 per kilogram. On the street, that same kilogram could realize $100,000 to $200,000 depending on how much it was cut, or diluted.

His father managed the sale of roughly one hundred thousand kilograms every single year. One billion US dollars. Sure, the old man incurred costs for distribution, and he needed to pay off quite a number of officials and politicians, both in Colombia and overseas. For their part, the farmers received very little, but chemists required paying and a small army was on the payroll to protect the bush labs and their property. They also lost about 15 percent to law enforcement and needed to cleanse the money so that it could be banked and spent. Yes, many overheads. Nonetheless, Eduardo knew his father was a billionaire many times over with bank accounts in Europe, the Grand Caymans, and probably several other places he didn't know about.

"When was enough money enough?" Eduardo had asked him when last they spoke.

"This is our life," had been his father's reply.

There were two main ways in which his father's cocaine reached its markets. Specially commissioned freighters carrying a range of cargoes frequently took up to five metric tons at a time to small ports in Africa, where the cocaine traveled on by truck to destinations throughout Europe. The specially modified freighters incorporated hiding areas next to the hull for the valuable cargo, but otherwise took normal cargoes and crews. However, the sea route into the United States involved a much higher risk of interception by US Customs and the DEA. So the most reliable method involved taking smaller cargoes, up to two metric tons, and meeting with buyers at small bush airfields. This method also passed the risk of interception onto the buyers as his father was paid on delivery to the planes.

◊

Fabio was suddenly beside him. "Eduardo, it is time to take a break."

Eduardo looked around and saw they approached a small stream. "Yes, of course. Let's stop for ten minutes."

The mid-afternoon was still hot and humid, and men and beast alike sweated under the hot sun. The six men dismounted and the horses headed toward the stream to drink. Eduardo moved into some shade, unscrewed the cap on his water bottle, and tipped a good half liter into his mouth. He turned to Fabio, who was also drinking. "How much farther is it to go?"

Fabio had been working for his father for a long time, since before Eduardo was born. Eduardo placed a lot of trust and faith in his abilities, certainly more so than the other four men who accompanied them, which included Aristo. Fabio looked around. "We are now over the border. This stream marks a point approximately five kilometers from the airstrip. This track," he pointed north, "will take us almost directly there. We should arrive before dark, no problem."

10

El Alto Airport, La Paz, Bolivia

Mick Rogers walked around the Gulfstream G200 performing his preflight checks prior to their departure. Many pilots delegated this role to their co-pilots, but Mick believed the job required his experience and, in any case, Nigel supervised the loading of luggage into the luggage compartment aided by the embassy drivers and the three marines. They had refueled the jet on their arrival two days earlier and Mick's inspection of the jet provided an opportunity to examine all the visible surfaces for damage and a chance to look for leaks of oil or hydraulic fluids. The check also included opening engine hatches and checking the landing gear.

Nigel looked carefully inside the luggage space on his arrival, not seeing the well-placed package toward the forward bulkhead. Inside the device, its electronic clock counted the seconds and minutes and, if the display had been illuminated, it would have reported two hours and thirty-three minutes, the amount of time before an electronic signal would trigger a relay and allow an electrical current to flow from the batteries to the detonators.

Already aboard the jet were the four passengers: Special Agents Peter Murray and Karen Duffy, Emily Parker, and Jake. Emily's father often traveled with assistants and a chef, but with a flight time of just a little over four hours, the galley offered plenty of self-service drink options, and a plate of sandwiches from one of the local catering companies had been one of the last items brought aboard. Nigel and Mick came inside the cabin, the latter locking the main door, and they went up front to finalize the paperwork and prepare for departure.

Ten minutes later, Mick was taxiing onto the main runway. Radio clearance was obtained from air traffic control and, with a last check of the instruments, Mick brought the two Pratt and Whitney engines up to take-off power and released the brakes. The aircraft came slowly up to speed, and at 130 knots the front of the jet came off the tarmac. Nigel called, "Rotation," and Mick pulled back on the yoke. Within twenty minutes, the jet reached its cruising altitude of forty-one thousand feet and Nigel set the autopilot toward their destination.

Mick stretched and turned to his co-pilot "I'm going for a coffee, do you want one?"

"Not just at the moment, Mick."

Mick entered the cabin. Closest to the front, Pete read a crime novel. Karen and Emily faced each other over a table toward the rear starboard, and Jake lounged on the couch opposite the two women. He went down the aisle and sat next to Jake, who moved his feet to let him in. He looked at each of them. "We've just reached cruising altitude and the auto pilot has been set."

"How long to Houston?" asked Jake.

"There's a slight headwind but we should touch down at around quarter to seven, Houston time. We'll be flying over quite a number of countries, taking pretty much a straight line. The galley is fully stocked with food and drink. Karen or Pete can show you where everything is. I'll be in the flight deck so come and see me if you have any questions."

"Thanks for this," said Jake, looking at Mick and Emily. "I was starting to panic about getting back late and my father passing away before I could see him."

"That's okay, Jake." Mick patted him on the knee, stood up and went to the galley, busying himself with making a pot of coffee.

Jake took a moment to look at the pair of women across the aisle. They were a clear contrast to each other. Emily was younger, and her mannerisms, speech, and dress spelled money and a good education. He'd seen her picture in the media quite a number of times, but the real life person was always different, better in Emily's case. He could see the eyes of her father, Bill Parker, and could only guess at how different her upbringing had been compared to the children of ordinary folks.

Agent Duffy exuded coolness but Jake could somehow tell it was a well-rehearsed act, like the way he changed when he put on fatigues. If he hadn't known, he would have guessed law enforcement. Like her partner up front, she followed the Secret Service dress code and wore a suit of black pinstripe, a white blouse with two buttons undone and he could clearly see the butt of her Sig Sauer pistol in her shoulder holster. She looked like he thought a Secret Service Agent should look: smart, confident and so on. Jake also noticed that she possessed a natural beauty requiring very little make up. With her dark brown hair cut short in a fashionable bob, he'd also noticed her slim build and was trying to imagine what she looked like in her running gear.

All too late, Jake realized that Duffy returned his gaze through beautiful hazel eyes.

Duffy's eyes didn't waver from Jake's. "Mr. Walker, we weren't introduced earlier. My name is Karen Duffy, and I have been on President Parker's personal detail, and now his daughter's, for about four years. I'm sorry to hear about your father."

Jake composed himself and was forced to look away before responding. "Thank you, Agent Duffy—"

"Please, call me Karen."

Jake smiled at her. "Karen, I appreciate your kind words. You can call me Jake."

Now, Emily was looking in his direction. "How many times have you been to Bolivia, Jake?"

"This has been my first and only time, ma'am."

"Hey, let's all quit the formalities. My mother likes to be called ma'am." She smiled and her face opened and relaxed, revealing an expensive row of white, even teeth. "Mick said you are now in the security business. Did you two meet when he was still in the air force?"

Jake returned the smile. "Sorry, Emily. I've never met a former president's daughter, I guess. As to Mick, you are right. I first met him in Afghanistan in '01. My unit was one of the first into Kabul, and Mick was the pilot who flew us in and dropped us from about twenty-five thousand feet. I met him later in Afghanistan and then in Iraq during Operation Iraqi Freedom. We shared some good times together. This would be the fifth time I have flown with him, the first without a parachute and M4 carbine."

"That must have been an experience," said Duffy. "When did you get out of the forces?"

"About eight years ago."

◊

Jake remembered clearly the date of his discharge—January 17, 2004. Driving out of the gates from Fort Bragg for the last time was imprinted in his mind. Military bases had been his home his entire life, and he had felt apprehensive, almost ill, as a young recruit lifted the boom gate for him and he had left the life forever. As a civilian, he joined thousands of other veterans, relearning what it was like to lead a normal life.

The old man, his father, had been a major in the marines when his mother, Jessica, had given birth to him naturally in an army hospital in Manila in November of 1975. His father was away in Southeast Asia at the time, and a full ten years went by before he commenced any real father-son relationship. His father only took up the role because Jake's mother lost her life in an auto accident. His brother, Dan, was only three at the time and had little memory of that period, but Jake took his mother's death hard, and, as his father took up the role of both parents, he found it difficult to accept a man he hardly knew.

Over those years, they'd lived in the Philippines, Japan, Kuwait, Germany, and Africa, and, not surprisingly, Jake disliked school, mostly because he was always the new kid and his friendships never lasted. Jake's clear recollection of childhood was one of loneliness and a constant need to protect himself against the bullying and taunts that 'newbies' always attracted. So it was no surprise, at least to Jake, that he skipped a lot of school.

After he turned fourteen, his father sent him back to the States from Okinawa to board at the Valley Forge Military Academy in Wayne, Pennsylvania. Jake recognized a last ditch effort by his father to provide him with an education and an undisguised hope that he would follow in his father's footsteps toward a military career.

To his surprise, Jake found his calling at the Academy and forged real friendships of the kind that he'd never had before. Mature for his years, he bounced through the hazing and bullying that typified life in American military schools in the 90s. His schoolwork never really improved, but he enjoyed the physical exercise and showed leadership and courage. Ultimately, though, his lack of academic prowess caused him to run away shortly after his seventeenth birthday and enlist in the US Infantry, where he underwent basic combat training at Fort Benning, Georgia.

In 1998, Jake was posted to Kuwait to support Operation Desert Thunder, a response to Iraq's threat to shoot down U-2 spy planes. The Third Infantry Division saw little action that year and, toward the end of 1998, Jake applied for selection in the US Special Forces. They accepted him and he went back to Fort Benning for one of the toughest selection processes ever devised, a selection that Jake passed with only eight other men from an original intake of forty.

◊

Duffy was asking him a question. "So you saw action in the Middle East after 9/11, Jake? I was still in college during that period."

"What were you studying?" asked Jake.

"Studying to protect my father," broke in Emily.

Despite the lame joke, Duffy laughed. She had an infectious chuckle and Jake realized something he hadn't felt in a long time: attraction. He smiled back and Duffy added, "Hey, if I'd known where my criminology studies were going to take me, I would have joined the Army too. No, being on the president's protective detail was a terrific experience for a young Secret Service agent. I've traveled throughout the States and have been to Europe and Asia. And now I get to babysit when Emily travels too."

"Where's home?" asked Jake

"I was born in Boston, the youngest with three very protective brothers. My uncle James was a captain in the Boston Police Department, and I guess I took an interest in law enforcement from some of the tales he told me when I was young. Two of my brothers, Todd and William, are now in the Boston PD. Francis, the eldest, took a different route and works in banking."

The three continued chatting, blissfully unaware of the danger below them.

11

Panama, 5km north of the Colombian border

The men reached the airstrip late in the afternoon and tended to the horses as their first priority. Four crates, each of which contained 125 kilograms of cocaine, now sat on the ground—much to the delight of the horses that had carried them, who were now tethered in the shade of a sixty-foot Cativo tree, one of many bordering the airstrip. The airstrip ran for about eight hundred yards and was totally absent of vegetation. Several years ago, Eduardo's father had sent in a team of twenty men to construct it over a four week period, all by hand, but with the aid of horses to take away the larger trees and roots. Once removed of the trees, roots, and smaller bushes, a crop duster came in regularly to spray the strip with a chemical defoliant to keep the jungle on either side at bay. The airstrip ran roughly west to east in the middle of one of the least populated places on the planet, the Darién province.

Eduardo and his men sat or lay under the trees. The sun was past its peak but the temperature, even in the shade, was still in the nineties. They, too, had taken water and ate some of the bread, fruit, and cheese they'd brought with them. Fabio checked and cleaned his favorite possession, a Heckler and Koch MP 5 submachine gun. Eduardo and the others each carried M16 assault rifles, military issue, that he assumed his father had acquired in exchange for drugs or money. Eduardo also carried a Smith and Wesson revolver, but he was not planning on shooting and had never shot the gun out of anger.

"Eduardo," said Fabio, "what time is the pilot due?"

"The plane is due to land here at ten o'clock," replied Eduardo. "We have about six hours till then, and I suggest we try to get some rest as we'll be traveling back as soon as the exchange has been made." He stood up and went to get his satellite phone from a satchel. "I'm going to call my father."

◊

Back in the family home, some 40 miles northwest of Medellin, Leandro Ortiz stood in his conservatory, transplanting orchids. He loved their complexity, beauty, fragrance, and many colors. On a rare holiday in Fiji in the late 90s, when he could still travel, he traveled from Nadi to see the Garden of the Sleeping Giant, an orchid garden started in the 1970s by the late Raymond Burr, perhaps most famous for his portrayal of Perry Mason in the television series of the same name. That visit had started a new obsession for him, but one that he enjoyed immensely.

Leandro was somewhere in his sixties—no one knew exactly how old because he kept his past very secret. Nonetheless, he had been a ruthless enforcer when he was younger and his body remained fit and hard from a daily workout on the grounds of his property. He heard a knock on his door and one of his bodyguards came through. "Sorry to bother you, sir. It is Eduardo." He walked over and handed him a phone that was connected wirelessly to a satellite system and a dish on the roof of the sprawling fifty-room complex he called home.

"Eduardo."

"Papa, how are you?"

"I am well, a bit tired, perhaps. Working too hard. Where are you?"

"We are at the airstrip, waiting."

"How is Aristo?"

"He is sulking, but I have had a long talk with him. Our trip up here has been good for him, and I think he will stop his partying ways and learn the business."

"I will believe that when I see it. When do you think you will get back?"

"About two days, perhaps three. Much depends on the weather."

"Have you seen anyone?"

"No, it's been a very quiet trip."

"I am paying the fuckers up there a lot of money for protection. Promise me you will call me if you get any trouble."

"I will, Papa. Good night."

"Good night, Eduardo. Give your brother my love."

Leandro set the phone down. A tic started under his right eye and he brought up his hand to tend to it. This job didn't feel right and he regretted his haste at sending his only sons on such a trip. He had survived a long time by trusting his instincts, when many smarter men had perished or languished in prison. He brushed aside his negative thoughts and focused again on his orchids.

12

Gulfstream, Gulf of Panama

Mick checked their position from the onboard GPS and turned on the intercom. "Ladies and gentlemen, to the right of us is the border of Colombia and Panama. We have about two hours flying time to Houston and I'll be making a small course correction in about fifteen minutes. Any questions or needs, come and see me or Nigel in the cockpit." He turned the intercom off.

"Been smooth air today, Mick. Ever been to Panama?" asked Nigel, looking to the landmass off the starboard side.

"Never got the opportunity, and it still remains one of those countries I would least like to visit. I had a few pals that did some covert work there about twenty years ago. You remember Noriega?"

"Wasn't he some pot-shot dictator during Reagan's time?"

"In the late 80s. Yes, that's the one. A few high level people didn't appreciate his close proximity to the US and his anti-US sentiment. CIA went into Panama and dragged him back to the US. First ever case of rendition, if I recall. He's in a French jail now."

The men were silent for a few minutes, taking in the view. "I feel like that coffee now," said Nigel, getting out of his seat. "You want some? I think there are some sandwiches in the galley, too."

"Sounds good. If there's anything with mustard, it's got my name on it."

Nigel went aft into the cabin. He saw Agent Pete on the first seat on the starboard side, his head resting on a pillow as he attempted sleep. He considered making some coffee and food but thought twice and instead walked to the back of the cabin where Agent Duffy reclined in a club chair facing the rear, reading a novel. Opposite Duffy was his employer, Miss Emily, looking out of a starboard window. Their extra passenger, Mr. Walker, lay on the couch on the right with his head near the bulkhead adjacent to the bathroom, his eyes closed.

Emily looked up as Nigel approached and said, "Miss, I am just going to rustle up some coffee and sandwiches. Can I get you anything?"

"Some coffee would be good, Nigel. Thank you," she replied. "And yes, I am feeling hungry. Bring back a selection, could you? I am sure Karen and Jake here would like something, too."

Eight feet below, Qadir's device counted down its final seconds. Precisely twelve hours and fifty-three minutes since Qadir pushed the green arming button, a switch activated by the timing mechanism closed and, a millisecond later, an electrical current flowed from a nine volt battery to wires coiled around the detonator. As the current flowed, the wires immediately got hot, which was all that was needed to ignite the primary explosive in the detonator and the resulting shockwave caused the secondary high explosive to explode.

As Qadir had foreseen, but not corrected, the device had been placed with the red area pointed out toward the fuselage. So instead of directing most of its explosive force inwards and toward the cabin, most the energy and hundreds of ball bearings ripped through the fuselage and created a six foot wide hole in the port side and floor of the baggage compartment. As the explosive device was not adequately anchored to the spar that it was attached to, a large number of fragments of the casing were also directed through the cabin floor and forward against the bulkhead.

The cold air moving past the plane at six hundred knots offset much of the heat from the explosion. So although vital connections for fuel coming from the left fuel tanks were severed and aviation fuel spilled out, the fuel did not ignite. However, a number of electrical wiring looms were destroyed, and hydraulic fluid gushed out from a tangled mess of severed lines.

Reactions in the cabin were slow, but then everything is when a bomb explodes. Although not placed correctly, the device contained sufficient energy to create a large hole in the fuselage and the plane immediately depressurized. As the warm, pressurized air rushed out, anything loose or not tied down fell into the gap created by the bomb and into the thin air at forty-one thousand feet. This included all of the items in the luggage compartment and, even though the hole created in the cabin floor was a bit too small for him, Nigel went into the opening and out into the atmosphere before anyone could react. Nigel felt nothing during this time and splashed into ocean, already dead, three minutes later.

Jake nearly went out with the co-pilot, but he automatically reached for a handhold when the explosion triggered and held this grimly with both hands as the plane went into a steep dive.

"Oh my God!" cried Emily, not quite believing that she'd seen Nigel disappear through the hole in the floor. As the plane commenced into a steep descent, it took all her strength to hold herself in her seat, strength that faded within seconds as nearly all the oxygen and air in the cabin disappeared and the plane's remaining occupants started to experience anoxia.

Gulfstream G200s have an automatic oxygen system for crew and passengers. The system is triggered by a sudden change in pressure and, as its makers intended, masks automatically dropped down from the ceiling in the cabin. Still hanging by one hand, Jake held his breath and reached his left hand up and grabbed the nearest mask. He pulled it to his face and found that he could breathe.

Of the women, Duffy was the first to react. She was pinned to her seat facing upward to the rear, but found she could just reach her mask, which she pulled toward herself and placed over her mouth and nose. *Shit, shit,* she thought and then noticed Emily was slumped over the table between them, held there by her lap belt. Emily's eye had split —not badly, but there was blood on the table.

The noise and pressure was intense, but Duffy forced her torso upward and managed to grab the other mask. She lifted Emily's face and managed to place it over Emily's nose and mouth. Within about fifteen seconds, Emily started to stir. The plane remained in an almost vertical descent, and Duffy noticed that Jake had positioned himself with one foot wedged into the window area, holding his weight. She felt reassured by his presence.

In the front of the cabin, Pete slumped over the partition next to the galley. Without a seat belt and before he could attach his oxygen mask, his head had slammed into the partition in front of him as the plane went into its dive.

In the cockpit, his oxygen mask firmly attached, Mick struggled to bring the plane into level flight. In the thirty seconds or so since the loud bang, the plane dropped through twelve thousand feet. Multiple warnings, both audible and lit, were going off and the controls were sluggish, to say the least. He throttled the engines back and continued to pull hard on the steering yoke. At the same time, he went to the VHF radio and clicked "transmit" on the control panel. "Mayday, Mayday, Mayday. This is Captain Rogers, pilot of G200, registration November One Zero Five Five Alpha Zulu, en-route from La Paz to Houston. We have suffered major loss of control, currently at flight level One Zero Zero, ten miles east of Panama. Latitude seven nineteen zero north, longitude seventy seven fifty eight sixty west."

Slowly the atmosphere thickened and the controls started to respond, enabling Mick to level the plane out at just over five thousand feet. He started going through his emergency checks.

In the cabin, Jake was first to respond and relaxed his grip on the handhold beside him. "You two okay?" Both women nodded.

Jake removed his oxygen mask and moved quickly forward, avoiding the gaping hole in the floor. He reached Pete and lifted him back into the seat. He was bleeding heavily from a one-inch gash in his forehead and his right eye was bruised and starting to close, but the blood made it look worse than it was. Jake fastened Pete's seatbelt and pulled down an oxygen mask. He placed the mask over the man's nose and mouth and felt his neck for a pulse. It was just there, but quite feeble. Condensation started to appear in the mask, assuring him that the man was breathing. Jake moved to the cockpit and opened the door.

Mick looked back to the door, his face bathed in sweat. "What happened back there?"

"An explosion, cause unknown. There's a large hole in the fuselage to the rear of the port side wing. Nigel's gone. Sorry Mick, he went out before anyone could react. Peter is near the galley with a head wound, but is otherwise okay. Karen and Emily are fine. They were strapped in. Where are we?"

Mick took this in, and his thoughts went to his friend and colleague. He looked at the altimeter as it passed through five thousand feet. "Sorry, Jake. I think we're going down." He tapped the fuel gauges. "We are losing fuel and my air brakes and some of the other systems we need to remain airborne are no longer working." He looked to his right. "We're currently over the Gulf, but close to the southern coast of Panama." Mick pulled back on the controls and the jet went into a gradual bank to the right. "I think we can make land, but the nearest airport is too far away."

"What can I do?" asked Jake.

"Hold on a sec." Mick listened to a weak response on his headset. "Roger that, United Seven Two. We've had an explosion onboard, we are losing fuel and altitude and it looks like we will have to ditch. Am heading on course zero eight zero at flight level four five. Will call again if I get opportunity. Out." To Jake, he said, "Sorry, buddy. The good news is that I managed to get away a Mayday and this was picked up by a United flight heading to L.A.. The bad news is the terrain in this part of the world is pretty rocky." Mick pointed down. "Not real familiar with it. Over there," he pointed right, "is Colombia. We are just going over the coast of Panama. We are descending at five hundred feet per minute, roughly. The other good news is that I still have a rudder, but the ailerons are sluggish and we will be out of fuel very shortly. I don't know what is over that range ahead, but I figure it has to be better than what I can see right now. Go and brief the others and buckle up. I'll try my best and will call 'brace' when we are near to landing."

"Okay, Mick. No point wishing I'd gone commercial." Jake smiled, despite the fact that his joke could be his last. "If anyone can get us down in one piece, it's you. See you on the ground." He squeezed Mick's shoulder before moving aft into the cabin and closing the cockpit door.

The women looked toward him. "Don't worry," he called out. "Let me sort out Pete and I'll be with you."

Jake looked through the various overhead lockers and the wardrobe on the port side. He found several pillows and made Pete as comfortable as possible. He was still unconscious, so Jake placed the pillows on his lap and against the cabin wall and moved him into what he hoped would be the best position for a rough landing. He moved aft, looking for more pillows and blankets, which he gathered up and gave to Karen and Emily.

"We're going to crash aren't we, Mr. Walker?" asked Emily.

"Mick said he was going to *land*," replied Jake. "Pete's

unconscious—a blow to the head, but he's breathing okay and I've strapped him in. You should prepare as well." Noticing the blood on Emily's face, he went back into the washroom and came out with some tissues. He passed them over. "Here, put some pressure on your eye to stop the bleeding."

Emily took a tissue, applied it to the small gash above her eye and brought the tissue out to see it. "Well, would you look at that." She reapplied the tissue and sat back.

A loud bang reverberated through the cabin and they all flinched.

"What was that?" said Duffy.

Mick's voice came through the speakers. "I believe that was one of our engines. Good news—we have another."

Good news, thought Jake. Funny how some people could remain optimistic even when faced with danger. He looked through the window over his shoulder. The ground below loomed closer, and he saw a small range of hills fall away behind them. He contemplated taking one of the forward club chairs but sat down on the couch and fastened his seatbelt instead. *Everyone knows it's safer at the back of the bus.*

In the cockpit, Mick looked around for somewhere, *anywhere,* to land. There was jungle canopy as far as the eye could see, another range of hills to his front and, as he looked left, he spotted a valley that looked better for landing. He throttled back his remaining right engine and banked left. His airspeed was still over two hundred knots and yet they descended, no longer able to maintain level flight.

He spoke into the intercom. "Mick here, again. We are going to be on the ground within the next sixty seconds. Please, brace for impact."

In the cabin, both women adopted a brace position, leaning

forward with their arms on the table, their heads within inches of each other. Emily reached out, took Duffy's hand, and squeezed. "Have I told you how much I appreciate you, Karen?" Duffy squeezed back and tried to control her breathing.

Jake tightened his belt and said, "Hold on, you two." He grabbed the handhold that had saved him earlier.

Up front, Mick tried to keep the plane level. With four hundred feet of air to the top of the canopy, he spotted a bush strip to his right. Then, he lost power to the remaining engine.

Mick's passengers also noticed the lack of an engine, which stopped without any bang this time. The only sound was air whistling past and into the hole in the fuselage. Jake risked looking up and saw through the window opposite that the treetops were only a few feet below. He put his head down and held on tight.

13

Panama

Eduardo and his men heard the plane long before they saw it. They hadn't noticed the explosion twelve minutes earlier at forty-one thousand feet, but heard the plane's remaining engine as it crossed over the mountain range to their west.

José, the boy of the group at seventeen, turned to Fabio and remarked, "Boss, the plane is early."

"That's not our plane, you fool," said Luis before Fabio could say the same.

"No, it's not," Eduardo broke in. "Our plane is a single engine Cessna. That is the sound of a jet engine."

"Get everyone and everything under cover," Fabio barked to the men. Within thirty seconds, men, animals, and equipment were well under the canopy and the men peered skyward through the trees. Eduardo looked at Fabio and raised his eyebrows. "I have no idea," said Fabio. "It could be coincidence. It could be someone else using the strip. It could be an ambush or the military." He turned to the group and waved his hand urgently. "Men, be prepared to move if that plane lands. It shouldn't spot us if we stay right here."

As the plane came closer, they could tell that it was not on course to land and José spotted it through gaps in the canopy. "There!"

At that point, the plane's remaining engine fell silent and it became apparent, at least to the more intelligent of the group, that the plane was in trouble. Eduardo edged out into the airstrip and saw the jet coming down about a mile to the north of the airstrip. It went over the horizon created by the canopy and they all heard an enormous crash and tearing of metal and trees as the plane and the earth met each other. The noise seemed to go on and on, and then there was silence.

Fabio came out to join Eduardo. "Holy shit!" said the older man. "No one is surviving that."

"José and Jorge, stay here and mind the horses and our camp," said Eduardo. "The rest of you, come with me. Bring two of the horses," he said, addressing Luis and Aristo.

14

Air Traffic Control, Los Angeles Airport

Robbie Simpson, a junior controller at the flight tower at the Los Angeles airport (LAX) received the radio notification from United Seventy Two. He flicked a switch and spoke to his supervisor, John Wallis, two floors below him. "John, this is Robbie."

"Yes, Robbie."

"United Seventy Two out of Bogotá has just reported a Mayday over the Gulf of Panama. The aircraft is a Gulfstream G200, registration November One Zero Five Five Alpha Zulu. It was flying to Houston. They've been trying to raise the pilot again on radio, but have had no further contact. The last known position reported by the pilot was ten miles west of the Panama coast, near the border with Colombia. The pilot reported an explosion."

John Wallis was a thirty-year veteran of LAX. "Thanks, Robbie. Any further contact, let me know." He turned to his screen and punched in the registration number. When the details came up, he let out a gasp.

He turned around to his deputies, Spencer Dyson and Julian Sherman. "Gentleman!" he said, getting their attention. "We've received a Mayday from a Gulfstream G200 registered to former president Bill Parker. From the radio transmission received by a United flight, the pilot reported a major loss of control and an explosion. Last known position was ten miles west of the Panamanian coast, just north of the border with Colombia. The flight manifest shows his daughter Emily Parker is onboard."

Dyson said, "I knew something was going to happen today. I swear."

"Well, our day just got busier. Spence, get onto Houston, the plane's destination, and report this in. Make sure you talk to one of the top men." Wallis looked at Sherman and said, "Jules, get onto Washington and elevate this, NTSB and FAA only at this stage. I'm just going upstairs to brief the boss."

15

The White House, Washington, DC

President James Richard Watson was reviewing paperwork in the Oval Office. He rarely spent time alone these days and getting a few minutes of solitary time, even if it involved reviewing a report on the Federal Reserve Bank, was pure bliss. Into the fourth year of his first term, he was a Democrat and the former governor of New York, the only governor of that state to make it to president and the first of African descent. It was also an election year and the biggest debate was the economy. At forty-seven, he was young for a president, but not the youngest, and had entered politics after a successful career in law. He had a supportive wife and First Lady, Julia, and three children, Benjamin, William, and Andrea.

A number of issues troubled President Watson, not least how to extricate his country from the conflicts in the Middle East. He wanted faster progress and wished that his predecessor, Bill Parker, had been more cautious in his response to the events of September 11, 2001. The past was the past, however, including the state of the American economy he'd inherited. Publicly, America was the strongest, most resilient and innovative economy in the world. Privately, the president believed his beloved country was a potential basket case and technically insolvent. Put simply, the richest country in the world had been borrowing money, borrowings that had been ill-directed toward bailing out the financial sector. Unemployment was rising, the US dollar was barely holding its head up, and millions of Americans were facing, or currently experiencing, dire financial circumstances. To top things off, the election was only a few months away, and the press had been ruthless about the state of the economy, public debt levels, and public spending, particularly toward health and welfare. Inequality, the issue of gains going to the wealthy, while the middle class and poor went backwards, it was the new word in the media.

He tried again to focus on the report in front of him from a private think tank, proposing a breakup of the Federal Reserve Bank and the repayment of public debt by the simple act of crediting the bank accounts of bond holders. The secretary of the treasury, Paul Jameson— a man who had made his money and lots of it through private equity dealing—had warned him about the economist who had written the report, insisting that the man was without credibility within his own profession and telling him to ignore such theories, which had no basis in fact or fiction. Regardless of his own views, such radical change to the creation of money and debt would never suit the powerful interests he knew he now served.

A knock on his door brought him out of his thought processes, and, before he could say anything, his chief of staff, Bob Perry, entered and closed the door. "Sorry to barge in, James. We've just had a report from the FAA about a US-registered private jet going missing. I wouldn't normally bother you, but Bill Parker's daughter, Emily, was on board."

The President dropped the report. "Where and when, Bob? What do we know?"

Bob sat on the arm of one of the sofas and peered across the Resolute Desk at his boss. "It's Parker's own personal jet heading into Houston from Bolivia where his daughter had been visiting to open a school that Parker's foundation funded. A United jet flying to L.A. picked up a Mayday from the pilot. Its last location was over the Gulf of Panama, near the border with Colombia."

"Has it crashed?"

"We don't know; the pilot is off the air. If they've gone into the Gulf, there's probably no hope and the area of Panama and Colombia near to their last location is very remote and not plane or people friendly."

The president rose from his seat behind the desk. "Okay, who knows about this?"

"Me and one of my staff, United Airlines, controllers at Houston and LAX, and the FAA. There could be others and there no doubt will be before long. So far, no calls from the media, but you know how stories like these tend to get out quickly."

The president pressed his intercom and waited for his private secretary, Mary Daniels to respond. "Yes, Mr. President."

"Mary, ask the joint chiefs to meet me in the Situation Room, call the head of the FAA and get me a phone line to Bill Parker immediately." He looked at his chief of staff. "Bob, go and rustle up the necessary people. I want to know details, including what assets we have in that area, military or otherwise, and what satellites we can deploy to assist in a search."

16

Houston, Texas

Delia Parker sat in her drawing room at their ranch, southwest of Houston. The imposing forty-two room dwelling sat on seventy-five acres of prime real estate and had been in her husband's family for four generations. She was going over the proceedings for that night's fund raiser for the Foundation. It may have had Bill's name on it, and he did a great job as its figurehead, but all the real work in organizing, investing, managing, and raising money came down to Delia. Her thoughts were with Emily, who was flying back from Bolivia after a successful new school project that they had both nurtured over the last three years.

She knew that Emily was a reluctant participant in Bill's foundation. Bill had protected his youngest daughter since the day she was born. Their other daughter, Belinda, Emily's older sister by three years, had been given much more freedom. Freedom to choose her career, for example.

Bill was a politician and Emily's childhood had been affected around the realities of being the youngest daughter of the governor of Texas and then the US president for eight long years. This naturally restricted both Belinda and Emily as far as what they did and with whom. However, Bill was always more willing to allow Belinda to follow her own way than he had been with Emily.

Bill had never expressed disappointment at not siring a son, but he'd made it quite clear in his actions, if not words, that he wanted Emily to follow in his footsteps. He'd skillfully "guided" her toward studying political science in college and was even now working toward her nomination for the US Senate in three years' time.

Delia and Bill were both active supporters of the Foundation and what it had achieved. However, the Foundation was also a vehicle for raising Emily's profile and ambition toward entering politics. *I must have a long chat with her when she returns,* she thought.

Just then, Bill entered the room, followed by their two Jack Russell terriers, Allie and Denny, who were still chasing each other after a good walk with her husband around the property. "Hi, honey. Boy, can these two go. They never stopped for a second. What's happening?"

The dogs fussed around Delia and she patted them saying, "Hey, babies!" To her husband, she said, "We have to leave in about an hour and pick up Emily from the airport on our way." They heard a knock at the door and their housekeeper, Rose, opened it carrying a cordless phone in her hand.

"Mr. Parker, a phone call for you. She lowered her eyes. "From the president, I do believe."

Bill took the handset and Rose let herself out. "Jim, how the hell are you? You know that..."

"Hi, Bill, not a social call I'm afraid. I've just had word that your daughter's plane may, I repeat *may*, have gone missing." All the blood ran from Bill's face and Delia rushed to his side. "Bill, are you there? Bill?"

Bill Parker leaned on his wife. "It's Emily, honey. Yes, I'm here Jim; I'll just put the handset on speaker." He looked at the phone and pressed a button.

"What's happened, Jim?"

The president's voice came through the speaker. "Hi, Dee, sorry to be the bearer of bad news, but we think your daughter's plane may have hit some trouble earlier today. I just got word less than five minutes ago. I wanted you both to hear the news from me and I want to assure you that everything I can do, I will."

Parker felt his wife's legs buckle slightly and he held her tight. "Has the plane crashed?" he asked, trying to keep his voice level and calm.

"We don't know yet. I am getting my top people together as we speak. All we have is a Mayday call from your pilot saying that he was experiencing trouble and providing his position, just west of Panama, over the Gulf. He reported an explosion, but we have no way of confirming this at present. The Mayday was picked up by a United commercial flight on its way to L.A.. Anyway, I have to go and get organized. I don't yet know what we can do, but trust me, all the resources I have at my disposal will be deployed to locate your daughter and the others on the plane."

"Thanks, Jim. We appreciate your call. Please phone again when you have any further news."

Parker placed the phone on a nearby table and took his wife in his arms. They held onto each other for several minutes before Delia composed herself. "Bill, I think you need to call Anna. The Foundation can manage without us for one night."

17

Darién Province, Panama

Emily opened her eyes and realized she was still alive.

Her surroundings were unrecognizable. She could see trees and foliage, and everything that was left of the plane was covered in debris. She concentrated a bit more and recognized the cabin of the plane, but when she looked to the front of the cabin, she couldn't see the front anymore. It looked like, well, like the rain forest. She could smell aviation gasoline and hydraulic fluid, and she quickly made up her mind to get out of her seat. She unfastened her seatbelt and fell immediately to her left, cushioned by the sofa and, she realized, by Mr. Walker.

Winded and still disoriented, she then realized the wreckage sloped down toward the ground, slightly on its left side. She pushed herself up onto her feet by grabbing an overhead locker handle and inspected Duffy. She could see very minor cuts and abrasions around her face, but she otherwise looked okay. She shook her gently. "Karen, wake up. Come on, we have to get away from the wreckage."

Duffy started to come to and Emily unfastened her seatbelt, holding her into her seat.

Behind her, Jake stirred. He felt dizzy and sore, but a quick visual check told him that he had no serious injuries. He looked at the two women, assessing the situation, and unclipped his seat belt. He could no longer see the front of the plane, and there was a large hole where the tail section of the plane appeared to have come to rest against the base of a large tree. He moved past Emily and climbed down toward the opening, bracing his feet against a large tree root, once there.

He called back up, "Emily. How is she doing?"

"She's coming to." Then turning to Karen, "Karen, I'm going to help you up and I want you to hold onto my arms. I'll lower you down to Mr. Walker who appears to have found our exit. I think it's a good idea if we get out of here quickly."

Jake said, "I'm sorry, Emily, our positions should be reversed. Can you handle her?"

"Sure," replied Emily as she braced herself against the forward arm of the sofa and took Duffy's weight.

Jake reached up as Duffy slid on her bottom toward him. She came into his arms and he held her for a moment.

Duffy opened her eyes and gazed into the bluest eyes a mere six inches from her face, very conscious of Jake's strong arms around her. "Thanks, Jake. I'm starting to feel better." He let her go and she turned to Emily. "I don't know what you guys need from inside, but I need my handbag and backpack. They should be above my seat."

Miraculously, the overhead locker above Duffy's seat had not burst open, but Emily found she just couldn't open it. "Emily, slide down here. I'll see if I can get it," said Jake.

Emily slid down and, together, the two women slipped past the tree base into rain forest where they found a fallen log and sat down. As they looked at the wreckage, the tail end of the plane was barely recognizable. The tail fin and both engines had gone and there was no sign of the front end of the plane.

Jake crawled back up into the fuselage and managed to open the overhead locker and retrieve Duffy's gear. He emerged and made his way cautiously toward the cargo area where he looked inside. Empty, as expected, but he could clearly see scorch marks along the jagged edge of the hole in the fuselage. He called out, "Come over to this side, you two."

When they reached him, they could see the devastation caused by the fuselage as it had torn its way through the forest—a clear path of broken tree limbs and bushes stretched back about seventy-five yards or so, some twenty feet wide. Jake handed Duffy her belongings and she squatted down, sorting through what she needed.

"You have no idea how lucky we are," said Jake pointing to the jagged edge of the fuselage. "I'm no expert, but the scorch marks inside the hold there suggest an explosion and explosives. A bomb in other words."

"You're suggesting this wasn't an accident?" said Emily, still holding a tissue to her head.

"Can't be certain, but there will be traces of explosives if this was all due to a bomb of some sort."

"Let's face it," said Duffy, looking at Emily, "you've always been a target for extremists and nut jobs. That's why you have a protective detail."

"Some protection detail," said Emily, chuckling.

Jake did a personal inventory. Before leaving his hotel, he had changed out of his suit into jeans and was wearing his favorite Timberlands on his feet. Only a t-shirt covered his torso and he remembered that his jacket, which contained his cell and wallet, went out of the plane at around the same time as the co-pilot. He could remember putting it on the side of the sofa.

"Anyone got a cell?" said Jake.

"Here," said Duffy, retrieving hers from her handbag, which she then passed up to Jake.

"What about you, Emily?"

"Everything I had was in the baggage compartment. Stupid, I know. If the flight had been longer, my handbag would have been with me. Not that it contained anything particularly useful," she added.

Jake looked at the screen. There was no signal, but it had a full charge. He handed it back. "No signal, but keep it turned on. You never know."

Duffy slid the phone into the inside pocket of her jacket. It was hot and humid and she wiped her brow, contemplating whether to take her jacket off. The forest was very quiet and they looked around.

"Look," said Emily, pointing back to the wreck. "When we hit the ground, the plane must have sheared into two pieces, exactly at the point where the bomb detonated in the baggage compartment. Let's see if Mick and Pete made it. We need to find the rest of the plane."

"It could be anywhere," said Duffy.

"It can't be far," said Jake. "It's hard to remember…we were just gliding for the last thirty seconds or so and then a huge bang. But we know now that the plane split in two, and I figure the plane must have hit the ground or a tree or something and split apart back there." He pointed to the devastated pathway through the rain forest behind them.

"Sounds plausible," said Emily. She picked up a stick and held it in her fingers. "This is the plane coming in." She swept her arm across and pointed to a point on one side of the stick. "We know the plane was fractured here on the left side. If it split in two," she broke the stick, "it seems reasonable to suggest that the front part was deflected to the right, or at least to the right of the path that we took."

Jake couldn't quite follow Emily's theory but realized he had no better ideas. "The plane could have gone the other way as well, but as we can't remember the impact, that way seems as good a place to start as any." He pointed to their left. "I suggest we stick together and head that way. If we don't find the rest of the plane, or its path, we may then need to split up." He looked for the angle of the sun. "We've still got plenty of daylight left, but if anyone gets lost or cut off from the others, we should head back and meet up here."

Duffy picked up her backpack and put her handbag over her shoulder. The whole situation seemed surreal, without precedent, but she felt good that Jake was with them. His actions and presence gave her a confidence that would otherwise be absent. Wanting to lighten the mood, she said, "And what are you going to call me, Jake?"

Jake looked at her and remembered how good she had felt in his arms a few minutes ago, toned and fit as he'd surmised earlier. "Oh, I don't know," he said. "I kinda like Duffy. I take it you have a weapon in there?" He pointed to the bag around her shoulder.

Duffy smiled, "You and I both know my Sig is right here." She lifted her jacket to show her shoulder holster and Jake noticed the swell of her breast, his gaze lingering a second or so too long. Duffy pretended not to notice his attention, looked around, and unwrapped a mint she found in her bag. "Anyone want one?" she asked holding out the candy before popping it in her mouth.

Emily shook her head.

"I'm good," said Jake. He turned and led the way through the undergrowth in search of the rest of the plane.

18

The White House, Washington, DC

Five men assembled around the table in the Situation Room on the ground floor of the West Wing and a larger number of aides sat in chairs around the perimeter. Daniel Salzburg was the chairman of the joint chiefs and an admiral in the navy. General William P. Campbell of the army sat as the vice chair and General David King of the air force made up a quorum. Two other members of the joint chiefs were unavailable. Bob Perry, the White House chief of staff, and Secretary of State Amanda Nichols also sat at the table.

President Watson strode into the room and the attendees rose. "Sit, sit, we don't have time for that." The president took his seat at the top end of the long table. "Has Bob briefed you on what we know?"

Salzburg spoke. "Yes, Mr. President, but it's not much."

"What are we doing to find out more? We got any ships out that way? How long will it take us to get out there?"

"We don't have many assets in the area, Mr. President," replied Salzburg. "If we are looking around the southern end of Panama, the closest ship we have is the *USS Peleliu*, an amphibious assault ship coming back from a six-month mission in the Indian Ocean. She's old, but has great capabilities for air search and rescue. She is steaming home to San Diego and is currently in the Panama Canal. Due to exit into the Gulf in around three hours."

"Okay, what say we get her commander on the line now?"

Salzburg turned around and locked eyes with a young lieutenant sitting behind them with a group of other assistants. "Jerry, get hold of Captain James via sat phone and patch it through here." The young man stood up and headed away to talk to the communications staff to see if they could raise the ship.

King addressed the table. "Mr. President, we have several satellites in the area, but the nearest can only provide a low angle, low resolution picture of the area in question. If there is a flaming wreck, we might have a better chance, but it will be difficult for us to pinpoint where things are. I have two satellites being moved closer, but it'll be morning before these can be of much use to us."

"Don't these planes have radar and transponders?" asked the president.

"Yes," said King, "both, but only the emergency locator transmitter, or ELT, is of any use to us. All general aviation aircraft have them and they are designed to activate in the event of a crash. The range of the ELT will depend on a number of factors, but if we get within twenty to thirty miles of the crash site, we will be able to pick it up."

"Amanda, call the director, what's-his-name, of the Secret Service. I also want the CIA contacted and to know exactly what human assets we have down in that part of the world."

As Nichols headed for the door to make her calls, Salzburg's aide came back into the room. "Captain Peter James is on line three, sir."

Salzburg pulled the wireless speaker phone toward him and pressed a button. "Captain James, are you there? This is Admiral Salzburg."

James voice came through clearly. "Yes, Admiral, I can hear you well."

"I have the president and some of the joint chiefs with me. What is your current location and situation?"

"Admiral, Mr. President," acknowledged James. "Well, we're on our way home to San Diego, in the canal and scheduled to exit in about two and half hours. Roughly twenty-five nautical miles to the Gulf exit."

"Hi, Captain James, this is Jim Watson. We have received a Mayday from a private jet, which was last reported ten miles or so west of the Panama coast, the part that borders Colombia." He paused. "On board that jet is Emily Parker, Bill Parker's daughter."

James's voice came through the speaker. "That's a remote part of the world, Mr. President. Not a place I would choose to ditch a plane. I take it you would like me to steam down there and have a look?"

"Captain James," said Salzburg, "you are our closest response. How soon before you can get aircraft in that vicinity?"

"I have some jets that can be overhead within the hour," replied James. "But someone is going to have to clear this with the Panamanians. For our choppers, I think we could manage to be fifty or so nautical miles from the southern tip of Panama by the morning, well within range. Again, we'll need the Panamanians' support, but our rotary aircraft are much more effective in search and recovery operations and we should be able to deploy them at first light."

"Thanks, Captain James," said the president. "I will personally make the call to President Rivera as soon as I can. Meanwhile, make preparations and go as quickly as is legal and safe. Admiral Salzburg will get back to you about launching any planes later tonight."

The president turned to Perry. "Bob, rustle up some Panama experts and brief me in the next hour. I'll then make a call to Rivera."

"Will do, Mr. President," he replied.

"I assume the Panamanians will already have received a report about the Mayday?" asked the president.

"There are mandatory reporting requirements under our obligations to the International Civil Aviation Organization, Mr. President," said King. "So yes, their FAA equivalent should be aware and might be able to assist in the search operation."

"Thanks, David. Okay, everyone, time to get moving. Bob, please keep Bill Parker in the loop about what we are doing. If you need me to call him, let me know."

19

Darién Province, Panama

With the two horses bringing up the rear, the four men moved cautiously toward the crash site. They only had a general idea of its location and Eduardo figured they had traveled about a thousand yards from the northern edge of the airstrip. Eduardo estimated they still had at least three hours of sunlight left. Ten yards ahead, Fabio held up his hand as a signal to stop. He turned around and gestured for Eduardo to join him.

Eduardo moved up and looked past Fabio. About five yards to Fabio's front, Eduardo could clearly see the area where the plane had come down. Fabio pointed to his right indicating what appeared to be the tail section about fifty yards away.

"I suggest we go up this way," whispered Fabio, pointing up through the trees.

"Okay, I'll lead; tell Aristo to stay here with the horses."

Eduardo moved off placing his feet carefully and, three minutes later, he crouched about ten yards from the wreck, staying hidden and watched for any signs of life. Fabio joined him and said, "It looks quiet. Where's the front section, wings and so on?"

"Perhaps on the other side. I'll check things out."

Eduardo moved quietly to the wreck and peered inside. *Nothing and no one.* He signaled for Fabio and Luis to come up and he moved to the other side of the wreck. The entire forest was unusually quiet and he had a bad feeling about being there. He came back around the rear and saw Fabio examining the ground.

"Look here," said Fabio, pointing at a wrapper from a candy of some sort. "Nothing else. Nothing, no baggage, no bodies, but this here, suggests someone got out of there alive."

"I agree," said Eduardo, pointing into the body of the plane. "There is some blood on the window up there, but not a lot, which implies the person or persons are not badly wounded."

"We need to find the rest of it," said Fabio. He pointed back along the path created by the wreck. "Let's head back along there and see if we can get a clue to where the rest of the plane is."

Quickly, they retreated, picked up Aristo, and headed back along the trail created by the tail wreckage. Twenty yards beyond the spot where the jungle started again, they found the impact site. From the look of the broken trees and bits and pieces of the plane, it looked like the plane had hit the canopy, which was generally about sixty feet high, and had ploughed through until it hit a large tree.

Fabio patted what was left of its trunk. "Here's where it came in, struck this tree, left wing over there," he pointed to what was clearly a wing section about thirty yards away, "tail section there and the front looks like it headed that way." He pointed to the right of the path that the tail section had taken.

20

Darién Province, Panama

With Jake leading, they traveled about one hundred yards from the location of the tail section before bits of the plane, including one of the wings, started to appear. Then, to their left, was the final piece. The forward part of the cabin lay on its side. The front nose was crushed to about half its normal size and bits of wiring, pipes, and torn aluminum fuselage were everywhere.

"Let me go in first," said Jake.

Jake knew what he would find as soon as he climbed over the edge of the wreck and put his head inside. Death has its own smell and, although it was dark inside, he could still see Pete's body lying at an awkward angle, strapped into his seat, but hanging limply. He stepped on what used to be the wall or side of the cabin and climbed over what remained of the seating.

Jake recalled Pete's weakened state from the decompression, resulting lack of oxygen and the knock to his head. His seat appeared broken in several places and, judging by the angle of his head, Jake believed his neck was broken, probably from the impact. He felt for a pulse, but could feel nothing. Pete was dead.

He called out: "Mick, Mick, can you hear me?"

"He's gone, Jake," said Duffy from outside.

Jake moved to the cockpit door, but found he couldn't move it. It was wedged completely into the framework. "What can you see, Duffy?"

"I'm next to the cockpit windows and can reach inside as some of the glass has shattered. There is a lot of blood around his head and shoulders and I can't find a pulse."

"Okay. I'm sorry, but your partner, Pete, is gone as well. I'll see if I can salvage anything and meet you outside."

Duffy walked over to Emily who sat on the ground.

"I'm so sorry, Karen," said Emily. "You and Pete have been a team for quite some time. I'm really going to miss him and Mick."

"Nigel, too," said Karen.

"Damn, I'd forgotten. He was a nice man."

Jake came out of the cabin and walked toward them carrying some bottled water and wrapped sandwiches. "There should be enough here for a few days. I also grabbed this," he said, showing Pete's firearm, the standard Secret Service issue Sig Sauer, and a box of rounds. He passed around some of the water and sandwiches, placing the remainder, together with the pistol and rounds, into a black leather satchel he had found.

"I don't think you'll need Pete's firearm, Jake, unless you plan on finding us some fresh meat." Duffy smiled at him. "But keep it for the time being."

Jake squatted down and took the tissue from Emily. He peered at the wound, refolded the tissue and wet it with some of the water. He reached over and cleaned the dried blood from her cheek and around her eye. "Needs a stitch, but should be okay for now."

"Thanks, Jake. What should we do?" said Emily. "Anyone have any idea how far to the nearest town or road?"

"I'm not really sure, but the little bit of geography I know tells me this part of the world is pretty remote," said Jake. "As for what to do, our worst choice would be to try and walk our way out of here. There could be help nearby, but we have no idea which direction to go. These planes have black boxes that are designed to withstand impact and record the conditions within the plane, including the last few words of the pilots."

"Jake's right," said Duffy. "The plane should also have an emergency beacon that'll keep pinging, or whatever they do, so that search crews can locate the wreckage."

"Well, I'm not sleeping in there," said Emily.

"It doesn't look like it's going to rain," said Jake, "but it might get colder. Duffy, why don't you see if you can find some blankets inside the plane? Emily, there is plenty of wood around." He pointed back to the track laid down by the wreck. "Nature's calling, but I'll give you a hand when I get back. We'll get a fire going." He headed past the wreckage and into the canopy.

Duffy moved over to the plane wreckage and climbed inside the cabin. She tried not to look at her friend and stifled tears as she peered into the wardrobe. There were a couple of blankets there, which she grabbed along with some pillows that had fallen out of the overhead lockers. She found a third blanket and headed back outside.

As she stepped out, someone struck her between the shoulder blades. She crashed to the ground and her assailant pressed her down with his foot against her neck. "Do not move," he said in accented English and pressed home his point by pressing the muzzle of his rifle against the side of her head.

Another man came over, armed with a machine gun of some

kind, and he roughly searched her. *"Tiene un arma,"* he said.

He pulled her onto her feet and she considered taking action, but the rifle pointed at her didn't waver. The second man reached in and took her pistol, tucking it into his pants. "Sit," he said.

Duffy realized that she still had her cell phone. She turned to her left and saw that another two men held Emily and were bringing her over. She thought of Jake. *Stay down, Jake.*

Forty yards away, Jake watched on from his place hidden within the canopy. He'd heard voices and immediately went into hiding. He counted four armed men and figured that the most probable purpose of armed men being in the vicinity was drug running. He needed to proceed very cautiously.

21

The White House, Washington DC

In the Oval Office, Amanda Nichols said to the president, "This is a bad situation, Mr. President. If the plane has gone down in the Gulf, there is very little hope for the passengers and crew."

"The chances aren't much better if they made land in that part of the world," said Bob Perry. "There is very little in the way of flat land—lots of hills and valleys, mangrove and semi-tropical rain forest. Walter here can tell you more," he said, pointing to Walter Cornwell, an analyst with the State Department that specialized in Central America.

"Yes, thanks for coming on short notice, Walter," said the president. "As Bob may have mentioned, we have a navy vessel on its way through the canal as we speak. I am going to call President Rivera and ask him for permission to fly a search and rescue mission, starting with a flight over the site by jets this evening. It's 8:00 p.m. now and will be dark down there soon, so the jets can only achieve an initial reconnaissance, but with any luck we should be able to pick up the emergency beacon. We will send a much larger force, including helicopters and medical teams, at first light and bring in some satellite support if it is needed."

Walter Cornwell took a sip of water. "First, Mr. President, Rivera is likely to be helpful. Panama is very reliant upon us for aid and financial support. He is only one year into the job, but relations with the country are pretty good. If we explain the situation, I am sure they will cooperate, but I wouldn't be surprised if Rivera asked for concessions. They do have fixed and rotary wing aircraft, but the navy has more than enough assets to do a thorough search in that area. If he insists, however, we should permit him to assist in the search operation." The president wrote a few notes as Cornwell continued. "Now, Darién province. This is a large area, over a hundred square miles, but the same remoteness extends into Colombia. It's a national park and there are few people who actually live there—a few indigenous populations and a couple of coastal villages. Cocalita is one quite close to the search zone. It's not my area of expertise, but I suspect that speed is critical if survivors are to be found.

"Darién and the area to the south of the border with Colombia is a major area for guerrillas, insurgents, and the drug trade. It is the only area where the Pan-American highway stops. There are no roads in or out, just a few logging trails. How familiar are you with the FARC?"

"Bunch of guerrillas, opposed to the Colombian government, operate out of remote areas, responsible for kidnapping and a lot of the narcotics trade," said Nichols.

"Yes, Secretary, you are well briefed," said Cornwell. "FARC stands for *Fuerzas Armadas Revolucionarias de Colombia*, excuse my pronunciation. Roughly translated, The Revolutionary Armed Forces of Colombia. They have long history dating back to the sixties and have Communist roots. Due to the remoteness of the area around the crash site, FARC has a major presence in the area. It is a definite no-go zone for any foreigners and kidnapping and extortion are commonplace. Even tourists in the major cities are taken there while the guerrillas negotiate ransoms. If any of the people on the plane survived, they may have very little time before someone finds them."

"Thanks Walter. Please stay while I call Rivera." He picked up a handset and pressed a button. "Mary, could you please call President

Rivera in Panama and see if he will take my call."

He turned to his chief of staff. "How're Bill and Delia Parker holding up, Bob?"

"I spoke to Bill twenty minutes ago. He's all for flying down there straight away. I didn't speak to Delia and Bill said she was resting. I gave him all the facts we have and that we should have an air search underway commencing tonight. He was obviously upset, but he thanked me for what we are doing."

The president's handset rang and he picked it up. "Thanks, Mary. President Rivera?"

At the other end, President Rivera was in his home. "Yes, James, it is me, please call me Martin. What can I do for you?"

"My call is about a missing plane, Martin. I am sorry we have not yet had the chance to talk, let alone meet. Something I will rectify."

"Don't think of it, James, you are the busiest man on the planet. I was expecting your call as I was briefed by my aviation people only an hour ago."

"So you already know a US-registered jet has gone missing in the south of your country?"

"Yes, we have a lot of commercial flights which are approved to overfly us and we track most of them by radar. Our operators also picked up the pilot's Mayday."

"The plane was a private jet, Martin. We don't know what happened to it, but it was flying from Bolivia to Houston and it happened to have Bill Parker's daughter aboard."

"Oh no, that is really bad news. What can I do to help?"

"As your people would know from the Mayday, the pilot

reported that there had been an explosion on board and that he was unable to make the nearest airport. Given its last known location was just off the southern tip of your country, we would like your permission to commence a search and rescue. We have a navy vessel just coming through the canal as we speak, and I want to fly a couple of jets over the area tonight, and at first light send a larger number of helicopters over the area to search for the wreckage and, hopefully, survivors."

"I am very sorry this has happened, James. Of course we will help. If we weren't such a poor country, I would send a fleet of our own helicopters down there to help."

The president frowned and looked toward Amanda Nichols, who gave him a nod. "I am sure we have enough aircraft and people to do this, Martin. How much financial support are we providing under the bilateral aid program this year?"

"I believe we will receive fifteen million dollars this year, James. It is very generous, but we could always do with some more."

"I appreciate your help, Martin. I am going to authorize a special, one-off payment of ten million, as a sign of the excellent relations we have with Panama. It's nothing when I think of all the gas and time we save going through your canal."

"That is excellent," said Rivera. "I will make the necessary calls now. Naturally, liaise with our aviation authorities so that we avoid any further accidents."

"Thank you, Martin. How about you fly up for a formal visit later this year? I'll have my people call yours, okay? Good-bye."

"Have a good night, James."

The president placed his receiver back on its cradle. He stood up and walked toward the window, spending a few seconds looking at Washington at night. He turned. "Ten million! Ah well...Walter, thanks for your briefing. It was very helpful."

"A pleasure to help, Mr. President." Walter Cornwell stood up and left the room.

"Bob, get onto Admiral Salzburg and get those jets in the air."

As Bob rose, the president turned to Amanda Nichols. "Amanda, how did you go with the Secret Service?"

"I spoke to Phil Venables, the director, earlier. Naturally, they are concerned about their two agents and he offered whatever assistance he could. But get this. He later called me back and told me that one of the agents on the flight, Pete Murray, had called his boss in Houston before they departed. A security consultant asked for a lift and permission was granted. I have few details, but the guy is security cleared. He's been working down there for the embassy and the pilot vouched for him. On that basis, he was allowed onboard."

"You don't think this guy had anything to do with this?"

"Too early to tell, but I don't like coincidences. Name of the guy is Jake Walker and Venables said they were checking him out and would let us know more as soon as possible."

"Okay. What did you get from the CIA?"

"I finally got onto McBride an hour ago. He said the nearest human assets were in Colombia and he promised to call me again in the morning."

"Alright, Amanda. I'm going to be up for a while. Come and see me if anything further develops."

22

Panama Canal, Panama

Scott Davis breathed in deeply and looked over the starboard rail of the *USS Peleliu,* an amphibious assault ship, which steamed through the Panama Canal to its home port of San Diego. As the sun set, the sky revealed colors of red, orange, and violet. At the end of almost six months in the Arabian Sea and the Indian Ocean supporting a number of regional efforts, including piracy off the coast of Somalia and providing air support and heavy lifting capacity to US forces in the Middle East, Scott was tired and thinking about home. The ship was about four days from port and it was Scott's first time through the canal.

A marine helicopter pilot, Scott had been flying for three years and he was looking forward to getting home to his wife, Charlotte, and his two daughters, Louise and Abbie. This tour had been rewarding, particularly when compared with the six months he had spent in air support operations in Afghanistan. Nonetheless, he wanted to be back home with his family and was thinking about asking for a training role or something that would keep him stateside for a while. As he watched the sun setting, he reflected on his career in the marines and his misfortune at being led by a man he truly hated, Captain Jason Copperton.

Put simply, Scott believed that the man was a coward and had caused the death of two of his friends. The problem with a belief like this was that Copperton also knew he had failed in combat and, as he didn't like someone knowing this, he'd taken a personal dislike to Scott.

Just over two years ago, Scott went straight from flight school into air support operations in Afghanistan with the Third Marine Aircraft Wing. Although Scott only trained fifteen hours on the AH1 Super Cobra, a further couple of months flying time resulted in a reasonable pilot and he successfully supported ground operations.

In September 2009, three Super Cobras (affectionately called Snakes by their crews) were tasked to support the 5th MEU (Marine Expeditionary Unit), who were under sustained enemy fire in a mission in the Herat province. Scott was on call that morning, with his co-pilot and gunner, Walt Kennedy. Copperton was in one of the other Cobras and Dianne Stanworth and her co-pilot, Andy Edwards, were in the third.

Dianne had been in Scott's flight training course and they were good friends, not only because they'd both gone through the same hurdles, but also because there was a level of trust between them; as one of the mature trainees, he had treated her with respect. She was the baby of the unit, the youngest Super Cobra pilot in the marines at twenty-two years, and a female to top off her reputation.

Their support mission that morning had been successful, supporting a squad of marines that had been pinned down by enemy mortar and machine guns. The officer on the ground called in the fire accurately with smoke to show their location and the location of the enemy, and it only took a couple of fly-pasts to neutralize the threat with a mixture of rockets and guns. The Cobras stayed on station for another fifteen minutes and then Copperton ordered the flight back to Bagram airbase.

They flew in arrow formation at about two hundred knots and Scott estimated a further fifteen minutes flying time to Bagram when Dianne's voice came over the communications channel. "This is

Whiskey Two, small arms coming from the ground at ten o'clock."

Scott looked down to their left and saw a number of figures firing at them. Small arms couldn't penetrate the Super Cobra's armor, so Scott didn't worry, but he saw a flash in his peripheral, and as he turned and looked left, he saw Dianne's Cobra head toward the ground, auto rotating as it went, smoke spewing from the engine cowling. Dianne kept her cool, reporting her experience over the radio even as she descended, but her Cobra had sustained a mortal blow and it went into the ground hard in a cloud of dust.

"Christ, what happened, Walt?" asked Scott.

"Pretty sure it was an RPG."

Scott called in the incident to Copperton and, as he watched, he half heard the man call her position through to flight control. About two hundred yards to the north of the crashed Cobra, Scott saw a small settlement, roughly fifty or so buildings, and he banked left and took position ready to provide support.

Dianne's Cobra had not exploded on impact, but a fire quickly started and, from about five hundred feet, Scott watched as Dianne exited the Cobra and went to attend her co-pilot, Andy Edwards, who remained in the front gunner's seat. At that point, a number of rounds hit their Cobra and Walt responded letting fly with sustained bursts from the Cobra's dual 20 mm machine guns.

"She's not going to last till a rescue bird arrives, Scott," said Walt.

Scott called Copperton over the radio, "Whisky One, suggest we continue to provide support, Whiskey Two is taking hits. Over."

Scott noticed that Copperton was above him and to his rear. "Scott," said Walt, "take her down and I'll lay down some covering fire."

Over the radio Copperton's voice was unequivocal, "Negative, Whisky Three, I have taken a hit from small arms and am losing hydraulics. There is nothing we can do here. Return to base. Over."

Scott flew past the wreckage about one hundred feet off the deck and Walt sent two rockets toward one of the larger buildings. He could clearly see armed men on the roof and about a dozen or so figures on the ground, directing fire at him and Dianne.

Scott flew over the settlement and heard the two rockets impact. He circled around and could see in the distance Copperton's Cobra heading back toward Bagram. On the ground, Dianne's Cobra had caught fire and she was lying on the ground, returning fire with her service pistol.

"Whisky One, this is Whiskey Three. Roger your difficulties, I am staying here as long as I can. How long till we can get support? Over."

The Super Cobra is a fine attack helicopter, but there is only room for two people. Scott knew that it was only a matter of time before he ran out of fuel, or ammunition, or both. *Where was that support?*

Copperton's voice came in his ear. "Whisky Three, you are ordered back to base. Over."

To Walt: "That guy is a jerk, coming round for another pass."

"Roger that," said Walt, "we have two rockets left and about enough rounds for a couple more passes."

Scott watched the targeting by Walt on his heads up display and their last two rockets detached and lit up toward the settlement. Out of her helicopter, Dianne was unable to communicate and, as they flew over and Walt opened up the guns, he could see sand and rock being blown up from rounds that were coming in her direction.

Copperton's voice again. "Whisky Three, I gave you a direct order to return to base. Over."

Scott replied, "Negative. We will remain for as long as we can."

Armed figures were creeping closer to Dianne and Scott brought the Cobra into a hover and they laid down some fire with the guns. He turned to the right with the intention of laying down some cross fire and, as he brought the Cobra around, they saw three figures run toward Dianne, who had moved further away from the wreck, which was starting to burn fiercely.

"It looks like Andy's gone, Scott," said Walt.

Walt tried to target the running figures, but only succeeded in putting one down. In a flash, two men reached her and put her down on the ground.

Several more figures broke cover and still more small arms fire peppered the front of the Cobra.

Walt targeted the running targets and managed to hit several, but his guns fell silent after only a couple of bursts. The men brought Dianne to her feet taking her toward the small settlement. Scott knew they could do no more. *Damn Copperton*, he thought and turned the Cobra around.

Back at Bagram, they were just going through their post flight checks, when Copperton wrenched open Scott's door, his face a mask of rage. "Davis, I gave you an order to return to base. You are a fool and could have gotten all of us killed there today."

Scott couldn't control himself. "You should have stayed on station with us. Dianne was alive and we could have supported her until help arrived. Instead, I watched them capture her and she will soon be dead, if she isn't already." He clambered out and put his face right up to Copperton.

Walt was already out of the Cobra and grabbed his friend's shoulders. "Scott, come with me."

Scott glared at Copperton and shrugged off Walt. He moved closer so that their faces were inches apart and whispered: "You spineless cunt."

As Walt pulled Scott away, a red-faced Copperton retorted, "Get him out of my sight, Kennedy, before I put him on a charge."

Later that night, Scott went over to the maintenance area and spoke to his ground crew chief. Yes, Copperton's Cobra had sustained hits, but there was no major mechanical damage, certainly no loss of hydraulics. *Copperton had been lying.*

Ground troops were quickly deployed to the accident site, but despite an extensive search of the settlement, they found no sign of the missing pilot. They did retrieve the charred remains of Dianne's gunner, Andrew Edwards.

Seven weeks later, Dianne Stanworth was executed by al-Qaeda for propaganda purposes, her head removed from her body by machete. Her execution had been videoed and uploaded to the internet. Scott couldn't watch the video and never would, but when he heard of her death and the manner in which it had happened, he had wept for the young girl and the gutsy, gallant way she had served her country.

That day was imprinted in Scott's mind and Copperton never forgot their altercation, the situation working itself to the point where Copperton used his rank at every opportunity to put Scott down and make his life hell. After six months on tour, he and Walt rotated back to the States and had then been posted to the *USS Peleliu*. Scott started to believe in himself and his country again. Then, three months into the tour, Copperton reappeared and was again their flight leader.

◊

Walt joined him at the rail. "Briefing in fifteen, Scott. Something's up—all crews are required to attend."

23

Caribbean Sea

The Cessna headed almost due south toward Panama. Wayne Costello checked his instruments once again and looked at his watch: almost eight thirty. His instruments indicated twenty thousand feet and a cruising speed of 230 knots. He'd taken off from Grand Cayman at seven and he was due over the landing site at ten. The onboard GPS was working fine and would take him right there. This was the easy part of the journey; the tricky part was the return.

The plane was new, although Wayne didn't own it. As far as he knew, it was owned by a shell corporation and his cover was that he was a business man checking his investment portfolio and doing business in the Caymans. He'd flown to the Caymans from Florida the previous day and met two men he knew only as Doug and Carl at the NCB Bank in George Town, their usual rendezvous. The two aluminum brief cases behind him contained five million dollars. His pay, four hundred thousand dollars for each trip, was in his own numbered account back at the bank. Sure, the thought had crossed his mind to simply take off with the money, but he knew that he would be looking over his shoulder for the rest of his life if he did.

The Cessna Corvalis TT had a range of about fourteen hundred miles, so the trip to the southern tip of Panama was well within its capacity. His return journey, though, was back to Florida where he would drop his packages about twenty miles offshore at a predetermined place programmed into his GPS. Not enough fuel for the round trip, so part of the deal was a refuel from the Colombians, pumped by hand from drums at the airfield.

On the flights to the Grand Caymans and from Panama to Florida, it was necessary to fly over Cuba, but Wayne easily obtained the necessary permits via a corrupt official in George Town.

This was Wayne's fifteenth trip to Panama. The US Coast Guard had captured the previous occupant of his position, who was currently in prison—twenty plus at Pensacola, he'd heard. *Ah well, at least the climate was pretty good there.* Wayne had no intention of being caught though, and he had been thinking about an exit strategy for several months now. He knew that he could not do this line of work forever, and he'd been planning for the future. From the trips he'd done over the past two years, he had more than four million in the bank and he figured it was time to retire.

Wayne's father was a Brit and Wayne had been able to get a British passport, which he intended to use to settle in the Bahamas. Flying a few rich tourists around had to have less risk than this. He wasn't going to push his luck.

24

Atlanta, Georgia

Tania Olsen sat in her office overlooking the largely empty newsroom of CNN at its headquarters in Atlanta. She was flipping between online news sites looking for new stories, which she could then tailor and then feed through to the producers. Tania had worked for the company for over ten years and had cultivated some of the best contacts over that period. She managed a team of ten juniors and was a valuable source of exclusives for the broadcaster. Almost 9:00 p.m., three hours to go before her shift ended and she could go home for some rest.

She was reading about yet another roadside bomb blast in Iraq, another four US soldiers dead, and she contemplated whether this one had any unique features to make it worthy of news. Her phone rang and she picked it up.

"Tania Olsen."

"Tania, this is Casey."

"Hi, Casey," said Tania. She knew Casey as a contact from the Washington Post. "What are you doing working at this hour?"

"Got a call from a friend. It's a hot story, so I came in to write it up."

"So hot you want to give it to me?"

"Well, we'll be posting it online in the next hour and it will make tomorrow's print run, as an exclusive if we time it right. So yeah, I owe you, but you can't broadcast it until after ten, okay?"

"Sure."

"A plane has gone down in the Gulf of Panama."

"Okay."

"Bill Parker's personal, private jet."

"Shiiit, you sure of this?"

"Impeccable source, five-nine, hazel eyes. I'm sure."

Tania laughed. "Tell me more."

Casey's voice became serious again. "Later. Anyway, it's not Bill himself. It's his youngest daughter, Emily. She was onboard returning from Bolivia where she's just opened a new school, funded by her father's charity."

"Survivors?"

"Too early to say. Pilot got off a Mayday and is no longer transmitting. Last known position was over the Gulf at the southern end of Panama. Couple of Secret Service agents aboard as well."

"You been able to verify this?"

"Can't reach anyone at the FAA. Our White House guy is chasing it down from his end, but this is the real deal, I'm sure of it. Plane was due in Houston just after six. Didn't arrive. I went online to check on Parker and found there is a fund raiser in Houston tonight. It's gone ahead, but none of the Parkers are there."

"Alright. Thanks, Casey, we'll do some checking as well, and if it's verified, we'll run it. I appreciate you thinking of me."

"No problem. Ciao."

Tania put her phone back on its cradle. Outside in the newsroom, Nick Porter was writing up a background story on the New York Federal Reserve chairman. Tania's unmistakable New York twang broadcasted from her office. "Nicky, in here please." The young man quit reading, got up and went into her office. "Thanks, Nick. You have an hour to verify that Bill Parker's personal, private jet crashed into the Gulf of Panama earlier today. Call the FAA, Houston airport. Try and reach Parker himself, if you can. My source tells me that his daughter Emily was on board, but we can't broadcast this if it's not one hundred per cent."

"I'll get onto it."

As Nick reached the doorway: "Send Trish in."

A moment later and her assistant appeared in her doorway. "Hi, boss, what's up?"

"A plane crash in the Gulf of Panama. Bill Parker's jet, daughter Emily aboard. Get me as much background as you can." Trish sat down and started to take notes. "Type of plane? How old is it? Who was on board? What's Emily Parker's involvement here? When did she leave Bolivia?" Trish's pen kept scratching as questions flooded from Tania's mouth.

25

Darién Province, Panama

The men made a cursory search of the wreck. They found some beer and spirits, which they loaded into saddle bags on the horses. They left the sandwiches and non-alcoholic drinks they also found. Jake watched as Duffy's handbag and backpack were searched. One of the men held up items of underwear and said something that caused a lot of laughter. He scattered everything, finding nothing of interest. From her handbag, one of the men cut the straps, which he then used to bind the women's wrists.

One of the men stooped, picking something up from the ground, and there was a hurried conference between him and another. It was difficult to see in the setting sun, but Jake made out an older man with dark hair and a beard. He was carrying some sort of submachine gun. The man he was talking to was younger, possibly in his twenties. He was the one that had taken Duffy's Sig Sauer and was now pointing it toward Duffy and Emily.

The younger one summoned a third man over who proceeded back inside the wreck. The fourth man covered the two women with an assault rifle. It wasn't too hard to figure out that Duffy's identity as a Secret Service agent was probably now known to the men. *What else did they know or suspect?* The third man came out from the wreck and he walked over to the two, whom Jake now thought were the leaders, and showed them something, which Jake couldn't see. The older one spoke to him and he raised his arms, showing what looked like an id card in one of his hands. The gesture was universal: "I don't know." *Don't know where his weapon is,* surmised Jake, gripping the very pistol they'd been looking for.

A bit of an argument ensued and the older man went over to Duffy and asked her something. Jake couldn't hear, but her response was obviously not the one they wanted, and he hit her face with the back of his hand. Some of the men were now facing outward, and Jake wondered if they now suspected there'd been other survivors. The two leaders conversed again and the younger one pointed back through the tree line.

Jake surmised their search was now over and they prepared to move. The women were hoisted onto the horses and the group made its way through the trees.

Jake followed the party and, after thirty minutes, they came to a large cleared area, which revealed itself as an airstrip. Jake's previous guess that they were drug runners of a sort now seemed certain.

They met a smaller group and Jake could count six men. All were armed. Duffy and Emily were assisted down from the horses and told to sit down, which they did. They were about halfway along the airstrip and Jake had positioned himself on the other side of the strip, roughly thirty yards or so away. The fact that they were here and it was getting dark suggested they still had a rendezvous to make. If they'd already done their business, they would have been elsewhere. It was possible they'd seen the crash and had simply come back to the airstrip as a place to stay overnight, but their rendezvous with two other members of their group told Jake otherwise.

The older man called the group together and two of the men headed back into the tree line and two others went fifty yards or so up and down the airstrip, settling down just inside the tree line. *Sentries.*

Jake realized he was tired and rested his head against the tree behind him. He closed his eyes. The women needed his help. Run or fight? He'd been here before…

◊

A seasoned sergeant in the Special Forces, Iraq had been Jake's home since Operation Iraqi Freedom in March '03. The coalition forces had captured Baghdad in the first week of April and he'd spent the rest of the year helping the coalition forces consolidate their position within the country.

Jake's unit, the 4th Special Forces Group, had been operating in Iraq since late 2002, well before Operation Iraqi Freedom commenced. However, he was not involved in the earlier phase and joined elements of his unit in March '03 after spending six months in Afghanistan pursuing elements of the Taliban. At the end of the six month tour, he'd been eligible for leave, but volunteered instead to join his unit in the push to capture Baghdad. The Iraqi resistance was token and ineffective, but the coalition forces throughout the country were soon to understand that the battle was far from over.

In December '03, well after Jake should have gone back home for a rest, he found himself in a fierce street battle in northern Baghdad, which had escalated following the capture of several Ba'ath party members and militants. At about 1900, he and his small team received orders to return to Camp Victory, a large base established at the airport on the edge of Baghdad. Their recall was not unusual and he fully expected his team would be deployed elsewhere, if not that night, then in the morning.

With Jake (Luke) that afternoon were demolitions Sergeant First Class Eddie "Frogman" Martinez, a tough twenty-four year old from Boston; a weapons sergeant and rookie, Kevin "Calvin" Klein, a twenty-three year old who hailed from Iowa; and another rookie and medical sergeant, Frank "Tony" Bennett, who was only twenty and hailed from

Kentucky. Frank had served in the Rangers before completing USSF selection and took on the call sign of Tony, a good voice, Luke'd heard. He'd fought with these guys for several weeks and they were forming into a good team.

Under the cover of air support from Apache helicopters and F16s, two Blackhawks arrived and they boarded the first one, which took off immediately. There were two gunners manning M60D machine guns on each side and two pilots. They hung on as the Blackhawk flew at full power only a hundred feet or so from the rooftops, the twin General Electric turbo-powered engines screaming at full speed.

Luke was watching the gunner on his right and thought, *How young is this guy?* Sensing this perhaps, the young man turned toward Luke and smiled. He started to say something, but there was a huge bang and the helicopter lurched to the side. When Luke opened his eyes, the door gunner was gone, his harness and the mount for his 60 severed in the explosion. As smoke filled the cabin, he suspected they'd been hit by an RPG.

There was no time to react or even think as the Blackhawk dropped out of the sky and they hit the ground hard and fast. Somehow the pilot managed to find a square of some sort and the wreckage hit the ground, bounced and then came to rest next to a dry fountain to one side of the square. Luke and his team scrambled out the nearest door and he checked them each: no visible injuries. He ducked his head back inside and saw one of the pilots had been injured and was being tended to by the other pilot.

Suddenly, the Blackhawk came under direct fire and several rounds punched through the open windows at the front as the armored glass was no longer there. Blood splattered as the pilot was hit in the head and chest and, as the second pilot recoiled, Luke could see from his wounds that the seated pilot was dead. The other pilot took cover and scrambled back to Luke's location at the door. The gunner on the other side opened fire with a long burst at the buildings opposite the square.

He locked eyes with the pilot and realized she was a woman. "Hi there, ma'am," he said, "Luke."

She slithered out of the door and squatted next to him. "Lieutenant Shaw—Paula." She pointed up to the cockpit. "We've lost Jerry."

He noticed that the door gunner was still firing and jumped into the cabin and tapped him on his helmet. "Hey, gunny, save some."

Luke moved back to the door and focused on their surroundings. His men, Tony, Frogman, and the new guy Calvin, were down behind a low wall about ten feet away. A few more shooters had joined others on the opposite side of the square and the helicopter was now coming under regular fire with rounds seeming to hit the crippled Blackhawk every ten seconds or so. He turned back to the gunner and called out, "Bring the 60, we can't stay in here." The gunner detached the 60 from its mount and scrambled back towards him.

Luke turned to the pilot, who remained low by the door, and touched her on the shoulder. She looked up and he could see the raw fear in her eyes. "Paula, can you get on the radio?"

The woman looked at him and said: "Sure." Her helmet was still connected to the Blackhawk's communications systems and she moved her mask over her face and started to converse with her unit.

Luke stepped down out of the wreck and pulled the gunner with him over to his men. It was only a small space, but they were managing to keep their heads down. As Frogman and Calvin returned fire with their M4 carbines, Luke noticed the rate of fire coming in their direction diminished accordingly. The sun had now set and muzzle flashes they could see in the windows provided some indication of the threat they faced; Luke noticed figures were also seeking to enfilade their position from positions on the rooftops.

Frogman also noticed the threat and turned round to Tony.

"Tony, get your head up and direct some fire to the building over there."

Luke looked at the door gunner. "Gunny, what's your name?"

The kid looked like his helmet was going to swallow him. "Private Ortega."

"Well, Ortega, we need your 60 to start doing its job. Set up the bipod over there," he pointed to a space between the helicopter and the fountain structure. "How many rounds do you have?"

"Just this box here, Sarge," he replied, tapping the ammunition box which was attached to the machine gun.

Luke looked in and saw it was about half full, about two hundred and fifty rounds. He ducked his head inside the cabin but couldn't see more. He dropped down beside the gunner. "Ortega, we don't know how long we are going to be here. Three to five round bursts maximum. Watch for muzzle flashes on the rooftops, windows, and doors. Tell me when you have used half of your ammo, okay?"

He moved back to what remained of the Blackhawk. The pilot joined him on the ground. The Blackhawk had lost its skids in the crash and a lot of everything else and sat on its belly. Jake noticed some fuel was leaking, spilling down into the cabin and trickling toward the ground. He looked at what remained of the engine and rotors and pointed up. "Rocket propelled grenade. Did you see it?"

"No. One minute we were flying along at about 150 knots, next we were here." She paused. "I just got onto my unit, not good news. The nearest ground troops are a unit from the 15th MEU. They are about twelve clicks away to our southeast and are making their way here, but we can't get an air extraction until the morning. 'Other priorities,' I was told. They have asked us to hold out until then."

"Okay, Paula. Keep your head down behind that wall over there." Luke went over to Frogman, who was looking through the scope on his M4, and got down next to him.

He fired one round, and Luke saw a figure in a window fall back. "How much ammo you got left, Frog?"

Frogman remained focused on his front. "Only three mags."

Luke got down prone next to him and commenced firing toward the rooftops. "Can't stay here." Frogman looked at him. "Only a matter of time before the guys with the RPG launcher join the party." He pointed back with his thumb. "Bird's leaking gas. Can't get an extract. Cavalry are on their way, a marine unit about twelve clicks to our southeast and facing resistance."

"What's the bad news?" asked Frogman.

"Once we leave, we have no comms. Oh, and I'm down to this one," he indicated the magazine in his M4, "and one in my pouch."

◊

Something woke Jake from a troubled sleep and a familiar dream. He opened his eyes and noticed light that, when he sat up and looked, came from lit oil drums at either end of the runway. He figured a plane was coming in.

26

Panama Canal, Panama

Captain James walked into the briefing room which contained all navy and marine pilots on the ship who weren't required elsewhere. His executive officer, Command Master Chief Peter Boswell, shouted "Ten hut!" and the assembled officers stopped talking and stood up.

"At ease, gentlemen, ," said James. He walked up to the lectern and looked over the faces before him. He placed some notes before him and looked up.

"Earlier this evening, a US-registered Gulfstream G200, traveling from La Paz in Bolivia to Houston, reported a Mayday over the Gulf of Panama to our south. On board were six people, including two pilots and Emily Parker, the daughter of Bill Parker. There were two Secret Service agents, Peter Murray and Karen Duffy and, finally, a security consultant, Jake Walker, who was aboard getting a lift back to the States."

There was some brief chatter and James continued. "We don't know a lot more at present; we just know that the plane reported trouble and has not been heard or seen since. Its last known location was here," he pointed at a map of the region, "approximately ten miles off the Panama coast, near the border with Colombia.

"We're pretty sure it came down, but whether it went into the Gulf or made land we just don't know at present. As we are the nearest ship with search and rescue capabilities, we have been tasked to divert to the area and search for the wreckage and any survivors.

"Lieutenants Watson and Burgess?"

Two men raised their arms and said, "Sir!"

"We are not going to commence a proper rotary wing search until daybreak when we will be much closer. However, we have permission to do a preliminary fly over the area this evening, which I am tasking to you two.

"Your main focus will be to identify the crash site by homing in on the ELT and to take some photographs. Your first job will be to visually search the area offshore for wreckage and, if you get no sightings, you are then to move inland and see if you can pick up the ELT. That's all we can hope for tonight.

"By morning, we should be around fifty nautical miles from the last known position. Squads two and six will lift off at 0700 and head directly to the wreckage, if we have picked up the ELT, or to search visually both on and offshore if not.

"Burgess and Watson, come with me. The rest of you get some sleep; there will be a pre-flight briefing at 0430."

Walt turned to Scott next to him. "Something to relieve the boredom."

"Yes, let's get some shut eye." Privately, Scott was wondering if the Jake Walker mentioned was an ex-Special Forces, Medal of Honor recipient whom he had known before he joined up. He hoped so.

27

Darién Province, Panama

Eduardo squatted down next to the women. It was almost 10:00 p.m. and he'd sent Jorge and Juan to both ends of the airstrip to light the oil drums, which would serve as crude, but effective, landing lights.

"My name is Eduardo." He looked at Emily. "You are someone, no? Someone important?"

Emily looked away and stayed silent.

"You are very lucky. Unlucky to have crashed your plane, but lucky to have survived the crash, and lucky to have been rescued by me. This area is called Darién province and extends south to my country in Colombia. You could have been found by the FARC, revolutionaries, mercenaries, kidnappers, you understand? Instead, you have me." He looked at two women and pulled Duffy's security pass out of his breast pocket.

"Special Agent Karen Duffy." He tapped the pass against the knuckles of his left hand. "This is a good picture, a good likeness." He shuffled over, took Duffy's chin with his left hand and moved her face from side to side.

Duffy felt powerless; her bonds were really tight. She was determined that Emily's identity be kept secret for as long as possible.

Eduardo sat down and relieved his legs. "And you." He looked at Emily. "I don't think you are Special Agent. Too skinny and you have that rich girl look about you. What sort of woman has two Secret Service agents with her, huh?"

He looked at Duffy. "I am sorry about the loss of your partner. As I am sure you are aware, we couldn't find his weapon and this raises the probability that there is a third survivor, no? A person who has gone into the rain forest?" He spread his arms wide. "Perhaps the co-pilot?"

Fabio called him from the side of the airstrip and he stood up. "Anyway, we will talk some more. You will have figured we are not here by coincidence and have a transaction to complete."

28

Gulf of Panama

The two AV-8B Harriers were ten nautical miles out from the Gulfstream's last known position. Their flight paths had been quickly cleared by the Panamanians and it had taken just twenty-five minutes to reach this far south. They carried sufficient fuel to remain in the area for eighty minutes, if required.

Pipers One and Two were piloted by Navy Lieutenants Greg Burgess and Tim Watson, both on their second overseas tour and their first with Harriers. Their brief was to quickly quarter the area offshore, and if nothing was sighted, they were to move onshore. Special receivers were tuned to listen for the plane's ELT, which would be absent if the plane had hit the Gulf, as radio waves don't transmit well in two hundred yards of water. If the plane had gone into the water, they would have to rely on water-based search teams who would listen for the ping of the locator beacon in the plane's black box.

Both pilots used night vision. "Piper Two, this is One. Over," said Watson, who had been appointed the lead.

"Roger One. Over."

"Piper Two, we are approaching last known position. I will search the area to the west and you remain east. If nothing is sighted, we will then head onshore. Over."

"Roger One, nothing from the ELT. Out."

About two hundred feet above the water, both planes throttled back and began a visual search of the water using night vision equipment. Watson could see a couple of fishing vessels, but no wreckage of any sort. By the time he had searched a rectangle ten miles by five west of the last location, he spoke into his mike. "Piper Two, negative sighting. Will rejoin you, remain on station at flight deck five. Over."

"Roger One. I see signs of wreckage in the water, a suitcase and what looks like clothing. Join me to confirm. Out."

Watson vectored in on his partner and Burgess's voice came over the radio. "One, you are approaching the area now. Over."

"Roger that. Yes, that looks like it went into the Gulf. Over."

"One, I am also getting a faint signal which appears to be coming from onshore. There is a chance it made land. Over."

"Thanks Two, I have same reading. Suggest we go do a recce[7]. Out."

7   Reconnaissance

29

Darién Province, Panama

After the man calling himself Eduardo left them, Emily said, "Who are these guys?"

"Almost certainly in the drug business," replied Duffy. "We're pretty close to Colombia here, so they are probably dealing in cocaine. Given the airstrip, I figure there's probably a plane coming in with cash and, once the exchange is made, it will load up with fuel and drugs."

"Well, there's one thing he said that's true: we're in a bad spot. But rather these guys than the FARC. Have you read anything about them?"

"Not much more than what you see on the news," said Duffy. "Some sort of insurgents that don't like their government too much?"

"Yes, something like that."

The women sat still for a few moments, both wondering what they could do. "I can't shift these bonds," said Emily. "What do you think they're going to do with us?"

"As he said," replied Duffy, "their presence here was no coincidence. I figure they were probably waiting when our plane came down and thought they would see if there was anything of value they could salvage. If they hadn't found my security pass, we would probably have been shot."

"So you think they know about me?"

"Not yet, but it's only a matter of time. It's not every day you find a Secret Service agent. Not around here anyway. Regardless, you're worth far more to them alive than dead, so I'm not worried at the moment."

"What about a search party?"

"It's dark and remote," said Duffy. "I don't think we can expect a rescue mission tonight."

"Why not?"

"Well, my geography isn't so good south of New Mexico, but this looks about as remote as you'd want to be. Jake said that Mick got a Mayday across, but we're still likely to be hundreds of miles away from any friendly people who can search for us."

"I guess you're right," agreed Emily. "I imagine at first light, though, someone is going to be looking for the plane. When they don't find us…"

"Don't worry too much. If we do end up being kidnapped, your father will pay a ransom and you'll be released. And there's still our Mr. Walker."

"Assuming he hasn't bugged out already."

"At least you have some value to these guys," observed Duffy.

Ten minutes later, they heard an approaching aircraft and watched as a single engine plane with no lights came down smoothly from their left and touched down on the makeshift runway. After a couple of minutes, the engine noise built up loudly as it taxied toward the man called Eduardo, who was holding a torch. The engine shut down and they saw the pilot exit from a side door. He reached inside and brought out two aluminum suitcases, which he placed on the ground. Eduardo shook hands with him.

Even after fifteen trips, Wayne still felt at his most vulnerable during the exchange. After shaking hands, Eduardo offered him a hipflask, which he declined. "No thanks, Eduardo. It's hard enough flying in the dark when I'm sober."

The young man he knew only as Eduardo motioned to one of his men, who brought over a fuel handle, which connected via a hand pump to a drum containing aviation gasoline.

"Thanks," said Wayne. He moved to the fueling port on the Cessna so that they could begin to replace the fuel used on the journey. He would need a full tank to reach Florida.

As the fuel was being pumped by hand, Eduardo took the cases and handed them to the man he knew as Fabio, who sat on the edge of the airstrip and began to count the contents. Wayne wasn't worried; the money was always right. The past six trips had involved the same amount—$5,000,000 in used $100 bills in exchange for 500 kilos of cocaine, shrink-wrapped and waterproof in four packages. Wayne figured the weight of the money at around 50 kilos, based on about a gram for every $100 note. So the deal broke down to one kilo of money for ten kilos of drugs. By the time it was cut and on the street, that ratio would be much more even.

Suddenly, the sound of two jets came from nowhere and, within seconds, all could clearly see the jets' lights and hear and feel the roar of their twin jet engines as they passed overhead at about four hundred feet.

Eduardo spoke rapidly in Spanish with the older man on the ground.

"What the fuck was that?" said Wayne. "The Panamanians never come down this way. What's going on?"

Eduardo came over and motioned to the younger guy on the pump to keep going. "About three hours ago, we were sitting here waiting when a private jet came from there," he pointed into the sky, "and crashed into the forest over there.

"We had some time on our hands so we went to look. There were some survivors and I suspect those jets are on a search mission. You have nothing to worry about. It's got nothing to do with what's happening here."

The sound of the jets became louder and they overflew the airstrip again, at a lower altitude. Wayne had some experience with planes and turned to Eduardo. "They're Harriers. There is only one country around here that flies them and it ain't Colombia. Could we hurry this up? They're able to land vertically right here and now if they wanted."

"Relax, Mr. Wayne. I'm pretty sure they have been looking for the crash site. We'll load your plane up and you can be on your way shortly."

"I hope you're right."

Fabio came over and spoke to the younger man in Spanish. "The money is all there."

"*Gracias*," said Eduardo. "Give Mr. Wayne his packages."

Eduardo turned back to Wayne. "While we load up your plane," said Eduardo, "I wonder if you can help with an identity problem?" He guided Wayne over to Duffy and Emily.

"We found very little at the crash site," explained Eduardo. "Private jet, US-registered, two dead and these two here." He gestured to the women and shone his torch in their faces.

132

Wayne was feeling anxious and wanted to be out of here, but he dutifully examined the two and suddenly felt more anxious.

"I think you can imagine, my friend," began Eduardo, "that in the ordinary course of events, I would have no use for two Yankee women in the middle of nowhere. What has made me interested, very interested, is that the one on the left is a Special Agent in the US Secret Service. Her name is Karen Duffy and one of the bodies on the plane also carried a card identifying him as US Secret Service.

"So, I have a private jet, two US Secret Service agents and this woman here," he pointed at Emily. Turning to Wayne, he said, "Do you recognize her?"

Wayne looked at the woman and could see the silent plea in her eyes. "Sorry, honey," he said. "He'll find out anyway..."

He turned to Eduardo. "Do you remember the last US president?"

"Of course, who doesn't remember Bill Parker?"

"I'm pretty certain that this woman is his daughter, Emily Parker."

30

Gulf of Panama

Watson and Burgess left the crash site and flew north back to the ship at about five hundred knots, one thousand feet above the Gulf.

Watson called the tower back on the ship "November Mike X-ray Golf, this is Piper One. Over"

"Roger, Piper One. What news? Over."

"Base, we found some evidence of the plane in the Gulf, baggage and clothing, but we also picked up the ELT and found the wreckage of the plane about ten miles inland and just north of the Colombian border. It was difficult to get a visual on the wreckage, but it appears to be in several large pieces. Over."

"Roger Piper One. Any sign of survivors. Over?"

"Negative, base. But, given the nature of the wreck, it's possible someone may have survived. Of interest was an airstrip about a click or so southwest of the crash site. The strip was lit for a landing and there was a single-engine plane refueling. On the strip, we saw several people. We activated the cameras over both areas, so should have something when we get back. Over."

"Thanks, Piper One. What is your ETA? Over."

"We're about seventeen minutes away, base. Over."

"Roger that. Piper One, report to the captain when you get in. Out."

31

White House, Washington DC

President Watson walked with Bob Perry toward the residential part of the big white building. It was almost half past ten and the president was feeling tired. It was a familiar feeling and reflected the long days and nights dealing with the issues of office. Bob was taking him through his itinerary for the following day, but the president was only half listening. Bob's phone rang.

"Hello," he answered and then listened for about ten seconds.

"We'll be right there." He ended the call and looked at his boss. "The navy has located the crash site."

The president raised his eyes and thought for a second. "See if you can raise Admiral Salzburg and apologize for the lateness of the hour. I'll be in the Oval Office. Oh yes, Bob, please tell my wife I won't be up for a while, could you?"

Four minutes later, the president sat behind his desk and had barely started to get his thoughts in order before there was a knock at the door and Salzburg entered.

"Thanks for coming, Dan," said the president. "Sorry about the late hour."

"That's okay. I've been with my senior guys and we have the latest from Captain James."

"Great, fill me in."

"The *Peleliu* has just exited the Panama Canal and is steaming south toward the area where the plane was last seen. Two Harrier jets were sent to fly over the area. Offshore, there was some sign of wreckage; I understand some baggage and clothing were spotted in the water. However, they also picked up a signal from the plane's emergency locator transmitter coming from onshore. These things have a range of up to fifty kilometers in the right conditions. So, the pilots flew inland, vectored in on the transmitter and were able to get a visual on the wreckage, which is in several large pieces."

"Where exactly?"

"It's about ten miles off the coast and about ten from the Colombian border. Hilly country, coastal rain forest, so it's going to be difficult to get in and out. The pilots use night vision, but at the speed they were traveling and given the light conditions, they were unable to detect any sign of survivors. That said, one of the pilots suggested the nature of the wreckage looked survivable. The planes also carry high speed cameras and infrared, so there may be something from the prints when we get them."

"I see. That doesn't look too bad."

There was another knock at the door and Bob Perry walked in and sat down on one of the sofas opposite the admiral.

Salzburg continued. "By first light, James will have two marine Super Cobras and three navy Sea Knights in the air heading to the crash site. The *Peleliu* has a fully equipped hospital, and we will have a full medical trauma team in one of the Sea Knights and two full squads of marines in the others. If there are any survivors, they'll be in the best of hands."

"That's good, but why the fire power of the Super Cobras?"

"Well, the Harrier pilots found something else on their flight. About a half-mile south west of the crash site, they overflew a small airstrip. This was lit up for a night landing and they saw a single engine plane and some people on the ground. Our assumption is a rendezvous to smuggle drugs, but we are concerned about the proximity to Colombia and the possibility that the people on that airstrip may have found and, perhaps, detained any survivors."

"Surely not, Dan?"

"I know, I know, but we would be wise to take precautions. Remember, there's been over a five-hour gap between receiving the Mayday and the fly past by the navy. Until we get there, we just don't know what we are going to find."

"There's more news, James," said Perry. Both men turned to look at him. "The other passenger on the plane, Walker. I think we can rule him out as a threat.

"I spoke with Jen Barnett, the Bolivian Embassy's head of security," Perry continued. "It seems that Walker has just finished providing advice on security at the embassy and works for a respected firm, Jerico Security, based in L.A.. He is security cleared by Homeland and has a good record within the company.

"Also, Ms. Barnett told me that the pilot, Rogers, knew Walker from his days in the forces. I pulled his service record and here's an overview." Perry handed over a sheaf of pages in a clear plastic sleeve.

The president leafed through the pages quickly. "Special Forces, distinguished himself in Somalia, the Balkans, Afghanistan and Iraq. Medal of Honor..."

Perry intervened. "Yes, a distinguished record, a war hero. But he never did his twenty, got out in oh three. Anyway, Walker's in Bolivia and it appears that he needed to get back to the States quickly as his father has had a stroke and is in the Good Samaritan in L.A.. The pilot, Rogers, vouched for him and he got his lift. Probably wishing he hadn't now."

"So what does this bring us?" asked Salzburg.

"Who knows," said Perry. "But if there are survivors, Mr. Walker would be a handy man to have on your side."

Perry's cell rang and he punched the green button. "This is Bob." He listened for about twenty seconds. "Okay. I'll see you shortly." He picked up the remote for the TV and switched it on. "How do you get CNN?"

"Pass it here," said the president. He pressed several switches and the pleasant voice of Hala Gorani came over the speakers; behind her was a file shot of a Gulfstream jet. "Just repeating breaking news, we have confirmed that the former US president's private jet has crashed off the coast of Panama. On board was Bill Parker's youngest daughter, Emily, who was returning to Houston following the opening of a school in La Paz, Bolivia…"

"Didn't think they'd get it this soon," said Salzburg.

"They've got better sources than the CIA," said the president. "Bob, get onto this, could you? Issue a brief statement, just what we know at this stage and that we will be searching for survivors at first light. Get onto Parker as well and make sure he is in the loop. We'll send him some more security if he starts to get harassed."

"Will do."

"Dan, please call Captain James and fill him in. I wouldn't be at all surprised at the press getting into helicopters and flying down to the tip of Panama tomorrow. Last thing we need."

"Oh, Bob, organize some coffee, could you? This could be long night."

32

La Paz, Bolivia

Qadir sat on his bed in his hotel in La Paz. An older hotel, he'd chosen it because it had internet access and cable TV, the kind of place a businessman from Pakistan would stay in. He sipped some hot tea and regarded the remains of his dinner sitting on the small table near the window. The television was tuned to CNN but muted, and he glanced over. His English was basic, enough to get by, but he didn't need English to understand the montage of a Gulfstream jet over a map of Panama. He reached for the remote and listened to the newsreader.

The report didn't reveal a lot of detail, but it seemed clear that the bomb had done its job. He would have preferred to have seen the jet crash into the Gulf, but he knew that the chance of survival of a plane crash into land was very remote. He clapped his hands and made a silent prayer of thanks.

Qadir got off the bed and plugged his laptop into the internet socket in the wall. In due course, he gained a connection and opened a Gmail account. There was the usual junk in his in-box: people offering him cheap Viagra, links to great bargains—"I make $70,000 a month and only work four hours a day"—and so on. He never opened any incoming messages and he never sent any.

He opened his draft folder and there was one message in it. He opened it and quickly read the contents. It had been written by his superior, Mahmood Ali Zadran, and informed him to be cautious on his return and to use an overland route. Several of Qadir's own men had been captured by US forces. Qadir knew their tactics and the risk it entailed for his own security.

Qadir went over his itinerary. La Paz to Peru tomorrow at 9:30 a.m., then to Spain and connecting flights all the way through to Karachi in Pakistan. A long trip, it would take two days, but it avoided going through the US. He couldn't use the same passport that he'd used to enter Peru, as it had no entry stamp for Bolivia. So he'd gone back to his contact at the Pakistani restaurant who provided him with a new passport with the required entry stamp to Bolivia and a valid visa. His new name was Imran Bajar, and he'd decided to use the same cover that he had used on his way over. Earlier that day he had walked to the local markets and bought some wool samples from a merchant.

The CNN woman was onto other news and he tuned out. He deleted the draft email and clicked on the compose button. A new window appeared and Qadir drafted a response and an estimate of when he would be back in Kabul. He also relayed the news of the downed aircraft and suggested that they claim responsibility. After all, it was a great day for him and al-Qaeda, a bad one for Parker and the Americans.

He saved the email and ensured it was in the draft folder for Zadran to open the next time he opened the Gmail account. *Whoever devised this simple communication method was a genius,* he thought. He never suspected that for several years the US had been reading the draft emails from Gmail, Yahoo, and other internet accounts, particularly accounts that had been accessed from different IP addresses.

He switched off the television and prepared for his bed. As he lay down, he went over his route again, comparing it to the alternative of traveling back via Peru, pretty much a reverse of his original journey, and then flying to Europe and into Pakistan. He had weighed the risks and because he'd been able to obtain another passport, he assessed them as low.

And he didn't want to ride a horse over that mountain again.

33

Darién Province, Panama

Eduardo watched as the Cessna took off with its cargo and a full tank of fuel, its engine note fading as the pilot gained distance and altitude. After the fly over by the jets, Costello had been in a hurry to be gone and Eduardo wanted to get on his way also. He looked at the older man next to him. "Okay, it's time to finish up here. I want to be on the other side of the border by morning."

"What about the women?" asked Fabio.

"We take them with us."

"Why?"

"Fabio, you heard who the blond woman is. Bill Parker is a wealthy man and will pay well to get her back."

Fabio looked up at the younger man. "Wealthy, yes, but he is also very powerful. Do you think two military planes would have been up there so fast," he pointed up, "if she was not who she is? We have our money, Eduardo. This is not our business."

"Relax. Within hours, we'll be long gone from here. Untraceable. I know of a place west of Chigorodo where we can keep her while I negotiate a payment from her father."

"Your father isn't going to like this."

"Let me worry about him. He's always telling me I should show more initiative. Well, here it is. Aristo and I can look after her." He pointed up and down the runway. "We'll split up closer to home and you can take the cash back. Anyway, get those fires out and ask my brother to come here."

Aristo came back after moving the part-full fuel drum back under the canopy. "We are leaving now, Lalo? The men are tired and hungry."

"I know. I am tired as well. You saw the two military jets. More will be here soon looking for the blond woman. So we cannot stay a moment longer. Get your things together and then prepare the women to depart. Give them some water and help them up onto the two spare horses. Rope the horses together and bring them back here as soon as possible."

"Who is she?"

"She is our ticket, little brother. I am tired of this business and I sense a great opportunity." He picked up one of the aluminum cases. "Take the money from these and put it securely in the saddle bags on the spare horses. Do that before you help the women."

Aristo picked up the heavy cases of money and moved off to get his gear and the horses. Eduardo went to gather up the others for departure.

◊

About fifty yards away from the group of men, on the other side of the airstrip, Jake watched them prepare to depart. He had seen the interchange between the pilot of the Cessna and the young, tall Colombian and was just as surprised as the others when the two Harriers flew past. If he'd been up at the crash site, he reflected whether he might have been able to signal them under different circumstances.

Anyway, the jets were evidence that Emily's daddy still possessed the influence to mobilize the United States Navy to come and look for his daughter. He was pretty sure there were few US bases in this area, certainly nothing in Panama or Colombia, so the jets almost certainly came from a carrier or other flight-enabled warship, either in the Gulf or the Caribbean. Jake's mental map of the area was sketchy, but he was sure the land mass between the Gulf and the Caribbean was thin at this point. That's why they could build the Panama Canal in the first place.

He checked the luminous dial on his Seamaster: 22:47. The men opposite him were almost certainly preparing to head back into Colombia. They'd be tired, but they would also have figured the link between the plane crash and the two US jets. If the ship was close, they might even dispatch some helicopters tonight.

He took another sip from the bottle of water he carried. Only a few drops remained. His best option was to lie low and head up to the crash site after the men had gone. By morning, he'd be heading back to a US ship and might even be stateside by tomorrow night, given the circumstances with his father. No one would blame him for taking such action. After all, he was up against six men with automatic weapons. Emily would be ransomed and be back with her family in no time. He checked the Sig Sauer pistol again and his thoughts turned to Duffy and how good she'd felt in his arms back at the crash site.

Who was he kidding? They might know who Emily was, or they might only suspect that she was someone important. Regardless, at some point, Agent Karen Duffy was going to be of no use to them, a potential liability even. He had to at least have a crack. Even if he just shadowed them and was able to get help later.

Or he could just stay here and take the safe option.

◊

Eight figures on horseback headed south on the runway and disappeared into the tree line. Fabio led, followed by Aristo, who'd roped his and the captives' horses into a single file of three. Eduardo was behind the women and José, Jorge, and Luis made up the rear of the group.

A half-moon had risen, providing some light to the trail ahead. Emily's head slumped as the enormity of the day and the events of the past twenty-four hours sank in. The rainforest consisted of light vegetation, bushes, small trees, and ferns, with a clear trail taking them south and away from rescue. A light drizzle persisted and she wished for a jacket to go with her thin blouse. *If I get out of this, I am always going to keep a handbag and some essentials with me when I fly again. If I fly again...*

Earlier, the youngest of the group had come to her and Karen and given them water. He was well dressed in clean khakis and had smiled at them. She and Karen had a hurried conversation while he readied his own horse and they concluded that he and Eduardo were related, if not brothers. The younger man had not tried to hide the transfer of bundles of cash from the aluminum suitcases into the saddlebags and she was conscious of the large amount of money that was now behind her and Karen.

She could sense the tension in the air, especially after the jets flew over, but the men were not overly alert, and Emily figured they traveled along a well-worn path, one they'd used many times before. After the exchange with the pilot, she knew that Eduardo had quickly assessed her worth to her parents and he intended to hold her somewhere for ransom, unless they could somehow find a way to escape. She knew the stories of westerners being kidnapped in this part of the world. She again tried to loosen the leather bonds around her wrists. She found some extra freedom as the leather stretched, but not enough. Perhaps later, when they rested, she could try to cut her bonds on something sharp.

Astride the horse ahead, Duffy's thoughts also turned to escape. From her training, she knew that the longer they remained captive, the harder it would become for them to escape their captors. She thought back to her basic training and remembered sitting in a classroom during agent school listening to a lecture on escape and evasion. The instructor, a former major from the marines, told them of his own capture and escape from the first Iraq war.

The man, she forgot his name, sat on the front of the desk in one of the many lecture theaters at the Academy, just outside Washington, DC. "No one ever expects to be taken captive in law enforcement. In the military, in the theater of war, it is an ever-present risk, albeit a low one for all but those who go into the enemy's midst. For you, and your career in the US Secret Service, it is highly unlikely that you will ever need the advice I am going to give you today. But one day, what you remember may very well save your life.

"The very, very, very best time for escape," he emphasized, "is right after capture. I repeat, *right* after. Your captors will have spent effort and energy in your capture and getting you to submit and be compliant. It is likely they will be feeling euphoric and the last thing they will expect is resistance. Your submission, even if it costs you a beating, will give your captors a feeling of power and superiority and, right at that point, they will consider you to be a low threat.

"Once you have been a captive for a day, you will be weaker as it is likely you will not receive food or water. Each hour you are captive, your alertness and ability to form an escape plan deteriorates. That first hour after capture is your best moment. Look for weaknesses, wait for their attention to slip and prepare yourself to run and to fight..."

Duffy thought back to their capture at the plane. Theory was good, but these men had been alert and the forest belonged to them. She didn't think there had been a realistic chance to get away. She had no doubt that her worth to her captors had been assessed and they'd brought her along solely because her death might harden Emily's resolve and cause difficulties for them and their plans.

She reflected back to Jake Walker, who would know by now of their fate. With each passing mile, her hopes faded that he would attempt some sort of rescue. Former military or not, he was on foot, on unfamiliar ground, with no back up, against six armed drug traffickers. She wouldn't blame him a bit for hanging back and waiting for rescue, but part of her wanted him to follow.

Both she and Emily wore pants. Duffy wore her jacket, but Emily was only wearing a blouse. Light drizzle dripped through her hair and down her neck, not heavy, but annoying nonetheless. Balancing the rain, she figured the temperature was still around ninety. The Service regulations forbade her from wearing heels while on protection detail and both women had sensible, if not sturdy, footwear. They needed every advantage and Duffy was determined to use every skill she possessed to find a way out of here.

If she didn't do it soon, however…Well, she didn't want to think about that.

34

White House, Washington DC

Bob Perry and the president heard a knock at the door and Admiral Salzburg entered the Oval Office. Bob looked at his wristwatch and sighed: 1:25 a.m. His wife would give him trouble when he got home.

"Hi, Dan," said the president. "Come and sit down. Did you get any results from the Harriers?"

Dan Salzberg gratefully sat down on one of the thick, comfortable sofas and turned to his boss. "Well as you know, the pilots reported a plane on the airstrip and could see people as well. We figure their presence was coincidental to the plane crash, but the proximity to the crash site of what appear to be people involved in the drug trade causes us some concern."

The president stood. "I know. It worries me, too. Let me get you a coffee."

"Okay."

He moved over to the coffee service. "How do you have it?" He looked over to Bob and could see the tiredness in his eyes. He felt it too.

"Just black would be great.

"This is our current thinking: the Mayday was received at about 16:30 yesterday, suggesting the crash occurred between 16:30 and 17:00." Salzburg accepted the coffee and the president sat down on the opposite sofa, next to Perry.

"Go on."

"Well, the Harriers saw the plane and some people on the airstrip just after 22:00 hours—five hours after the plane hit the ground and some one thousand yards to the southwest of the crash site."

"So, you figure," intervened Perry, "that there was ample time for the men at the airstrip to investigate the crash site?"

"Our analysis assumes they were there, or thereabouts, when the crash happened," said Salzburg. "But you are right, we figure they probably had time, motive, and opportunity to travel to the wreckage and see what they could salvage."

"Where does this take us then, Dan?" said the president.

Salzburg referred to a folder he had with him and extracted some photographs, which he handed across. "These shots were taken by the Harriers on their fly past the airstrip—they carry high resolution, infrared cameras on the underside. We weren't able to make out much detail with the people. However, we have some good shots of the plane on the ground, which appears to be refueling from drums of avgas. I have had our analysts look at the photos."

Perry and the president looked through the four, A4-sized prints. "And?" said the president.

"We are pretty sure the plane is a single engine Cessna Corvalis TT. Relatively new model. And modern. We don't quite have the right angle to read all of the registration number, but we are sure the last letter is a U preceded by a seven. This helps us to narrow it down."

"For what purpose?" asked Bob.

"Well, we are figuring that this plane took off shortly after the Harriers left and is carrying a load of drugs, probably cocaine, but it could be cannabis as well. If we can intercept the plane and talk to the pilot, we may get some idea as to whether the drug gang, or whatever they are, actually did go up to the crash site. We might also get a lead on where they are heading."

"I see where you're going," said the president. "If there were any survivors, the pilot of this plane may have seen them, or at least talked with the gang about the crash site. What are the chances of an intercept? He could be headed anywhere."

"That's where we've had a bit of luck. We are almost certain the plane is registered in the US and checking registrations of this type of plane leads to only three possible registrations. One plane is operating out of Minnesota, doing regular passenger and postal service runs around the state. Another is owned and operated by a well-known celebrity in L.A.. The final one is owned by an offshore company, and it's this one that we are focusing on.

"According to the latest flight records, a Mr. Wayne Costello, who cites his occupation as a businessman, logged a flight plan two weeks ago and left Miami the day before yesterday to the Grand Caymans, with a scheduled return flight to Miami later this morning."

"So…" said Perry.

"This type of plane has a range of twelve hundred nautical miles, adequate to fly nonstop from southern Panama to Miami. We haven't been able to get on to the Caymanians and they may not help us anyway, but we suggest he may have flown to the Caymans, picked up some cash from any of dozens of private banks and then flew on to this airstrip in Panama. He exchanges the cash for drugs, refuels and heads back to Florida."

"Don't the coastguard and Customs have routine ways to stop this happening?" asked the president.

"I'm no expert, Mr. President, but I'm told that a lot of drug shipments are dropped into the ocean and then picked up by fast jet boats that are capable of outrunning our enforcement agencies. He could even fly the shipment straight into any of the general aviation airports and take his chances. Customs only searches a fraction of the aircraft coming in and out of the Florida. They just don't have enough resources."

"Okay, Dan. Good work. I assume you also have photos of the crash site?"

"Yes, here." Salzburg passed over some more prints. "As you can see, no evidence of bodies or survivors. Two major pieces, the nose and the tail. The absence of fire suggests the crash might have been survivable, but the absence of survivors on or near the site does not look good. Captain James will have some choppers down there at first light. We'll know more then."

"Thanks, Dan, this is good work." He turned to his chief of staff. "Bob, get onto Customs and also wake up General King. I want air traffic control, the navy, Customs, and the air force vigilant and ready. If that plane is heading into Florida, I want that pilot. I am going to put my head down for a few hours. Wake me if there's anything important."

35

Colombia-Panama Border

Four hours had passed since they'd left the airstrip. Moving through this part of the world was always dangerous and Eduardo knew of the insurgents living and operating in the area. There were also rival drug gangs which regularly moved cannabis and cocaine north because the region was sparsely populated and the border totally unprotected. He hadn't been worried when he was carrying the cocaine, but five million in cash posed quite a different risk. Nonetheless, the FARC groups in the area didn't worry him. They had a financial arrangement with his father.

With the unexpected arrival of the Harrier jets, they'd needed to get as much distance as they could away from the airstrip and the crash site and he figured they'd covered about fifteen kilometers or so from the airstrip and were now in Colombia. He believed the theory of another survivor, as the missing weapon from the other Secret Service agent suggested this. He intended to talk to the women again on this matter.

Now over the border, he started to feel more relaxed, but he would not truly relax until they were farther into Colombia. From the border, they faced a seventy-kilometer ride to make it into safer territory, property under his father's protection, and only forty kilometers to the hideaway near Chigorodo. Eduardo figured they could do this easily in two days and would split up with Fabio tomorrow morning. Nearly all the route was under cover and he was unworried about any pursuit from helicopters. The farther away they traveled, the greater the area any rescuers would need to quarter to find them. When they were well into Colombia, they would be safe.

36

Gulf of Panama

Scott Davis awoke to the sound of his alarm at 03:45. He quickly washed and shaved and dressed in his combat flight suit. Twenty minutes later, he strode into the officer's mess to get some breakfast before their 04:30 briefing.

He loaded a plate up with some eggs, bacon, and tomato and turned just as Walt Kennedy came up with an empty plate in his hand. "Hey, buddy. Looks like we are going to be late getting home. Did you get onto Charlotte?" he asked, referring to Scott's wife.

"Morning, Walt. Yes, I managed to call her last night. She wasn't happy to hear about a delay. I also talked to the kids. They seemed okay that I wasn't going to be there for a few days; I miss them."

They moved along the self-service area, Walt also selecting a cooked breakfast for the carbs and energy it provided, and they proceeded to one of the many spare tables at this early hour.

"Don't worry too much about home," said Walt, with a mouthful of beans and toast. "A lot will depend upon what we find out there today. As you know, there are very few plane crashes into this sort of terrain in which people walk away. If there are no survivors, they'll call in the crash investigators and we could be on our way shortly after."

"I think you're being optimistic, Walt. Even if there are no survivors, we will probably be tasked offshore to provide support until the wreck is thoroughly investigated, bodies removed and, if necessary, we will then be tasked to lift the wreckage out for transport back to the States. It could be a couple of weeks before we are home."

They ate their breakfast in silence for a few minutes.

"There was a guy on the flight that I think I know," said Scott.

"Yeah, who?"

"In his briefing, the captain mentioned a passenger, Jake Walker, a security consultant. I knew a Jake Walker from before I joined up. Got introduced to him at a friend's party, talked for while, shared a few drinks. He was in security and I remember him taking interest in my own plans to join the marines and fly helos. Nice guy, modest and unassuming. Well, he mentioned his own service and I was interested enough to do a bit of research on him. I found out later he had been awarded the Medal of Honor during Operation Anaconda in '02. He's been out of the military for about eight years or so. Apparently, he applied for a discharge following the downing of a marine Blackhawk in Baghdad."

"You think this could the same guy?"

"Don't know, but if there were any survivors from this plane crash and Jake Walker is one of them, Emily Parker couldn't be in better hands."

The men fell silent for a moment and focused on getting their breakfasts eaten. Scott's hairs bristled as he felt a figure come up behind him.

"Davis and Kennedy." Scott didn't need to turn around; he knew

Copperton's voice well.

Walt looked up. "Morning, sir," he said cordially.

"Briefing in five minutes, you two." He moved around the table, sat down, and looked at Scott, who returned his gaze. "There'll be four Whiskys in the air today supporting two Sea Knights. You'll be my wingman, Davis, and I fully expect you to keep to the task, understand?"

Scott's eyes never wavered. "Fully." He added, "Sir."

Copperton moved off.

Walt looked at his friend, who said, "Walt, I know, I know, but I just can't help it. I don't respect the man; he knows I don't respect him. And he knows why."

"Agreed, he's a creep and poor officer. But he is still our boss and will continue to make trouble for you and for me while we are under his command. Just a couple of weeks and you can apply for a stateside posting again."

"The bastard is likely to follow me," said Scott. "Come on, let's make that briefing."

37

Darién Province, Colombia

Fabio rode up to join Eduardo. They were now navigating by starlight and they could hardly see. "Eduardo."

"Yes, Fabio? You are going to tell me it is time to halt, no?"

"We've been riding now for over six hours, without break. Yesterday, as well. The horses are clearly weakening, as are the men. We need a couple of hours."

"Okay," said Eduardo. "We've come about fifteen kilometers or so and are just into Colombia. At the next source of water, call a halt."

Small streams flowed throughout the area and, before long, one appeared and the men dismounted. Although the rain had stopped, the humidity remained high and contributed to everyone's tiredness.

"Look after the horses first," ordered Fabio, addressing Jorge and Luiz.

Jorge and Luiz took the horses and, after they drank deeply from the stream, they roped them together and took them about thirty meters away to a clearing where they could forage and recuperate.

Back at the side of the stream, Eduardo and Fabio were talking and the women sat on the ground nearby, still trussed. Jorge and Luiz returned and Eduardo spoke to the men. "Get some food, water, and rest. I will take the women over there," he pointed in the direction they had come, "and give them some food and water. Until I come back, stay alert and listen for any sign of pursuit."

He went over to Jorge and tapped him on the shoulder. "You can rest later. We have to feed the women and will need to watch them. Luiz, you can take over in about an hour." To Jorge: "Bring your rifle."

Jorge and Eduardo helped the women to their feet. They gave little resistance as they were guided back up the trail about twenty meters from the stream where a small piece of open ground appeared and some starlight filtered through a gap in the canopy. "Sit," said Eduardo in English. "Jorge, untie their hands."

Their hands free, the women rubbed their wrists to restore some circulation. Eduardo took some dried fruits and nuts from a shoulder bag and gave them a handful each. Jorge stood a couple of yards away and kept his rifle pointed in their general direction.

Eduardo reached into his satchel. "Here is some cheese as well," he said, handing them each a small portion farm cheese made locally on his father's property. "Not the best, but it is all we have." He also set down a water bottle on the ground and the women ate in silence.

He went a short way into the canopy to relieve himself before returning and sitting down on the ground. "Miss Parker, we know there was another passenger on the plane that survived."

Emily looked at Eduardo, but didn't speak. Eduardo turned to Duffy. "You had a partner on the plane who died, unfortunately. Like you, he carried his government credentials and a service holster for his pistol. We did not find the pistol, as you know, and I want to know who else was aboard. Was it the co-pilot?"

Duffy thought quickly. If she said yes, they might relax their guard. However, why would a pilot be back in the cabin during an emergency? Surely, he would have been upfront with Mick Rogers and, if so, they would have found his body. No, she would deflect attention for a while longer.

Before she could respond, Emily replied for her. "No, it was not the co-pilot. We had another passenger aboard, an embassy staffer who was going home on leave. He was also in the tail section when we impacted the ground and survived the crash. I asked him to retrieve the pistol."

"So where is he now?" said Eduardo.

"He had gone into the forest to gather firewood when you found us," replied Emily. "We haven't seen him since and have assumed that he saw our capture by your men and is right at this minute telling the authorities which way we have gone."

Eduardo considered the response. No one was after them; they were too far and over the border. "So what happened to the co-pilot then?"

"He died," said Emily, "in the initial explosion."

"What explosion?"

"We don't know what caused it," said Emily. "One minute we were flying along, next there was a huge bang down in the cargo bay and the plane depressurized. Some of the explosion was directed into the cabin and, before we knew what had happened, the co-pilot was sucked out of the plane. He'd been talking to us at the back when it happened."

Eduardo stood up and looked around. Probably not the whole truth, but most of the story made sense. "Okay, we are going to rest here for a couple of hours. We are now in Colombia and heading for a place where we can rest up. You know who we are and what was going on back at the airstrip. We don't carry weapons for fun and will use them to defend ourselves if necessary. You will be kept tied up. This is a dangerous area. If you do as we say, you will live."

"Both of us need to go to the toilet," said Emily.

Eduardo conversed with Jorge in Spanish. "Stay here and I will send up Aristo. One at a time, you are to take them where they can have some privacy. Keep your rifles on them at all times. When they are done, retie their bonds and bring them back down to the stream."

A couple of minutes later, Aristo joined them. "Take her," said Jorge, pointing at Emily. "When she has finished, come back and I will take the other." He jerked his rifle upwards and motioned to Emily to go with Aristo.

Duffy watched them go and figured they had gone no more than fifteen yards or so back along the trail. Despite the dark, she could see her captor watched her closely, his rifle not wavering from her head. She didn't like this and wished that the younger brother of the leader had chosen her.

Shortly, Emily returned and Jorge waited while Aristo retied her wrists behind her back. He jerked his rifle up again and said: "You, first." Duffy got to her feet and headed slowly back up the trail. In Spanish, he said to Aristo, "Stay here. I will be back within ten minutes."

Duffy stood still and Jorge jabbed his rifle between her shoulder blades. After about twenty yards, Duffy stopped and turned, about to tell the man that she was okay to go here.

38

Gulf of Mexico

Wayne Costello felt the tension leave him as he passed over the coast of Cuba. His flight had been uneventful and, before long, he watched as Key West drifted beneath the plane. Slowly, he descended until he was a mere 150 feet above the waves and throttled back to 120 knots. He'd had plenty of time to prepare his packages during the five-hour flight. He looked at the four 125-kilogram cubes behind him, each designed to withstand impact into water and containing the same number of vacuum-wrapped, one-kilo packages of cocaine.

The packages were watertight and designed to sink, and Wayne's only task had been to attach sonar beacons that enabled divers to locate them and bring them to the surface and into a speedboat via a winch. Someone had found that the best way to do this was to use truck straps, to which the beacons were attached. As he would be dropping the packages at two-second intervals (or thereabouts) in waters of about one hundred feet in depth, it was unlikely that any would be lost, even if one of the beacons failed to operate.

With the plane's settings locked, Wayne climbed into the back. The rear seats had been removed and special doors had been fabricated into the floor and lower in the fuselage to enable him to drop the packages through. He opened the panels and put them aside, watching the waves 150 feet beneath rush by below the plane. The plane was flying a predetermined course toward his GPS drop off point and he could see it coming up rapidly. He maneuvered the first package and sent it down, tumbling toward the Gulf. Three more packages and one minute later, he sat back in his seat and commenced a climb to three thousand feet.

Suddenly, there was an enormous roar and the plane pulsed from a shockwave as a very fast jet flew over his starboard wing. His radio was tuned into the General Aviation frequency and it came to life: "Mr. Wayne Costello, this is Lieutenant Sutherland from the United States Air Force. You are ordered to follow us to Southwest Florida and land. Do you copy? Over."

Wayne started to sweat and then remembered that there was nothing incriminating on the plane. He looked to his right and saw what he knew to be an F16 flying next to him, about one hundred feet away. He couldn't see the pilot's face behind his visor, but could feel his eyes looking directly at him.

"Mr. Costello, we know that is you piloting the Cessna. Please acknowledge. You have twenty seconds to comply or we will open fire on you. Over."

Wayne leveled out at fifteen hundred feet. He pressed the presell switch on his radio handset. "This is Wayne Costello. What do you want? Over."

"Mr. Costello, I have orders from the chief of the air force himself. All will be revealed upon your landing. Please indicate you will comply. Over."

Wayne figured that they wanted him for exactly what he had been doing. *But evidence? No way.* "Roger, I will follow you. Out."

39

Darién Province, Colombia

Duffy stood still and turned, about to tell the man that she was okay here, when the man punched her in the stomach.

She was totally unprepared and, as all the air left her lungs, she collapsed onto the ground on her knees, unable to breathe let alone call out. Jorge pushed her head roughly and she fell onto the ground behind her. Still fighting to breathe, he climbed on top of her, turned her onto her front and pushed her head into the soil and leaf litter on the forest floor. She tried to struggle, but he twisted her left arm behind her and she felt a prick as he pushed the point of a knife into the area beneath her jaw.

The man brought his face close to hers and she could smell his foulness, a mixture of bad breath and awful body odor. He spoke in heavily accented English. "No fight. No cry." He pushed her arm higher for emphasis. "Okay?"

Duffy nodded. She started to breathe again and thought back to her training in unarmed combat. She retained a good level of fitness, ran several times a week and, at 130 pounds, still managed to punch above her weight.

Keeping her left arm up behind her back, Jorge stabbed his knife into the ground in front of her face. Duffy felt and heard him loosening his belt and then his hand was lifting her jacket and blouse. She brought her right arm upward and he punched her in the back of the head. "Don't move," he hissed.

The punch landed on a thick part of her skull, but it hurt nonetheless and Duffy went limp, hoping for a chance to throw him off. Jorge got his pants down off his hips and Duffy felt him start to tug at the back of her pants. She desperately thought for a solution, but the man was strong. Tears formed in her eyes. *Don't you dare, Karen. Think, girl, think!*

40

Darién Province, Panama, earlier

After the men headed south from the airstrip, Jake had two minds about what to do. He possessed a pistol and a full magazine of twelve 9 mm rounds. For most people, such a gun was only good for short, close combat, good for around twenty-five feet. In his hands, Jake knew he could hit targets one hundred feet away, but the small rounds would not put a man down unless he was able to hit a man's head—an outcome that was almost impossible at night.

He faced six armed men, almost certainly not combat-trained, but five of them were carrying M16s—the standard rifle for much of the US forces. With a thirty round magazine and 5.56 mm, high velocity rounds, M16s were accurate, could fire single shots or be on full automatic and, even in poor hands, were well able to hit a man one hundred yards away. The rounds were small, but their high velocity caused them to tumble and they could cause lethal damage once they impacted a human being. One of the other men, the oldest and probably the leader, carried a Heckler and Koch 9 mm submachine gun—a great close-quarters weapon in the right hands. In other words, they outnumbered and outgunned him.

They also had the advantage of horses. Jake didn't doubt he could keep some sort of pace with them. Across a prairie or grasslands, no. But he was still fit enough to make thirty miles a day in a semi-tropical rain forest. He would need to keep refreshing his one and only water bottle, but he'd seen several streams in the area, so he didn't see this as a problem. His only food consisted of two sandwiches, one of which he'd just consumed, so if he decided to engage them, he must do this in the next twenty-four hours. He didn't doubt his ability to find food and he could survive for quite some time out here, but he couldn't feed himself *and* track men on horseback. No, he would need to catch them quickly and by surprise.

He again considered staying, but he just couldn't imagine waiting for rescue by the plane wreck and the shame he would feel at doing nothing. *President's daughter kidnapped while ex Special Forces, Medal of Honor…*He could already see the headlines.

Twenty minutes after they left, Jake got up and followed. He knew they would not be going fast, given the rain and lack of light. Speed under such conditions would involve too much risk for the riders and the horses. With the light from the half moon, even one filtered through cloud cover, he maintained a steady pace for about thirty minutes. Eight horses made a trail of smells, dung, broken foliage and large hoof prints, which Jake easily followed, even at night.

After thirty minutes, Jake slowed to a fast walk. The tracks told him the group was not hurrying, the gaps between the hoof marks suggested they traveled at walking pace. He thought back to the women's capture at the plane. He felt sure that the group knew that a third person survived, but unless the women had revealed his identity, it was very possible they considered he would remain at the wreck for rescuers to arrive. All would depend upon the answers the women gave, or had given, when questioned.

Jake could feel their confidence. The arrival of the Harriers no doubt confirmed the importance of one of their captives and they would know to put some distance between the wreck and themselves as quickly as possible. With no survivors to tell any rescuers what had happened, the subsequent search team would concentrate on the area around the wreck, perhaps only an area covering nine square miles and, by morning, there would be little chance of them finding the small band of horse riders as they headed out of the search cordon.

Jake still had no feeling about how far they were from Colombia, but he figured that once the group had crossed the border they would be feeling relatively safe and lower their guard.

As he went along, he found plenty of water sources as numerous small streams brought water down from the mountain ranges. The temperature was mild, but the rain created a high level of humidity and made the going uncomfortable. His watch showed 2:45 and he figured they'd traveled about ten miles from the crash site, probably only eight as the crow flies. Even though he felt certain they would stop soon for a rest break, Jake increased his pace, keeping a careful watch and stopping every five hundred paces to listen.

Another hour and roughly three miles farther, he again stopped to listen and felt certain he could hear the faint sounds of the group moving through the forest. He moved off the trail and started to move more cautiously. He heard voices and stopped, got on his stomach and started to crawl forward. It was very dark and he was going by touch and sound alone. Only a small amount of starlight came through the gaps in the canopy above. Yet his night vision was acute and he constantly looked for movement.

Presently, he came over a small rise and, from the conversation he could hear, Jake figured they'd stopped, perhaps only thirty yards away. He kept perfectly still. He could hear the trickling of a small stream and, when one of the men tethered the horses together and took them up and into the forest, Jake became certain that they'd stopped for a rest.

For the tenth time, he checked his pistol: safety off and one round in the chamber. *But what the hell was he going to do?*

After five minutes, he couldn't believe it when the two women headed back up the trail about ten feet to his right accompanied by two of the men. They stopped on the trail, about fifteen feet or so away. He checked the other men, down by the stream, chatting quietly. *More relaxed than they should be*, he thought.

One of the men spoke to the women in English, telling them to sit down. He untied their hands and gave them some food and water before heading into the forest on the other side of the trail to urinate. On his return, Jake saw him sit and he proceeded to question them about the crash, telling them that he knew a third survivor existed and asked if it was the co-pilot, whom Jake knew would never be found.

He felt sure that Duffy made the connection, but before she could reply, Emily lied to the man telling him the other person was an embassy staffer. *Clever girl!* A couple of minutes passed and then Emily told the man they needed to relieve themselves and the man left to fetch another of the group.

Jake felt he would never have a better opportunity and, as another man came back up the trail, he was contemplating taking them both on. In the end, he decided to wait, given the proximity of the larger group only thirty yards away.

The new man arrived and took Emily back up the trail. Jake turned around slowly and began crawling through the bush adjacent to the trail. The forest slept soundly and Jake thanked his training as he moved silently across the forest floor, testing each new patch of ground for things that could give his presence away. Emily finished her business and the man took her back. Jake watched and waited.

Presently, Duffy appeared with the other man directly behind her, but far enough away to avoid any sudden movements from her. Jake had to crawl again to catch up. Duffy stopped and said something Jake didn't catch, but he clearly saw the man ready himself and, when Duffy turned, he gave her an enormous punch in the stomach. Jake tensed as she collapsed and watched as the man laid his rifle and a satchel against a nearby tree.

The man pushed her onto her back and roughly rolled her over. Duffy attempted something Jake couldn't see and got another punch in the head for her trouble. Jake got within ten feet and crept toward them, closer, closer. He could see the man tugging on his belt and his intentions became clear. A yard or so away and in striking distance, he climbed into a crouch, held the pistol in his right hand and brought it down hard on the man's skull. His opponent slumped forward and, as his head hit Duffy's, she cried out.

Quickly, Jake pushed the man off her and held his left hand over her mouth. "Duffy, it's okay. It's me, Jake."

He took a quick glance back along the trail. He was sure her cry had not gone unnoticed and, sure enough, the other man hissed out a question in Spanish. Receiving no response, he called out again. "Jorge? Jorge?"

Jake noticed the man's knife in the dirt and picked it up. Duffy sat up and he picked up the rifle and satchel from the ground and handed her Murray's Sig. The man groaned. "Hurry. We're leaving."

As Duffy watched, Jake took the knife, plunged it into the man's neck, and severed his windpipe. Blood gushed over his hand and the man's body shook as he died.

Jake wiped his hands on the man's shirt, and they heard the other man call out to the group down at the stream. "We can't leave, Jake. They still have Emily," she whispered.

"We'll risk everything if we try to get her now," replied Jake. "Don't worry, we won't leave her. Follow me, quickly." He hurried back up the trail and Duffy went after him.

41

Gulf of Panama

Three dual-rotor Sea Knights, piloted by navy pilots, headed south from the deck of the ship. To their front were the two Super Cobras, carrying Hellfire missiles, rockets, and 20 mm cannon, although the marines had been clearly briefed that they were unauthorized to use their weapons unless lives were at risk.

Captain James had managed to make good progress after leaving the Panama Canal and they'd left the *USS Peleliu* at a point about forty nautical miles south of the Isla del Rey, the largest of the Pearl Islands in the Gulf. The flight over the Gulf took twenty minutes before the coast appeared, and they headed for the GPS coordinates identified by the Harrier pilots the previous evening.

Behind Copperton's Cobra, Scott felt good to be doing something after weeks of inactivity. He and Walt were quiet with their own thoughts and they watched as the sky got brighter to their front and they could make out features on the coast.

Onboard one of the Sea Knights was a medical team, staffed by navy personnel, and the second and third Sea Knight each contained a squad of twelve marines. It would be their job to rappel from the helicopters and secure the site and the airstrip. The medical team had a full equipment load and were fully trained and prepared to treat multiple trauma victims should that be necessary.

At the appointed moment, Copperton called over the radio, "Pilots, this is Whisky One. Am crossing the coast and heading direct to the site of the wreckage. Maintain formation. Out."

The four helicopters followed him and within minutes were over land, still traveling at about two thousand feet. Copperton altered course to the northwest and the flight followed. Scott watched his GPS and estimated the site to be about five miles away as they came in through a wide valley. The sun had yet to rise, but there was enough light emerging to make out clear features ahead and on the ground.

Copperton dropped toward the treetops. "This is Whisky One, stay behind Two. When I make a visual, I will go in with Knight Two, which is to deploy and secure the accident site. Knight Three, you are to land on the airstrip and secure. Whisky Two and Knight One are to maintain station to my rear. Over."

One by one the pilots acknowledged their understanding and Scott took note when they passed over the airstrip. According to the Harrier pilots, the wreckage should be straight ahead, about five hundred yards or so. One of the Sea Knights fell out of formation and went down to land on the airstrip. Even before it hit the ground, a dozen armed marines jumped out and moved to the safety of the canopy on either side. The pilot then lifted off and gained some altitude until the marines could investigate the situation on ground.

Presently, Scott and Walt could clearly see the direction the plane's impact had taken. They saw two clear parts, the nose and the tail, and both wings were clearly visible, as well as the usual thousands of other parts, big and small, that are typical when a passenger jet makes a high velocity impact with terrain. Scott brought the Cobra into a hover and they waited for the marines to deploy and secure the site.

"Knight Two, this is Whisky One. Over."

"Roger Whisky One," replied the pilot of the Sea Knight.

"We will hold station. Deploy and secure. Over."

"Roger. Out."

The pilot maneuvered the Sea Knight over the clearing created by the nose section of the Gulfstream as it had slammed through the forest. Side doors opened and six marines quickly dropped over the side and onto the ground. They cleared their lines and, with a thumbs-up, quickly dispersed and took cover. A second six men came down. Once clear of the lines, the lines were quickly retrieved and the pilot gained some altitude.

"Whisky One, this is Knight Two, men are on the ground. Over."

"Roger that," came Copperton's reply.

Lieutenant Mortensen's voice came over the radio. "Whisky One. Site is secure. We await further instructions."

"Roger One, all head over to the airstrip. Out."

The remaining helicopters headed southwest to the airstrip.

As the rotors stopped turning, Copperton lifted his canopy and emerged from the Cobra. All five helicopters sat on the ground, and he headed over to the head of the medical team, Lieutenant Commander Valerie Booth. Both were wearing a wireless headset. Mortensen's voice came over the net. "Knight One. We have completed an initial recce. There are two deceased in the nose section, one of the pilots and a male passenger. No further persons, alive or deceased, have been located. Over."

"Roger that," replied Copperton. "We are setting out now and should be in your location in two zero. Out."

He looked at Booth. "Ma'am?"

"Yes, I got that, Captain. Looks like we won't be needed. I'll come with you to the crash site nonetheless. We will need to extract the bodies and then await the crash investigators. I suggest we take half of the marines and leave everyone else here for the time being."

Copperton looked around him. The only marine he could see was Lieutenant Weston. His men had formed a perimeter as planned. "Weston and Davis?"

Scott and the marine lieutenant came over and stood before Copperton.

"We are heading over to the crash site on foot. I want six of your men to accompany us," said Copperton, looking at Weston. "Davis, while we are gone, I want a thorough search of the area and to be briefed when we return."

"Sir," chorused the two lieutenants.

Weston went off speaking into his headset and Scott headed back over to Walt, who waited next to their Cobra.

Twenty minutes later and flanked by the six marines, Booth and Copperton approached the nose cone of the plane.

Lieutenant Mortenson came over to them and addressed Booth. "Nothing alive out here, ma'am."

"Thanks, Lieutenant. Please show us around."

It took them all of thirty minutes to properly examine the nose and tail sections of the wreckage. That done, the three officers took some shade about twenty yards from the tail section and sat down.

"Well, this is all very strange," said Booth. "At the briefing, we were told there were two pilots, two Secret Service Agents, the security consultant, Walker, and Emily Parker. We have found some sign of blood, consistent with the impact, but no bodies, nothing."

"I agree," said Copperton. "Two very different situations. The nose of the plane clearly took a big hit with the pilot, still in his seat, and one of the Secret Service agents, Pete Murray, both dead, and with injuries which look consistent with the crash."

Booth looked around her. "So, we are missing four people. Lieutenant, we need to establish a perimeter. What are your thoughts?"

The twenty-two-year-old Mortensen pondered for a few seconds. "I will set up a perimeter at around one hundred yards or so. Probably use eight of my squad. This will leave the balance to go over the area thoroughly."

"Sounds good," said Copperton. "Please brief your men to stay well away from the wreckage and not to touch anything."

"There's one thing I noticed," said Mortenson. "Not an expert is this, but I know what C4 smells like."

"And?" said Copperton.

"At the tail section, the bottom of the fuselage has clear scorch marks. I didn't touch anything, but my nose told me enough."

"Thanks for that," said Copperton. "I guess we will have to wait to see if the NTSB[8] can confirm. In the interim, why don't you go and get a small sample of the fuselage and the residue."

Mortensen acknowledged and headed off toward the wreckage.

"We'll need to get those bodies out, Captain, and back to the *Peleliu*," said Booth. "Probably best if my people do that. From the look of things, there are likely to be survivors out here and I can't figure out

8   The US air crash investigation unit, the National Transport Safety Bureau.

why they didn't just stay here. Maybe they went looking for help, but I doubt it. They would have known their best chance was to stay with the wreckage. I suggest you radio back and send over my team. We'll winch them down, as we will need some of our kit. You can then take a ride back to the airstrip. I'm going to call James and give him a sitrep."

42

Darién Province, Colombia

Jake and Duffy ran back up the trail. A few shots were fired in their direction but were well wide. After a couple of minutes, Jake stopped and said, "This way," and they went right, following a narrow trail probably laid down by some of the larger mammals that populated the region.

After a few more minutes, Jake stopped and took Duffy's hand and they moved into the scrub and sat down.

Duffy's heart rate was fast and it took some time for her to recover. Jake passed her the water bottle. "Here, take a few sips." Duffy took the water and took too much in, coughing some of it back up. Jake lowered the bottle. "Take it easy."

There was a faint glow from the sunrise and Duffy watched Jake as he also took a drink. He was shirtless and had covered his body and face with mud. He looked like Rambo with short hair. He certainly had Stallone's physique, and she wanted to reach out and touch him.

"I thought you were never coming." She slapped him, not too hard, across the chest, letting her hand rest a second or so on his shoulder. "Why didn't you just stay at the plane? You'd be safe by now."

"Which is it, Duffy? You wanted me to follow or stay at the

plane?" He smiled. "Hey, the thought crossed my mind, but at the end of the day, I knew that the only option, the right option, was to follow and hope that my chance would come, which it did."

"What now?" asked Duffy.

"Well, we should rest here a bit. They might suspect that there are two of us, but, given your, I mean Emily's, explanation of the other passenger being an embassy staffer—I was only a few feet away when that guy was talking to you—I am hoping they are thinking that you managed to escape that guy's attempted assault and have escaped alone and on foot."

"You killed him."

"He deserved it for what he was going to do to you. You know that Emily is their bonus and, at some point, you were going to be a liability to them. What do you know about them?"

"Well, there are five in total now, Colombians all I am sure. Eduardo is the guy who is leading them. Speaks good English. I get the impression he is a bit of an aristocrat, or at least well educated. There is a young guy there, sixteen or seventeen years old, very handsome. We figure he is Eduardo's brother. There is a guy in his forties, looks very fit, Eduardo called him Fabio. Two others in their twenties or thereabouts. All are armed with M16s; Eduardo also has a pistol and the older man has some sort of machine pistol."

"Any idea where they are going?"

"We overheard Eduardo talk about a place he had, Chig-something or other. But to be honest, no idea, other than they have a large amount of cash and, as they know who Emily is, we were pretty sure they have ransom in mind."

Two shots rang out and Jake stood up. "Let's go. I hope that wasn't Emily."

43

Southwest Florida International Airport

The air conditioner hummed and Wayne sweated even as the icy air swirled around him. It gushed out of him and stung his eyes. Accompanied all the way by the two F16s, he'd landed on the main runway at Southwest Florida without trouble and FBI agents arrested him as soon as his propeller stopped. They impounded his plane and took him to this room, a Customs' interview room by the look of it. He looked around and saw plain walls, linoleum floor, one door, and a mirror that had to be two-way.

Wayne sat on the only chair in the room next to a bolted-to-the-floor table. A camera pointed down at him from the corner above the door and Wayne tried to give his best tough guy look as he waited and waited.

After at least an hour of waiting, two men entered the room. Wayne guessed one to be in his thirties, the other younger. *Dark gray suits, regulation haircuts, parted on the same side...Have to be Feds*, thought Wayne.

The two men remained standing, as there were no other seats. "Mr. Costello," said the older one. "I am Special Agent Frank Dawson from the Federal Bureau of Investigation. My partner here is Special Agent Phil Jackson. I assume you know why you are here?"

"I have no idea. I am a businessman and I want to talk to a lawyer. I know my rights."

"You have just been on a business trip to the Grand Caymans, Mr. Costello?" said Jackson.

Wayne looked at him. "I repeat, I want a lawyer."

"Mr. Costello," said Jackson. "We know a lot more than you think. Right now, you are facing up to twenty-five years in a Federal prison for importation of narcotics."

Wayne kept his silence. "Quite frankly," said Dawson, "we don't really care as much about the narcotics as we do about your movements over the past twenty-four hours. But if you don't cooperate, things will turn very bad for you. Now, the Grand Caymans—we know you were there. Flight records confirm it."

"That's right."

"What sort of business are you in?" asked Dawson.

"My business."

"Okay, okay," said Dawson. "When did you leave the Grand Caymans?"

"I want a lawyer, okay?"

"Truth is, Mr. Costello, you didn't fly from the Grand Caymans to here, did you?" said Jackson.

Wayne started to have an uneasy feeling, but he kept quiet, wary about where this was heading.

"In fact, Mr. Costello, we have a clear photograph of you and your plane on a jungle airstrip in Panama," said Dawson.

"Impossible. I have never been to Panama."

"Photographs don't lie, Mr. Costello," said Jackson. He pulled an A4 print out of an envelope and dropped it on the table, face up.

Wayne glanced down at the photograph and saw his plane photographed from above. A trickle of sweat fell down the bridge of his nose and dropped onto his lap.

"I know. You're going to say that plane could be anyone's. But we know it was you, Wayne," said Jackson. He continued, "Fact is, Wayne, you are in a lot of trouble. Your plane was observed by the air force and the Coastguard dropping four packages into the Gulf of Mexico this morning. As we speak, divers are looking for those four packages and we're pretty sure that, when we do retrieve them, they are going to contain enough Class A drugs to put you in a federal prison for a long, long time."

"But, to be honest, that's not why we are here," said Dawson.

"No," said Jackson. "Sure, you are going to be indicted and you will go to jail, but a little incident happened down in that part of Panama in the last twenty-four hours and, if you help us, I am sure we can put a good word in for you with the federal prosecutors."

"We're pretty sure we know who your employers are. But we are also certain that you are not going to confirm what we know. So let's skip that," said Dawson.

The two-guy routine was giving Wayne a headache. *Probably why they did it*, he thought.

Dawson put his hands on the table edge and looked at him. "Wayne, there was a plane crash last night. Went down not one mile from the airstrip you visited last night. What we want, what we need to know, is whether you saw, or heard talk of, any survivors?"

Wayne kept his head down, weighing up his options. They weren't good.

Dawson stood up. "Wayne, I can promise you two things," said Jackson. "If you keep this silence up, I will do everything in my power to ensure you come out of prison an old man. However, if you tell us what you know, and admit what we both know about your visit to Panama, I will talk to the president himself about your cooperation. Come on, you know what we want. Help us and we will help you."

Wayne wiped his face on his sleeve. "Okay, I hear you." Another bead of sweat ran down his nose. "I'm not admitting to anything, but the Colombians had two US women with them at the airstrip and, yes, one of them was the former president's daughter."

44

Darién Province, Colombia

Both Emily and her captor had heard a noise, a thud, followed by a muffled scream from Karen. Her hands had been retied, and she had tried to get up but was held down by the young man.

He had called out "Jorge? Jorge?" but there was no response, and he had then shouted out to the larger group. Within seconds, Eduardo and Fabio had come running up the trail and went past them. The men let off a couple of bursts from their weapons and Emily feared the worst.

Eduardo came back, anger written over his face. He said something to Aristo. Emily had some Spanish and caught the words *muerto* and *estupido*—dead and stupid.

"Where's Karen?" she asked Eduardo.

"She is gone," he replied. "She escaped and killed one of my men." To the younger man, he said, "Take her down to the stream and get ready to go."

The younger man led Emily back down the trail to the stream. The horses were brought back from their rest by one and the man helped her up onto her horse. The others prepared to depart and, presently, Fabio and Eduardo came back down the trail and Eduardo said something to the younger man. He moved over to Karen's horse, removed the saddlebags and handed them to Eduardo before leading the horse and another away up the stream.

Eduardo mounted his horse and the group started moving. After they had gone a hundred yards or so uphill, two shots rang out and, a short while later, the younger man joined them and rode up to Eduardo. The foliage became thicker and the trail was less distinct. Fallen trees littered the trail and, several times, one of the men needed to dismount and clear the way forward by using a machete.

As the sun climbed higher, the temperature rose until it was well into the nineties. Emily felt uncomfortable, tired, hungry, and frightened. The farther they went, the more she feared for her life. She'd been surprised that Karen fought that man, even more that she'd killed him. What would she do now? With a weapon, would Karen attempt to follow? Emily couldn't see how she could overcome five armed men. Hopefully she would be heading back to the crash site to let the right people know what had happened, and then they could make a plan to get her out of this mess.

45

Darién Province, Panama

After Copperton and Booth left, Scott and Walt looked around their immediate area. Walt noticed several oil drums just under the canopy and went over the check them out. Scott went with him.

Three forty-four gallon drums. Walt gave them a kick. "Two are empty," he remarked as he undid the cap on the third. "Avgas."

"Never get out of here without it," said Scott, putting his nose near the opening to confirm his friend's assessment. "Someone must fly in regularly, just to replace the fuel." He wandered deeper into the canopy and Walt followed.

After about five minutes, Walt crouched down and beckoned Scott over. "Here, take a look at this."

Scott joined him and saw a small footprint in a patch of sandy soil at their feet. "That's definitely not a man's footprint."

"No," agreed Walt.

They heard one of the Sea Knights starting up and went back to the edge of the airstrip. Copperton's gunner, Nick Forsyth was there. "Hey, Nick," said Walt. "What's happening?"

Forsyth turned and said, "Listening to the chatter, they've found two bodies, but no others at the crash site. The pilot and one of the Secret Service agents are deceased. I think the task now will be for the marines to cut a landing site, but before that, the focus will be on getting the bodies out of the wreckage and back to the ship."

"That means there are survivors, doesn't it?" said Scott.

"Not necessarily," replied Walt.

"No," agreed Forsyth. "There could be other bodies that somehow fell out of the plane on the way down. Anyway," he pointed to the departing Sea Knight, "once they winch down the medical team and their gear, the captain is going to come back. You guys find anything?"

"There are some interesting tracks and footprints back there," said Scott, pointing into the canopy. "I like the theory that there were people who survived the crash. One print in particular supports that. Let's see what the boss thinks."

After about forty-five minutes, Scott and Walt were sitting on a fallen log, having a break, when Copperton came back in the returning Sea Knight. Once the helicopter shut down, Copperton emerged and walked over to them, bringing Forsyth.

"Heat getting to you two, is it? Did you find anything?"

Scott ignored the jibe and stood up. He pointed over to the oil drums. "Three forty-fours, one of which is two-thirds full. They contain aviation fuel, consistent with the report from the Harriers that it saw a light plane here last night. We figure someone is making regular drop offs of fuel so that this strip can refuel planes for the return trip."

He pointed to the ground around him. "We've had a good look around. There are lots of footprints, military-type boots and no litter. Follow me." Scott headed away from the strip, into the canopy.

He stopped at a fallen tree. "All around here," he moved his arms around, "hoof prints and horse dung. So we are looking for people on horseback. And here," he crouched down. "I could be wrong, but these footprints in the soil, here and here, are different. They are smaller and look like the sort of shoes that women would wear."

Copperton crouched down and looked at the prints, poking them with a stick. "Forsyth?"

"Sir."

"Head back to the bird, get the camera and take some shots of the area, particularly these footprints here." Forsyth headed off.

"According to our briefing, the Harriers' sighting of the light plane was just after 22:00 last night," said Walt. "They could have as much as eight hours start on us."

"If that's the case, there's not much more we can do here. Nonetheless," said Copperton, holding up an evidence bag containing a small scorched piece of aluminum, "we think we might know how the plane came down. We'll get some photos of this area and then head back to the ship."

46

Fort George Meade, Maryland

Around the time the Cobra crews prepared to head back to the *Peleliu*, almost twenty-thousand employees of the National Security Agency (NSA) were heading into work at its headquarters in Fort George Meade in Maryland.

One of the early starters was Jane McKay, a twenty-two-year-old NSA analyst, who was analyzing photos of a man named Rahmattulah Sajadi. Sajadi was no longer living, having been shot dead by a British Special Air Service troop three days earlier in Kabul. However, Sajadi had been a known al-Qaeda operative and would have been captured by the SAS if he had not pulled a weapon when the SAS came into his home unannounced. Jane knew none of this. She didn't need to know. All she needed to know was that he was a person of interest and, as such, anyone he came into contact with was also of interest to her government.

Jane had graduated with degrees in science and IT and her specialty was digital photographs. On her desktop sat a digital image of Sajadi and another person. The photo had been taken one month earlier in Kabul by the CIA. The CIA had been watching Sajadi and his known associates for several months after they had intercepted a low level courier and obtained his name under "questioning." As a result, Sajadi had been monitored closely and a number of photographs had come into

Jane's in-tray having been passed directly to the NSA by the CIA.

The particular photograph before her showed the back of Sajadi as he talked with another person who faced toward the camera. The image showed them seated outside a café in Kabul drinking coffee. How the photograph was obtained was not Jane's concern. Her first task was to crop the image and enhance it. Luckily, the image was in sharp focus and had been taken using the telephoto lens of a fifteen-megapixel camera.

Nonetheless, as she cropped the photo to focus in on the man facing the camera, the image's clarity and sharpness declined. She saved the new image and then went into her tool kit and tried a number of interpolation algorithms to try and sharpen the image. The original digital image consisted of a number of pixels, or dots of color and spaces between them. Her cropped image had put the man's face into focus, but the spaces between the pixels were now more noticeable. Jane's algorithms would try to fill in the white spaces between pixels based on the properties of the surrounding pixels, attempting to guess what those missing pixels would be. Jane had a number of algorithms at her disposal, each with strengths and weaknesses. There were unique factors in every digital image and one of the algorithms would work better on this image than the others.

It took her four tries before she found the best improvement and saved the new file.

She brought up a second image of the two men. This one had been taken from the same position, but it had caught the second man looking at Sajadi. She went through the same process and saved the second, enhanced image of the man Sajadi had been speaking to.

She opened a facial recognition software application and opened the two digital images. Each face has a large number of distinguishable features, including the distance between the eyes, the size and shape of the ears and nose, and so on. The facial recognition software that Jane was using was able to create a 3D *faceprint* of the man, in essence a unique file of the person's facial attributes.

The software operated quickly and she saved the faceprint and loaded the three files into NSA's vast database. She clicked on search and went to get a coffee.

As Tariq Qadir had never been photographed before, the search came back without a result, but his photographs and faceprint were now part of NSA's database of persons of interest.

47

Darién Province, Colombia

Aristo led the two horses about fifty meters up the streambed. The horses were calm and enjoyed the cool feeling of the water over their legs. He wished that Eduardo had not given him the task of shooting the horses. Yet he fully understood his older brother's thinking: he was trying to put off the other woman from pursuing them. With Jorge now dead and the woman having escaped, they did not need the extra horses, which would only slow them down. Potentially, Eduardo had argued, she could use a horse to follow them or return to the airstrip and get help.

Aristo believed the chances that the woman would get on a horse and come after them were very remote. Sure, she was an agent of the US Secret Service, but she would understand the odds were against her and take her opportunity to head back to Panama and safety. This didn't worry him either. There was a reasonable chance that she would never make it, and even if she did, they would be so far away that they would never be found—particularly as they would be heading east soon, toward Chigarodo.

Aristo stopped and took the safety off his rifle. He walked back downstream and aimed his rifle. He shot once and then again.

48

Langley, Virginia

The CIA director, Bruce McBride, sat in his office and ran his eye over a report about the events in London in July 2005. At forty-seven, one of the youngest to sit in this office, he was reminded every day of those who'd held office before him whose photographs lined the famous foyer of the CIA's headquarters in Langley. His desk phone rang and he saw it was his personal assistant. He picked up the receiver.

"Yes, Julie?" he said.

"Dan Salzburg for you, sir."

"Thanks, put him through."

"Bruce, hi. Dan Salzburg here."

"Yes, Dan. What's new?"

"I've just been talking to Captain James on the *Peleliu*. A preliminary look at the crash site strongly suggests that there were four survivors, including Emily Parker."

"Any idea what happened to them?" asked McBride.

"There's a small airstrip near the crash site, almost certainly there so that drugs can be exchanged. And we know there was an exchange there last night and that Emily and one of the agents, Karen Duffy, were being held captive by a bunch of Colombians. We know this because we intercepted the pilot of the Cessna. He told us that the Colombians know Ms. Parker's identity. So we are assuming a kidnap situation. Of the remaining two, the co-pilot and the security consultant, Walker, there is no sign as yet."

"Okay. You want me to see what intel I can find on the Colombians?"

"Yes please, Bruce. The only info we have is a name: Eduardo. About twenty-four years, over six foot. Cocaine is his game. The shipment we intercepted tonight was half a metric ton. He had five men with him."

"I'll get my people onto it, see what we can turn over."

"There's more, Bruce. We can't confirm this until we test the samples, but James's men are convinced that the scorch marks and residues around the cargo bay of the downed jet show evidence of C4. They tell me it has an unmistakable odor."

"That changes things, Dan."

"I know."

"Look. We have good relations with the Bolivians and, given that Parker is directly involved, I am sure they will agree to hand over relevant border security data, including video and stills from their airports. Could you ask the president to call them? Once he has their agreement, let me know and I'll call their guy direct."

"Done."

"Thanks, Dan. Keep me in the loop. Anything I dig up from Colombia will be relayed as soon as possible. Talk soon."

49

White House, Washington DC

Seated on opposite sides of the big Resolute Desk in the Oval Office were the president and Admiral Salzburg, the latter talking. "I know we are only working on the judgment of a bunch of marines, Mr. President. However, James asked a number of his men who had worked with C4 to examine the residue sample brought back from the wreckage. He told me all were unanimous that the residues were consistent with a detonation of C4. I've never smelled C4, but I trust James's judgment on this."

"So we're dealing with a terrorist group on this one?"

"That's the likely option. I've heard no information on any group claiming responsibility, but we are watching."

"Right, so McBride said he could help?"

"We don't know what we are going to find. We don't know if the device, or whatever it was, was placed on the plane by one person or if we are dealing with many. We don't know if the perpetrators are still in Bolivia." Salzburg shrugged his shoulders. "It's a long shot, but if we can get the Bolivians' records, including images and video from their border crossings and the airport; we can look for people we know and compare images against our NSA database."

The president picked up the phone. "Mary, please call President Tores in Bolivia."

"There shouldn't be a problem with Tores," said Salzburg. "Particularly given the plane was Parker's own jet and his daughter was aboard."

The president held up his hand. "President Tores, this is Jim Watson. How are you? I hope my call is convenient."

In La Paz, President Juan Tores sat back into the golf cart to take the call. "Hello, Jim. I am well. Naturally very sorry to hear that Bill Parker's jet crashed. What news of his daughter?"

"We believe she is still alive and survived the plane crash. Unfortunately, she appears to be in the hands of a bunch of Colombians and we are not sure of their intentions."

"No!"

"Anyway, we've been able to establish that the plane was deliberately attacked, and the explosion reported by the pilot was caused by explosives."

"Not a Bolivian, Jim. I am sure of it."

"I think you are right, President Tores. Bill Parker still has a lot of enemies. My intelligence guys want a shot at looking through your border security data. We have a large database of people who are of interest to us and there's a chance we might be able to link something together. Catch these people."

"Of course, Jim. We'll make some calls to set things in motion and your guys in the US embassy here can take copies of anything we have."

The president put down the phone. "Done, Dan. Let McBride know. Tores said they would give their data to our people at the embassy."

"I'm on it."

50

El Alto Airport, La Paz, Bolivia

Qadir had pressed his cream suit and was waiting in a line to check in for his flight to Peru, from where he would join a connecting flight to Spain later that day. As he moved toward the front, he thought about what he would do when he got back to Kabul. Even with Emily Parker out of the way and his satisfaction at the grief this would cause her father, he remained unsatisfied and thought, even now, about ways in which he could kill him.

Above Qadir's head, in many locations, were sophisticated digital cameras that took stills and streamed video to a bank of servers in the airport's security room. From the initial exit from his taxi, through check in and to the departure lounge, the security system had photographed him dozens of times. Qadir remained unworried, confident of his anonymity, a nobody. Even if he had known that the Bolivian's equipment had actually been funded and installed by the US, this view would not have changed.

He reached the front of the line and handed over his passport. The young attendant checked his name and spoke good English. "Good morning, Mr. Bajar. Where are you traveling to today?"

"To Pakistan, Karachi," replied Qadir.

The woman checked her computer and smiled at him. "That is a long way. Have you got baggage you wish to check in?"

Qadir lifted his battered suitcase onto the scales.

"Was your visit to Bolivia enjoyable?" she asked.

"Yes, I have made many new business contacts."

The woman printed off a number of tickets and boarding passes and handed them over. "It is a long journey, Mr. Bajar. Two days in total, but I have confirmed your flights to Peru and Spain, all the way to Karachi. Have a great day."

Allahu Akbar! he thought.

51

White House, Washington DC

The same people sat around the table in the Situation Room less than twenty-four hours since their last meeting. Coffee and pastries sat on a buffet at the room's perimeter. On screen via satellite was Captain James, while Bill Parker was at his home in Houston patched through to a conference phone system.

"You heard me right, Bill," said the president. "A US-registered plane was there last night picking up five-hundred kilos of cocaine. The pilot has confirmed that he saw your daughter in good health. Special Agent Duffy was also there."

"So what has happened?" said Parker.

"If I may?" asked James.

"Go ahead, Captain James," said the president.

"At around 5:30 this morning, search and rescue teams were on the ground at the site of the plane crash. Crash investigators will confirm what happened in due course, but we believe the jet hit the canopy and the fuselage broke into two clear pieces: the nose section and the tail section behind the wing. Only two bodies were found, those of the pilot Michael Rogers and Special Agent Peter Murray. Both had injuries consistent with a high velocity aircraft impact and had been dead more than twelve hours. They were both in the nose section.

"The tail section took a different direction. From what we found on the ground, we figure that it separated on impact with a large tree and then slid through the forest tail first without hitting any major obstacles. The interior was empty, completely empty, no luggage or anything, but we did find some traces of blood. We aren't experts, but my people believe those inside had a good chance of survival and this has now been confirmed by the pilot of the Cessna who stated he personally saw Miss Parker and Agent Duffy. He was picked up this morning after dropping some large parcels of cocaine into the waters around the Florida Keys. He was positive that he saw the two women and told us they were in the company of armed Colombians. Moreover, he told us that the Colombians knew who they had, which doesn't look good."

"It's only the fucking kidnapping capital of the world," said Perry.

"Thanks, Bob," said the president, looking at him.

"Sorry," said Perry, and he loosened his tie.

James continued. "The marine officer that secured the crash site was absolutely positive that he could smell traces of C4 explosive, consistent with scorch marks found in and around the cargo area, which is in the tail section. The NTSB crash guys won't reach the crash site until later this evening, so I had some samples of the residues brought back to the ship. We don't have the means to test it, but I've got a lot of experienced guys here that have worked with C4, and they all confirm that the odor from this residue is unmistakably C4.

"We also had a number of people look over this airstrip this morning. Their visual inspection of the site revealed a number of footprints, including those of women, and drums of aviation fuel. This seems to corroborate everything. Of the other two people on the plane— the co-pilot, Saunders, and the passenger, Walker—there's been no sign. I have dispatched a further four Sea Knights, purely to conduct a visual search around the crash site. I have also deployed two squads of marines who are assisting on the ground to search."

"Thanks, David," said Salzburg, looking around the table. "I called the head of the NTSB this morning and they have sent a team of six air crash investigators to Panama. They will go to Panama City first, where they will join up with a team from the Panamanian Air Authority. It's a US plane and US citizens, but the Panamanians have jurisdiction over the wreckage under international law and our NTSB people will be there by invitation. Their task will be to locate the plane's black box, examine the wreckage and, ultimately, to determine the cause of the crash."

"Okay, thanks gentlemen," said the president. "What's our next step? It would appear that Emily Parker and Agent Duffy are in the hands of drug runners."

"The Cessna pilot, Costello, knows who his employers are, but he's not stupid and won't reveal who they are," said Salzburg. "However, what he did tell us about his Colombian contacts is that he normally meets with a man called Fabio. Just Fabio, no last name. This time, however, there was a man senior to this Fabio. He knows him by the name of Eduardo and has met him before. We are pretty sure they are Colombians and part of a large drug smuggling operation, one of the many groups operating out of the region north of Medellin. This doesn't have any of the signatures of FARC.

"I've asked the CIA director to look into the Colombian side of things," continued Salzburg. "There's nothing yet, however."

"What can we do to get her back? Can't we send some troops south of the border?" asked Bill Parker, who was patched through from his office in Houston.

"Sorry, Bill," said Nichols. "We just can't barge over the border in Colombia. Our relations with Colombia have strengthened over the last ten years and the current president Sanchez has been pro US and active against drug trafficking and kidnapping. But he won't let our troops into his country."

"Thanks, Amanda," said the president. "Captain James, please remain in place for the present. Maintain security around the crash site and provide assistance to the NTSB and the Panamanians when they arrive. Bill, I can't imagine how difficult this is for you and Delia. We are doing everything that we can to get Emily back."

Once Bill Parker's line was disconnected, the president resumed. "I have just got off the phone with President Tores. He has authorized us to look closely at his border security data. McBride is covering this." He looked at Salzburg. "Dan, keep liaising with McBride. We are going to have to work very fast if we are to have a chance of finding the person or people who did this."

"Amanda, get the Colombian ambassador in and see what they are prepared to do. If I need to call Sanchez, let me know."

52

El Alto Airport, La Paz, Bolivia

CIA agent-in-residence, George Newman, got out of his car, which he'd parked in the short-term car park at El Alto Airport. At forty-nine years old, he'd been in Bolivia for two years and loved the climate and the people. His job required very little of him, which suited him just fine. After almost thirty years in the agency, George liked the quiet life and didn't mind that his boss had probably sent him here because he was suited to it.

His morning had been interrupted by a phone call from the director of the South America Division in Langley. The news of the Parker's plane crash in Panama was all around the embassy, so Newman had not been too surprised to receive instructions to obtain the security footage of the airport for the past week. He had also been tasked to obtain border control data, including, where possible, digital imagery. However, being a land-locked nation, there were numerous crossing points to Peru, Chile, Argentina, Paraguay and Colombia. So his first priority was the airports at La Paz and Santa Cruz. Newman was not looking forward to the next few days.

He entered the administration building and showed his embassy pass to the man behind the security desk. "George Newman from the US embassy. I have an appointment with Manuel Teranes."

"Thank you. Please take a seat," came the response.

Teranes kept him waiting for fifteen minutes, but Newman held his annoyance in check when he finally arrived in the foyer. Teranes appeared to be in his early forties, medium build, wearing a white shirt, no tie, and gray slacks. He flashed Newman a wide smile as he greeted him. "Mr. Newman, I am so sorry, we have been working like bees to get things ready for you." He extended his hand and Newman shook it.

"Come, follow me." He headed off to the elevators.

They came up to Teranes's office, which overlooked the airport terminal. "Please sit down, Mr. Newman. Can I get you anything?"

"Thanks, Manuel, I am fine."

"You know I only got the request from our president two hours ago?"

"I know, it is not a lot of notice for you, but there is a strong possibility that the person who put a bomb on that plane entered the country on a commercial air flight."

"Don't worry, our systems are good here. After all, you paid for them." He smiled. "We have sixty-four cameras in the terminal, including the areas in customs, and twenty more in the baggage handling area. We have focused on the terminal data. The photographs we take are not high resolution; storage needs would be too high. Some of the cameras stream video, but most take images every two seconds."

"A week of data has been copied for you, many hundreds of gigabytes. Here," Teranes handed over three portable drives.

"Gee, thank you, Manuel. That was fast work."

"Each drive has up to one terabyte of data on it. You said you wanted everything. We are pleased that we could help you. It is a sad day for me that the plane left from this airport. You will let us know if you find anything, no?"

Newman stood. "Of course. Anyway, I'd better get this sent off."

Teranes escorted him out of the building. Newman was halfway back to his car when Teranes called to him. He retraced his steps. "Here," said Teranes when he reached him.

Newman took another portable drive from him and added it to his box. "That drive contains this morning's data. You never know."

53

Darién Province, Colombia

Jake and Duffy ran quickly back to the trail and then headed south. As they approached the area where Duffy had been attacked, they moved into the bush and approached more cautiously. "Stay here and watch our rear," said Jake. "I am going to look around. It looks like they have gone, but it could be a trap."

Jake moved forward on his front. He passed the point where the man was killed. He couldn't see the body, but he saw the trail where his body had been dragged into the scrub over to the other side. He inched forward until he could see the area where they had rested by the stream. He listened.

After five minutes or so, he got up on his feet, and keeping low, he headed down to the stream.

Duffy realized she was still in shock, but she was also angry, angry at herself for allowing herself and Emily to be put into such a position. *She was in the Secret Service on protection detail, goddammit!* If she hadn't cried out earlier, they might have been able to get Emily as well.

She simply couldn't imagine going back without Emily. She would have to leave the Service. An out-of-work, disgraced former agent, no longer young, unmarried, but with a criminology degree, no less! Now *that* would be useful…

She looked around. Past dawn, the sun still hid behind the thick undergrowth but it was getting warmer. She could hear birds, but no sounds of people. She took the opportunity to relieve herself, but she needn't have bothered, and she made a note to drink some water at the next opportunity.

Suddenly, she heard a voice. It was Jake calling her. She stood up and headed back down the trail. Before long, she could see him standing next to the stream. And the man had two horses. She smiled.

When she joined up with Jake, she patted the flank of the horse that had carried her to this point. "Good girl," she said. "Are you sure they are gone?"

"After listening for about five minutes and hearing nothing, I came down here and heard these two up stream. The two shots we heard? Fired into a tree. Whoever brought them up here was told to shoot them and couldn't go through with it. It's the only explanation I can think of."

Duffy took the water bottle from Jake and started to fill it. "It also means that they think I disarmed and killed that guy myself. You're in the clear." She drank deeply.

"I went to the top of this ridge," he pointed up. "The tracks indicate that they have continued onward. I figure they have about a thirty-minute start.

"The trail looks much less defined from here on. They will have to cut a way through in parts, so we should be quicker than them." Jake looked through the man's satchel and he found another water bottle, which he gave to Duffy to fill. Some dried fruit, nuts, and half a loaf of dark bread completed the inventory. He sniffed the bread and, finding it okay, broke off a piece and gave it to Duffy. The rifle had a sling and he put the bag and the rifle on his right shoulder. The knife was sitting in his belt loop.

Duffy approached her horse. "Give me a hand then."

Jake made a stirrup from his hands and Duffy climbed onto the horse's back. There was no saddle, just a blanket bound to the flanks, but both horses were bridled and there were reins to use.

"Put your pistol into your waistband, you will need two hands," said Jake. He climbed onto his horse and had a bite of the bread. *God, that tasted good.* He realized how hungry he was. "Let's go. I only have the beginnings of a plan, but we'll do our best to get her back."

54

White House, Washington DC

In the Oval Office, the president, Salzburg, Perry, and Nichols discussed the situation further. "We won't get permission to overfly Colombia, Jim," said Nichols. "I know the ambassador well and he was clear that, even if you call Sanchez personally, you won't get the go ahead.

"Sanchez has made significant progress against the FARC and several high ranking members have been captured over the last six months. His actions against the drug families and against FARC have been highly visible, successful and popular. Allowing the US to fly military aircraft across the border, regardless of the pressing reasons we have, is simply not an option."

"Well, it seems like they've managed to get away," said the president. "I can't think of anything further we can do."

"The *Peleliu* is now anchored about five miles off the coast," said Salzburg. "I have asked him to remain on station until the air crash investigators have completed their work and then they will lift out the wreckage and it will be brought back to the States for further analysis. The bodies of Michael Rogers and Peter Murray have been removed from the wreckage and will be taken by helicopter to Panama City later today. From there, they will be flown to Houston. The next of kin have been informed."

"Bob," said the president, "get onto the DEA and pass on the descriptions and intel we have about the people who have Emily and Agent Duffy. They also have contacts in Colombia and there is a good chance we will be able to find out who this Eduardo is. Keep me in the loop if anything further develops."

55

Darién Province, Colombia

The two riders steadily followed the trail made by Eduardo and his men. Jake could see steam rising from horse dung, and where they'd cut through the foliage, sap and water dripped, suggesting their close proximity.

Jake led, taking his time as different options swirled in his mind. Whatever happened, he wanted to do something before it got dark, which he figured was still ten hours away. The key issue was distance. Every additional mile into Colombia increased the risks of meeting insurgents or men associated with the drug trade.

"So how come you left the army, Jake?"

"It's a long story."

"We have time."

"I guess I'd had enough of the life. I was born in the army, or rather the marines. My dad was a marine officer and by the time I was fourteen, I'd lived on about seven military bases. I'd also been in ten different schools to that point."

"You served in Afghanistan?"

"Yes, right at the beginning. We were that close to capturing bin Laden. Could've saved a lot of lives...It was difficult terrain though, perhaps the worse the US has ever faced, very cold, high mountains, hard to support and get logistic lines in place. It was their territory and they'd spent years tunneling through mountains and getting ready for a fight. In the end, we just didn't throw enough resources at it. Now the Taliban and other groups are just waiting for us to leave. No different from what happened to the Russians and the English before them."

"I thought we were winning."

"It can't be won. The Afghanis have been fighting among themselves and against invading forces for centuries. No invading force has ever gained control for very long. It's very similar to what happened to us in Vietnam. We have tried by building new schools and infrastructure, training their police forces and military. A lot of US firms have made a fortune on contracts rebuilding roads and so on. And then the insurgents come and destroy what we make. Afghanis are not stupid. They know we don't have the political will for a long fight and things will all come full circle again."

"And Iraq?"

"Not much different, in terms of the likely outcome. But there will be a big struggle for power when we leave. In many ways, the Iraqis were better off with Saddam there. It's all about oil anyway, getting security of supply so that we can keep living beyond our means and drive around in SUVs."

"That's a pretty cynical view, Jake." They traveled in silence for a few minutes. "Tell me why you left and became a civilian again."

Boy, this woman is persistent. He thought for a moment. "I never was a civilian until I drove out of the gate at Fort Bragg seven years ago. Dad even sent me to military school in Virginia when I was fourteen. He hoped I would craft a career in the marines, as an officer. He was pretty pissed when I joined the grunts at seventeen.

"I guess in the end, I started to doubt myself, my ability to keep my team safe. Shortly after we won the first offensive in Iraq in '03, we moved into an occupation mode. We still had to get troops on the ground though, and there were plenty of hot areas where we attempted to crush the resistance. The Germans had the right approach. To occupy a country, you need to get large amounts of people on the ground, you need to be brutal, and you need to infiltrate every section of the community. You can't do that with a hundred thousand troops and with public attitudes being what they are. It requires ten times more resources and our government just doesn't have the political will, or the will of the people, to put that many young Americans over there. So, a decade on and we are just playing games, hoping that the Iraqis and the Afghanis can find the means to manage their own destiny, in time.

"Anyway, in late '03, we were supporting a marine task force on the outskirts of Baghdad and, late into the afternoon, my team got called back to base. A Blackhawk came and picked us up and we headed back to Bagram.

"On our way, we were shot down by a rocket propelled grenade and crashed into a square in the city. There were six survivors, myself and my team of three, one of the door gunners and one of the pilots, a young and very frightened woman. It was dusk and we were left there, no extraction possible until morning we were told. We were in some sort of square, you know, with a fountain to one side, and we were receiving fire from all sides. We kept our heads down, but our ammunition was running out and then the door gunner was killed. The other door gunner had been blown out of the chopper when we were initially hit."

Jake paused and a minute passed as they continued following the trail. "Go on," Duffy encouraged.

"I saw a lot of death when I was a soldier, Duffy. You never get used to it and I've seen many men sent home because they couldn't deal with it. As soldiers…as men, we can't show fear; the culture just doesn't allow for it. So like many, I internalized my feelings. It was a coping mechanism and I still hold a lot of bad experiences in here, and in here." Jake tapped the side of his head with his forefinger and then patted his chest.

"That day, in the chopper. We were just sitting there, a routine flight back to base for new orders. I remember the door gunner. There were two, but one of them turned to me, he caught me looking at him. And then, he smiled at me and I thought, *How young is this guy?* I guess he was no younger than I was when I joined up at seventeen. It's a moment that will stick with me till I die. One moment in time. I was about to ask his name and how long he'd been in and then he was gone, blown out the door as we were struck by the rocket-propelled grenade.

"Anyway, we were in the square and, once the other gunner took a round in the head, I made the decision to get out of there. The other factor was that we were partly using the cover provided by the Blackhawk. It was leaking gas and it was only a matter of time before it went up. I hate leaving dead behind, but we had no option. My team of three was still intact and we had the female pilot.

"We all had call signs in the Special Forces. My 2IC was a great guy from Jersey, named Eddie Martinez. We called him Frogman because he could hold his breath for minutes. I also had two rookies, Kevin Klein, call sign Calvin, and Frank Bennett, our medic who had the call sign Tony. Pretty obvious why they got those names. Anyway, I quickly briefed everyone and then we sprinted about one hundred feet toward some sort of warehouse I had spotted earlier, which led to a street of sorts out of the square. Frogman and Tony went first, then the pilot and Calvin. I brought up the rear, carrying the M60, which had about eighty rounds left. It was dark by then.

"Our strategy was simple, but dangerous nonetheless. Fight our way through the streets and, hopefully, rendezvous with the marines, which we understood were fighting to get to us. We made our way along that first street that led into the square. We would lay down covering fire while the others would run to gain distance, whereupon they would cover us. I don't know how many men were pursuing us—perhaps fifty or so. But it wasn't just the pursuit we had to deal with; even though we were gaining distance and keeping the pursuit at bay, more and more fighters were seeking to intervene from our front. The word had got out and people could smell our blood. Scariest situation I've ever been in.

"After about an hour, we'd probably put a couple of kilometers behind us. Frogman had taken a round in the arm and most of us had taken rounds in our vests. Those hurt like hell and you get a huge bruise, but we all would have died that night if we hadn't been wearing them. There were fewer and fewer people pursuing us and we found ourselves in this shopping area, closed and shuttered down at that time of night. Tony and the woman pilot took the lead. We were going roughly south at this point. There was a dimly lit crossroads we had to get through and Frogman, Calvin, and I were on opposite sides of the street. We were really low on ammunition and making every shot count.

"Suddenly, there was a screech of brakes and we started to receive fire from inside a van that had come to a stop in the middle of the intersection. We were also getting fired on from the pursuers. This was a bad situation and we could no longer see Tony and the pilot. I brought the M60 around, but before I could return fire, I felt like I'd been electrocuted. I'd taken a shot in the hand, could no longer operate the gun, and our pursuers were still making progress toward us."

Jake held up his right hand and Duffy could clearly see the rough scar tissue in the middle of his palm. "The van was there for about forty seconds or so and then it was gone. So were Tony and the pilot. We simply weren't able to put enough firepower on the van given what was going on."

Jake concentrated on his surroundings and Duffy gave him a moment. "What happened next, Jake?"

Jake remained silent and didn't speak for a couple of minutes. Duffy waited. "Well, we were three now and we just made the decision to run for it. We didn't have the ammunition or the numbers to keep fighting. We moved quickly and shot at everyone who got in our way. We probably ran about another four ks or so and then saw advance elements of the marines in armored vehicles. We made it out."

"And the pilot and your other team member?"

Jake stopped and Duffy came up beside him and put her hand on his shoulder. "They were never seen again," said Jake. "We figured that Tony was probably killed in the street. His body was never recovered, but he would not have allowed himself to be captured alive. For the pilot, we heard later that she was executed—animals cut her head off and uploaded the video to the net. Her name was Paula Shaw. Sure, I know that the chances of all five of us getting to safety were slim, but I just blamed myself, always have. Six weeks later, I was driving out of Fort Bragg."

Jake stopped and they listened. He could hear birds and other sounds to his front and figured they were still some distance away. "So there you have it, Duffy—a fallen hero."

"That's bullshit Jake, and you know it. Certainly not going to get my sympathy vote. What was your call sign?"

"Most men got a call sign during the Special Forces selection. I was no different. My people knew me as Luke."

"Luke?"

"As in Cool Hand. We had this guy in Selection, called him Marilyn, a name he wasn't too happy about, I can tell you. Anyway, he was a movie buff and he reckoned I had a good poker face. Paul Newman acted in this film in the 60s. It was called Cool Hand Luke. Never seen it, but I was known as Luke from then on." Jake encouraged his horse and they moved forward. "Anyway, what about you? Seven years is a long time to be doing the same stuff."

"It was great at first, straight out of the Academy, working beside guys who had years of experience in protecting presidents and other dignitaries. I was in a team and I earned respect, even from the men in time. Some of the old timers still refuse to believe that women can make it in their world, but there are fewer and fewer of them these days. Bit like the army, I would imagine.

"After about three years, I was asked to join the president's protection detail. I was thrilled. Many agents never get the chance. When Parker left the White House, I was given the option to stay on. I liked the family and took the job. I was happy at first but it's not the same as working on the current president's detail. I've been looking at options…"

They were quiet for a time.

"You got a man back in the world, Duffy?"

"I had one, Jake, but he turned out to be a bastard, and I found out he'd been cheating on me. My life can be lonely, and I guess that's why I put so much effort into my work. When I'm not working, I don't seem to meet many men, but then I don't seem to be in the right circle of friends. You would know that from being in the army. Plus, no one wants to date someone who is away so much of the time. And I haven't yet met anyone who can handle me," she challenged him.

"Perhaps you just haven't met the right guy yet."

Maybe I have, she thought.

Jake stopped and dismounted and they listened. "We are getting pretty close, perhaps only five hundred yards, perhaps less."

"You worked that plan out yet?"

"It's time for us to split up. I am going to try and get ahead of them. I can't do that on a horse. Find somewhere for the horses to rest and rope them somehow, so they can't wander off. Then follow the trail on foot. Don't let them see you, but you need to be close enough to be in a position to grab Emily.

"When you hear shots from an M16, you should assume it is me shooting. It should be a natural instinct for them to engage me; at least that's what I am hoping. In the confusion, I am hoping you will get the chance to release Emily. When you have her, head back here, grab the horses and then go back along the trail. We are about two miles from the stream where you were attacked. When you reach there, turn downstream and take the horses along the streambed. When you have gone about five hundred yards or so, wait and hide up. If I am not there in two hours, leave without me and keep heading north to get back into Panama."

Jake checked his M16 and handed over the satchel, which contained their only food supply. He moved to go. "Jake," said Duffy, "be careful."

"Don't worry," he smiled, which looked funny through all the mud and dirt he had on his face and body. "Whatever happens, shoot that thing to kill. This plan depends as much, if not more, on you to get Emily to safety."

56

Langley, Virginia

It had taken over two and a half hours for the data on Teranes's portable drives to be streamed by satellite to Langley from the US embassy. Newman left the data, all four one-terabyte drives, with the embassy's IT people before getting in his car and heading for Santa Cruz to get data from their airport.

In Langley, Michelle Williams sat in a secure room splitting the files into video and stills and preparing the data for a search through the NSA's database. A graduate in IT from Stanford, Michelle had been with the CIA for two years. Her specialty was data matching.

Michelle sorted the two groups of files. There were 420 gigabytes of video from twenty-four cameras. It was low resolution, but she still had 384 hours of footage.

Of the stills, there were over twenty-five million files, each about one hundred kilobytes—two and a half terabytes in all. She turned to Terry Abrams, her supervisor, who sat in the cubicle next to her.

"This is a huge amount of data, Terry."

"I know. We've got priority access to the supercomputers at NSA. All non-essential use has been suspended, but it's still going to take days to run those files through."

"What are the priorities?" asked Michelle.

"Well, Parker's Gulfstream left La Paz yesterday at 2:30 p.m. local time. We are hoping that our person or person either arrived on a commercial flight in the last week, or departed in the last forty-eight hours. Let's ignore the video for the time being. Can you sort the files by camera?"

"Sure. There is a date and time in the properties for each file, as well."

Terry turned to the terminal map, which Manuel Teranes had faxed through earlier in the day. "Let's run through the departures first. We are looking at a much smaller time window, so there will be a lower number of files. We can then load up the stock of files in customs to get the arrivals. I think we can ignore the other cameras. Cameras thirteen through twenty-six are the ones of interest; see if you can isolate them."

Michelle sorted the relevant files with a few clicks. "Done. I'll sort them in date order, like this. Now, how far back do we go?"

"Just today and yesterday."

Michelle, pasted the relevant images into a new folder on a shared drive. "Okay. That's still over four hundred thousand images."

"Better than twenty-five million."

Terry opened a new window and clicked on an icon. He was requested to place his thumb on the thumb reader, which he did. Satisfied, the application opened and he was now accessing one of the most powerful computers in the world, capable of over one gigaflops—10 floating point operations per second—and that was for each core of the multi-core computer. He brought up the comparison utility and selected the images that Michelle had isolated. "Here goes." He clicked on the submit button. "Let's get a coffee and then we'll prioritize the other images."

57

Darién Province, Colombia

Jake was lucky. As he moved out of the valley and up toward the ridge line, the vegetation thinned, and he found he was able to make good progress. It was still hard going, but his training kicked in and he found himself hurdling fallen trees, moving like his life depended on it. After about ten minutes, he figured he'd traveled about a mile. It had been difficult to anticipate where the trail was heading, but he managed to glimpse the party down and to his right and realized he was on the right track. His plan required that he get ahead of them and he kept up the pace for another five hundred yards.

He stopped at a small ledge overlooking the shallow valley below and caught his breath. Behind him was a large rock, perhaps five yards wide and similarly tall. A small clearing fronted the large rock and several smaller rocks were embedded into the dirt around it, and he looked past them to where he believed the trail lay. He couldn't have made a better position. He pulled apart the M16 and checked the mechanisms. He tested the magazine and figured twenty or twenty-five rounds. He put the rifle back together and pulled the breach to chamber a round.

It didn't take long before he heard the group finding their way along the trail below, and presently he could see figures on horseback moving from his right. He figured he had about a ten to fifteen yard elevation and guessed the range at between fifty and sixty yards. He checked that the gun sight was on its basic level, good for shots out to one hundred yards, and clicked off the safety.

His position still lay within a thick canopy of rain forest, with single trees reaching up from the forest floor to above his head and a thick ground cover of ferns and tropical plants, but he had picked a point where he had a clear line of sight through the tree line. He settled down to wait.

◊

They'd ridden for an hour, and the humidity was starting to hurt man and beast. Twice Emily had nearly fallen as her horse stumbled over the uneven terrain, and she frequently needed to duck under branches. Cobwebs matted her hair and mosquitoes and other small insects took their toll. As the group paused to navigate around a fallen tree, she turned around to Eduardo. "I need my hands untied." Eduardo looked at her, but did not reply. "Listen, please. Where am I going to go? There are five of you, all armed. Twice I have nearly fallen and I need to be able to hold onto something."

Eduardo regarded her disheveled state and relented. He whistled and the group halted. He moved up alongside Emily and undid the strap around her wrists, putting it into his saddle bag for later. "Don't think of trying anything," he said. "After the incident back at the stream, I am starting to wonder if taking you was worth the trouble."

"Thank you," she said. He handed her a water flask and she drank. Eduardo signaled to keep going and they moved off. *Why take me in the first place?* Sure, her mom and dad would pay to get her back, but her captors were in the drug business. Didn't these people earn billions? Perhaps Daddy needed to pay them better? Emily just couldn't work out the motivation. She was a liability. She had slowed them down and Karen had killed one of their men. She thought back to her work. Work? She wanted to do something else and would make her case clearly when she saw her father again. If she saw him again, she reminded herself.

No, it just wouldn't do anymore. She was twenty-four and still living at home. She knew that her father was hoping to get her into public life, but she'd seen what public life was about and it just didn't attract her.

Emily followed behind Juan and she watched as his head simply exploded and a plume of bone, blood, hair, and brain matter shot out of the right side of his head. He toppled onto the ground blood spurting like a fountain from the entry wound. Then her brain registered the sound of gunshot and the chattering of birds as they took flight.

In the next moment, Eduardo pulled her off the horse to the ground. The younger man, his brother, kept his head down and Eduardo motioned him over. He spoke to him in Spanish and Emily figured he had been told to watch over her.

The remaining two men took to the undergrowth to the left of the trail, returning fire towards a ridge. Eduardo also followed until she could no longer see him. She sat on the ground and watched the fear in the younger man's face as he pointed his rifle in her direction.

58

Over the Pacific

Qadir started to relax once they reached cruising altitude on his flight to Spain. The flight to Peru had been uneventful, although a little choppy as the small turboprop plane had negotiated the peaks and valleys over the journey. Now he was settled in a window seat aboard an Iberian jumbo jet. Qadir could have afforded business class but didn't want to draw undue attention to himself. So he purchased an economy ticket, or coach as the Americans liked to call it, and his three-seat row only had himself and another man in it, allowing for some space and comfort. *How good is this?* he thought as he adjusted his seat.

Once aboard, he declined the offer of alcohol and accepted only a juice. He reflected on a successful mission and considered his options when he got back to Kabul. He would still keep a watch on Bill Parker. Killing his daughter had been satisfying, but his desire for revenge was still not fully sated. *That* would take Parker himself.

In his meeting with Al-Zawahiri, the great man hinted that Qadir had a great future within the organization. Money had been getting tighter for the organization and Al-Zawahiri suggested that Qadir might move away from coordinating attacks to fund raising. "What do I know about fund raising?" Qadir had asked.

"You are a smart man and your courage is unquestioned, but we need someone who is unknown to the West. Someone who can meet with our supporters and encourage them to make a donation to the cause."

Perhaps the time had come for him to surrender his Kalashnikov? Qadir knew that he was tired of conflict, tired of hiding. Perhaps in traveling to the West he might get another chance to avenge his family's death?

A smiling, pretty flight attendant leaned over and picked up his empty glass. "Another juice for you, sir?"

Qadir was feeling buoyant. "No, thank you. Could I get a Scotch please?"

59

Darién Province, Colombia

Jake let the first rider go past and then had a two to three second window to make his shot. He aimed for the second rider's head and squeezed off one round, hitting the man within an inch or two of his aim point. He saw the round as it made impact and the man died, falling off the side of his horse.

He ducked down behind the natural ledge and waited. Within ten seconds, he received answering fire, an M16 and the submachine gun that he had seen with the oldest in the group back at the plane wreck. None of the rounds came anywhere near him, meaning they had no idea who was shooting at them and where he lay.

He risked looking over the top. He could see no movement, but after a minute some foliage moved. He took aim and let off a burst of three rounds. Whoever was down there moved quickly and Jake let off two more shots at the area where the foliage was moving. He heard a cry and then the sounds of a man in a lot of pain, his cries and screams filling the forest. Jake had heard such sounds before and knew that he'd shot another.

Nothing happened for several minutes, but Jake knew from experience that his friends would not be able to put up with the man's cries indefinitely and, sure enough, he saw a faint movement of the foliage close to where he believed the wounded man lay.

He took aim and fired two rounds and mentally counted that he'd fired eight rounds. At least sixteen bullets left.

The wounded man continued to cry and swear in Spanish and, for five minutes, Jake scanned the ground in front of him. Nothing moved.

As his thoughts turned to Duffy, he heard an M16 bark about one hundred yards to his right. On top of the M16, Jake clearly heard a pistol shoot twice. A figure rose out of the bush about forty yards to his front and ducked and weaved back toward the trail. Jake fired two shots, but knew he'd missed.

60

White House, Washington DC

President Watson sat at his desk in the Oval Office. It was getting late in the afternoon and the sun streamed through the windows, his favorite time of day. Alone for the first time in the last twenty-four hours, he turned his mind to budget issues, not his favorite topic. He'd done what he could for Parker's daughter, and he now felt that others would manage the wash-up. That said, he hoped she was recovered alive and safe.

He worked steadily through a speech he was to give in Congress in a few days' time and thought back to his inauguration. *Damn the timing of it all.* By the time he was president and in a position to do anything about the global financial crisis, Parker had already done deals that couldn't be undone. Now, three years later, the country had over fifteen trillion dollars in debt and a budget that could not be reined in without hurting a lot of people, people he'd made promises to. His wife told him to dismantle the Federal Reserve, told him a few facts that he hadn't known. He knew that he'd put the same people in charge of the financial system that had created the mess in the first place. Was that the sort of legacy he wanted? With his re-election coming up in a few months, he needed to be decisive, but over what?

His desk phone rang and he picked it up. It was his assistant, Mary. "Director McBride for you, Mr. President."

"Thanks Mary. Hi, Bruce, how are things progressing?"

McBride sat in his office in Virginia looking at three photographs on his desk, one of high quality. "Mr. President, some good news, we think."

"What have you got?"

"We've been running the data, the images from the security cameras at the La Paz airport in Bolivia, all afternoon. There's tons of it, but we've had an early break. On my desk is a high resolution photograph of an unknown man, Afghani we think, talking to a known al-Qaeda operative in Kabul about a month ago. An operative who is now deceased."

"And?"

"Well, our analysts decided to put through images from the departures from today and yesterday into NSA's computers first. There were less of them than arrivals over the past week. Only been running for an hour and up pops a match, ninety-five-point-seven per cent probability."

"Sorry, Bruce, what do you mean by match?"

"Well on my desk is a low resolution photograph of a male boarding a plane from La Paz to Lima, Peru, this morning. The photo was taken by one of the airport's security cameras in the ceiling at one of the check-in counters. We add millions of photos to its database every year, and each is put through facial recognition software to create a digital map of a person's features. We call it a faceprint. We are pretty certain that the guy who boarded a plane in Bolivia this morning is the same guy that we photographed in Kabul a month earlier talking with someone that we know for certain worked for al-Qaeda. The photo taken this morning matches the faceprint we created from the images we obtained in Afghanistan. It is the same man."

"So what's his name and where is he now?"

"He was using a Pakistan passport and was traveling under the name of Imran Bajar, but these guys never use their real names."

"Which guys?"

"Al-Qaeda."

"Where's the link? Seems pretty circumstantial so far."

"The link has just been reported on Al Jazeera."

"You're kidding?"

"Never have and never would, Mr. President. Al-Zawahiri himself has just uploaded a twenty-minute tirade on the West and particularly you and the former president. They have claimed responsibility for downing Parker's plane and Emily Parker's death and claim revenge for atrocities committed by the US over the past decade."

"So, a clear link between this Bajar guy and al-Qaeda? It seems clear he had opportunity?"

"Yes. We are going to continue to sift through the data the Bolivians have given us, but this is too much of a coincidence to pass up."

"Where is Bajar right now?"

"Sitting in seat 53A on an Iberian seven-four-seven, about three hours out from Lima. It's heading for Madrid, where he will change flights to Dubai. Eventual destination is Karachi."

"What do you suggest we do?"

"I suggest we ask the Spanish to detain him on suspicion of terrorism and then use the extradition treaty we have with Spain to get him back here on US soil."

"Do you think the Spanish will cooperate?"

"They will if you call them. We could let him pass through, but the risk of losing him is too great and there's no way we can trust the Pakistanis to do the right thing."

"Alright, Bruce, leave it to me."

"One more thing…"

"Yes."

"We are pretty sure that Emily Parker and Karen Duffy were taken by the son of a major person of interest in Colombia, Leandro Ortiz. His home is near Medellin and he has made billions from cocaine —Colombia's third largest exporter according to the DEA. We base this partly on the confession from our Cessna pilot, Costello, who claimed the guy in charge at the airstrip in Panama was named Eduardo. Plus, we intercepted a sat phone call between Ortiz and his son, who is named Eduardo. Time frame and origin of the call matches perfectly."

"So what can you do to assist in her return?"

"We have some assets down there, but it is a very hard country to operate in. In a few days, we should have some more information and I think the best idea is to simply bargain and pay Ortiz for a safe return. He is a business man after all."

"What about this Walker guy and the co-pilot?"

"Still no sign."

"Al-Zawahiri should have waited before telling the world about their success. Sooner or later, the media is going to find out that Emily Parker is still alive."

"Rivera has been very cooperative on that front. Denied all requests from reporters to fly down there. And there's been a few that have tried. I believe CNN is even trying to get down there by car. Let me know how you do with the Spanish, Mr. President. Get Amanda Nichols involved as we don't want to miss this opportunity. I think we have enough on this Bajar guy to detain him on suspicion of murder and conducting a terrorist act on Americans."

"Thanks, Bruce. This is good work."

"Oh yes, the guy that Bajar was talking to in Kabul. We have some of his associates in custody over there; pretty sure they are tied up with al-Qaeda somehow. Now we have this guy's photograph, we will be pulling all stops out to find out who he is."

61

Darién Province, Colombia

Duffy spent five minutes after Jake left finding a suitable resting spot for the horses and tying their reins together so that the horses would need to move as one to forage, thus preventing them from moving far.

She checked her Sig, moved the safety off, and walked down after Emily and her captors. The forest was very quiet and she put this down to the group ahead. It seemed the birds and animals knew when men came into their space and she had noticed the way the forest went quiet throughout the last twenty-four hours. It was nearly noon and the heat and humidity had built until her shirt stuck to her and perspiration ran into her eyes and down her nose. The trail was distinct and she wondered how often it was used and by whom.

A single shot rang out from her front and she crouched down to assess things. She found it hard to gauge how far ahead, but the sounds of horses and men scrambling for cover suggested perhaps two hundred yards distant, give or take.

She heard automatic fire and pictured men firing back at Jake and, as she thought of him, she remembered Emily; Duffy crouched down and started to move forward as quickly as she could.

More shots rang out and then she heard a terrible screaming and crying. She could tell it was one of the Colombians.

She came around a bend and spied several horses ahead through the foliage. She moved forward to a large tree to her right and peered around the edge.

Emily sat on a fallen log, looking toward her rear and not toward Duffy. She couldn't see anyone with her, so she cautiously moved around the tree, pistol first, with her left hand supporting the other, as her training kicked in.

Emily turned and saw her, her eyes widening in surprise. Duffy dropped her aim slightly and moved forward. Then she saw the younger Colombian hidden in the shade just behind Emily.

The man's M16 pointed straight at Duffy and her arms came up to adjust her aim. *Too slow*, she thought.

As the man's finger tightened on his trigger, Emily launched herself at the rifle and several rounds whizzed past Duffy's head. Emily wrestled with the man and his rifle and stood between Duffy and the man, giving her no shot.

The man was clearly stronger than Emily and twisted the rifle to his left and, as Emily went with the rifle, unwilling to let go, Duffy saw her shot and put two rounds into the center of the man's chest, just as she'd been taught. He went down quietly, leaving the M16 in Emily's hands.

Duffy moved forward quickly and put her arm around Emily. "I'm sorry I left you. Jake is with us. They will have heard our shots and we have very little time. Come with me, quickly."

Emily did not need further explanation and they ran back along the trail.

◊

After the first shot killed Juan, everyone's first instinct had been to get down. The shot came from their left and was clearly from a rifle. *Probably Jorge's*, thought Eduardo. He took Emily and Aristo farther back and told his brother to keep his head down and watch her. He heard Luiz and Fabio returning fire, and he crawled through the bush to where Fabio lay.

"How many are there?" said Eduardo.

"We have only had one shot," said Fabio, "so I don't think it is FARC, who wouldn't shoot at us anyway. It is one person. The woman?"

"I agree, it sounded like an M16, probably Jorge's. I never imagined the other woman would be able to follow us. Where is Luiz?"

Before Fabio could answer a further three shots rang out.

"He is over there. Luiz," Fabio hissed, "keep your head down."

Within seconds of saying this, they both heard a further two shots and it was clear that Luiz had been hit as he cried out and then started to sob, clearly in pain.

"You see ahead and up, below that large rock?" said Eduardo, peering through gaps in the foliage.

Fabio parted the foliage and looked through. "What did you see?"

"Smoke. Our shooter is up there."

Luiz continued to wail loudly and it was difficult to concentrate. "I am going over to check him out," said Fabio.

Fabio crawled away and Eduardo tried to line up his sights on where he thought the shooter lay. Sure enough, the muzzle of a rifle pointed downward and squeezed off two shots. Eduardo returned fire on automatic, spraying the rocks in and around the area where their opponent lay.

Luiz cried, but not as loudly. "Fabio? Fabio!" hissed Eduardo. *No response.*

A burst of gunfire came from Eduardo's rear, followed by two further shots from a different weapon. He didn't react immediately but suddenly realized the implications. Without worrying about the shooter, Eduardo jumped to his feet and ran through the foliage back to the trail. Several shots came in his direction, but they went wide.

Eduardo came upon Aristo and fell down where he lay. He held his brother's head and tears came to his eyes. He fingered the wounds on his chest and felt a body without life. *Why had he not listened to Fabio? How the fuck was he going to explain this to his father?*

He laid his brother's head back down gently. He could still hear Luiz crying, but he now knew what he had to do. Luiz would have to wait. He checked his rifle and took out the magazine. Depressing the spring, he figured he had about half a magazine left and put it back. He wiped his face with his sleeve and walked back along the trail, noticing the shells ejected by Duffy's Sig Sauer.

He slammed his palm into the side of his head and swore. It dawned on him that the person who had shot Juan and Luiz was not the person who had had just shot his brother and escaped. There must have been a third person all along. *Another Secret Service agent? The co-pilot?* There was a gap in the foliage to his right and Eduardo started to move upwards and away from the trail.

It was tough going uphill, and numerous plants and creepers tugged at Eduardo's face and clothing. He sweated buckets and when he reached a clearer area, he could see a faint track heading towards the rocky ledge where his opponent lay.

He rested for a moment and then moved along the track. *What was Fabio doing?* The foliage was still thick, but Eduardo had plenty of experience moving through rain forest and kept silent as he crept toward the rocky outcrop.

He never saw the man who killed him, never understood his reasons or his story. A high velocity round hit Eduardo just under his left eye and exited through the back of his head.

◊

Jake arose from his position on top of the large rock. He felt nothing about killing these men. They dealt in drugs and had evil intentions toward Duffy and Emily. They were amateurs, good for growing and selling drugs and paying for protection, but when it came to a life-or-death situation, they presented no match for someone with his experience and skills.

He climbed down from the rock and went over to Eduardo's body. Ignoring the bloody mess of his head and face, Jake took off his shirt, which he badly needed; his torso and arms were covered in cuts and scratches and he could also feel the effects of the sun, which was now into its descent toward the horizon. He checked his Seamaster and saw that it was a few minutes after one in the afternoon. The man had been slightly bigger than Jake, but the shirt felt good, even though it stunk like sweat and death.

He searched his jeans and found his wallet. Why did he need that here? A driver's license identified him as Eduardo Ortiz, a name that meant nothing to him, but he slid it into a pocket on the shirt. He would hand that over later, assuming they could now get out of this mess. He took the rounds out of the man's M16 and put them into his own magazine. He also had a Smith and Wesson revolver, which he checked —six rounds—and he put it into the waistband of his trousers.

He looked around. The man he'd shot was now silent and had probably bled to death, but there were two others. He hoped that Duffy had tackled one of them. He couldn't be sure, but the evidence from the discharge of her Sig suggested that one of the men was wounded or dead. The other man he'd last seen down beneath the foliage and he remembered taking a couple of shots at the movement. *Should he check or just get moving after the women?*

"Do not move," said a voice in accented English.

Jake froze. *Oh shit! You idiot, Jake!*

"Drop your rifle." Jake dropped it. "Now, turn around slowly." He did.

About twenty feet away stood the older one in the group. Blood streamed from a wound high on his left shoulder and Jake could see he felt pain. Not painful enough to prevent a fairly steady right hand holding a Heckler and Koch machine pistol straight at him, however.

"I see you have killed my employer. He was the son of one of the most powerful men in Colombia. Did you know that? He had a younger brother, who I suspect is also dead. I didn't particularly care for either of them, but their deaths will create a big problem for me. You understand?"

Jake's half listened as he focused on how to escape the situation. He looked at the man but did not respond.

"His father will not be pleased. His only children. Two sons! Can you imagine the rage he will be in? I know the man and I can't imagine it." Still holding the machine pistol steady, he reached up with his other arm and pulled out a packet of Marlboros from his shirt pocket. His eyes never left Jake as he shook out a cigarette and brought it to his mouth. He threw the packet to the ground and reached for a lighter in his pocket of his jeans, a Zippo. He lit his cigarette and took a deep lungful of the smoke. "To be honest, I am not sure I want to be the one to tell his father what has happened. Even if I brought you to him alive, I am not certain that I would live."

Jake's mind raced. He still had Ortiz's revolver in his waistband at the back, covered by his new shirt, but he had no chance to get it out and fire it before the man before him fired. A little closer? Maybe, but not from twenty feet.

"So, who are you? I am curious. The woman said you were an embassy employee, getting a lift back to America. I suspect you are more than that."

"I am no one and she was right. I work for the US Embassy in Bolivia."

"And your name?"

Jake thought hard. He needed a chance and talking might buy him some time. Easier to tell the truth. "My name is Jake Walker. I take it you work for a man by the surname of Ortiz?"

"My employer's name is of no concern to you, Mr. Walker. All that remains now is how to kill you: slowly or quickly."

A butterfly flew into sight between them. Orange and blue, about four inches, wing tip to wing tip. It darted around and then flew upward toward his opponent.

Jake knew that it took about one to two seconds for a man to react to something he sees and the man who stood before him was already distracted by the pain in his shoulder.

Jake's eyes never left the man's and, when his eyes briefly darted to observe the butterfly as it flew upward, Jake hurled himself down and to his right. The machine pistol barked and at least six rounds flew past his body, missing by inches.

◊

The women sprinted hard back along the trail. After they'd traveled about half a mile or so, they stopped to listen, but could hear no pursuit. Emily hoped that Jake would be all right and keep the men distracted until he could make his own escape.

After a half mile or so farther, Duffy went off the track. Emily followed and they found the two horses, just as she'd left them.

"I thought these two were dead," said Emily. "We heard the young man shoot them."

"I know. Jake found them. The guy obviously couldn't go through with it. Without them, we may not have been able to catch up."

The women mounted the horses and continued back along the trail. After about thirty minutes, they went down a decline and came to the stream. They dismounted and used their hands to drink deeply from the cool water.

"We go this way," said Duffy, pointing downstream. "If anyone does follow, our tracks will stop here. It won't prevent someone from putting two and two together, but it'll buy us some time. Jake said we should go about five hundred yards downstream and wait for him."

"What's his story, Karen?" said Emily as she mounted her horse and prepared to follow her protector and friend.

"He's actually ex Special Forces. You know the ones that wear those green berets in that film of the same name with John Wayne? We would have been toast without him, Em. Even now, I don't know why he came after us. I guess if he'd stayed with the plane crash, it wouldn't have looked good for him. Professionally, I mean."

They moved along the streambed. The horses were glad of the cool water over their hooves and they made reasonable time, despite a number of tree limbs and other foliage crossing their path every ten yards or so.

"Thanks for saving me back there," said Duffy.

"Hey, you were the one that came back for me. I'm just lucky that I'd asked for my hands to be untied, otherwise things could have been different."

A fairly steep valley on both sides started to level out and they came to a much clearer area, dominated by larger trees and ferns. They climbed out of the streambed onto the bank and dismounted.

"What now?" said Emily.

"We wait. Sit down. I still have some food we can share."

The women sat down and they shared some of the remaining food that Duffy had in her saddlebag.

"Jake said if he wasn't here in two hours, we are to leave without him and try and make it back into Panama."

They heard the unmistakable sound of a rifle being cocked, and when Duffy looked to her right, she saw two soldiers in combat fatigues ten yards away pointing assault rifles directly at them.

◊

Jake's momentum took him off the path and down a steep bank toward the floor of the forest below. He rolled with the impact and kept going as the machine pistol sent another volley of rounds in his direction. As he rolled, he grabbed for the revolver and came to rest behind a tree.

Another burst was fired toward him and, when the firing bolt hit on the empty chamber, Jake realized the man's weapon was out of ammunition. He heard the magazine being ejected and came to his feet quickly, looking around the tree. He'd traveled about forty feet, but could see the man upward and to his right. Jake adopted a two-handed firing position and took aim.

The man had just completed inserting a fresh magazine when Jake's pistol fired two aimed shots. The first hit him high in the chest;

the second he couldn't see. The man clutched at the fresh wound with his free hand and pointed the machine pistol vaguely in Jake's direction. Jake dived onto the ground as the whole magazine emptied in one continuous burst, perhaps seven seconds long. Leaves and other matter rained down, but none of the rounds came close.

Jake risked a look and watched as the man fell to his knees. Blood was coming out of his mouth and Jake knew only minutes remained for him. He stood up and headed in the opposite direction.

He quickly found the bodies of the men he'd shot and the younger guy farther back; two rounds from Duffy's Sig pistol had taken care of him. He searched the horses and men, conscious that he needed to get going. He found some more full M16 magazines, which he put in a bag around his shoulder. He found a larger canteen with some water and quickly drank about half a liter.

The money caused him to stop. It was all in $100 bills, bundled into $50,000 bricks, the weight spread over two horses, perhaps twenty-five kilos per horse. He thought briefly about taking it, but he would never spend drug money. Not ever. If he left it here though, it would find its way back into circulation in a way that he could not predict.

He led the two horses back toward where the younger man lay within a small clearing. He dropped the bags on the ground and took the horses farther back along the trail. He gathered some small pieces of wood and prepared the basis for a fire. This would attract attention and take time, but he believed it the best approach given his concerns about the money being found.

He lit the fire using a cigarette lighter he'd found on the body further up the trail, his first target. It took a few minutes to catch and then he laid larger and larger pieces until he had a good blaze going. He threw the money on the fire, amazed at just how much five million really was. He knew that much of the money would remain fully unburned, but he had to try.

Ten minutes later, he mounted one of the horses and went back along the trail, following in the footsteps of the two women. He looked back. There was a substantial amount of smoke and the risk of a larger fire. He put this out of his mind and focused on what they would need to do to get back into Panama.

62

Colombia

Shit, when was this ever going to end? thought Emily. After all we've been through over the last twenty-four hours, and now this.

Neither of the two women moved and before they knew it, five men and two women surrounded them, all wearing combat green with military boots and webbing. They looked like they were in an army. But whose army?

As seven rifles pointed at them, one of the men signaled for them to roll over on their fronts and the two women in the group came forward and searched them. They took Duffy's Sig and the M16 and, when they found no further personal possessions on them, the two were forced to their feet.

"Any idea who we are dealing with here?" whispered Duffy.

Someone behind her cuffed her head, signaling their silence.

The women heard a hurried conversation in Spanish and, while Emily picked up some of the words—women, drug traffickers and American—their renewed status as captives sank in and, by the look of them, they were captured by people who made Eduardo's team look like boy scouts.

The group moved off, first along the bank of the stream and then higher up to the right. Their hands were untied, but both women were conscious of the several rifles pointed in their direction. They both felt certain that these people would fire upon them if they didn't comply with directions.

At least we are going in the right direction, thought Duffy. She looked up and noted the sun heading toward the horizon, late afternoon. After an hour, they stopped and one of the men gave them some water. At that point, another group of three women and three men, similarly dressed and armed, joined them.

The terrain was becoming quite distinct from the rain forest they had left behind—tall trees with a covering of grass, small shrubs and ferns on the ground. The terrain also flattened and, after a while, Duffy noticed that they were traveling downhill, albeit at a shallow gradient.

Another hour and they came to a track that carried vehicles, judging from the tracks they could see. The group took a five-minute break and more water was given to Emily and Duffy, this time by one of the women in the group.

Emily tried to talk to her. "Hi, listen, we are Americans and we have become lost. Could you take us back to the border with Panama?"

"Shut up!" said a heavily bearded man in his thirties who came over and dismissed the woman who'd brought the water. "We will ask questions when we next stop. Till then, be quiet." He walked away and the women sat in silence.

After about five minutes, the woman who'd given them water approached again, this time with her rifle pointed at them. "Get up, moving now."

The group moved out. Duffy counted fifteen people in the group, spread out over one hundred yards or so. They walked on a roughly cleared trail, no more than a corridor hacked into the forest, and she suspected they could be logging tracks judging from the tire marks she saw. They followed a ridge line, and trees of a type she didn't recognize stood on each side, some as high as fifty or sixty feet.

After two miles or so, they arrived at a junction, with a smaller vehicle track leading to the left and down. They took the left fork and presently came upon the group's camp. This consisted of a cleared area close to a river with tents and tarpaulins scattered throughout. Several cooking fires were burning. Duffy could see two trucks and a four-wheel drive parked on a clearing next to the road and, as the group dispersed, Duffy and Emily were left with the bearded man who'd told them to be quiet. A short man with graying, short-cropped hair and bad teeth joined them. It was this new man who spoke.

"Follow me," he said as he headed toward the far side of the camp. With the bearded man following, they complied. At the other side of the camp, the short man told them to wait and ducked inside a large tent.

After five minutes, a figure came out of the tent, followed by the short man with the bad teeth. The new man led with a huge stomach that hung over his belt, dressed as they all were in combat fatigues. Emily guessed him to be in his forties. A jaunty, peaked cap sat on his head and he literally strutted around the two women. He looked at the short man and said: "*Consígales agua.*"

Another circuit of the two women ensued, before he stopped in front of them. "I am Ferdinand Morales. I am in charge of this *compañía*. You have already met Sergeant Cubrero." He gestured to the bearded man behind them who still had his rifle pointed in their direction. Duffy could see bad skin and teeth and he smelled unwashed and stale.

"We don't see many visitors around here. Do you know who we are?"

The short man came out of the tent carrying two tins of water, which he handed to the women.

Morales continued. "We are part of the People's Army of Colombia. You may have heard us referred to as the FARC. This is our home. We are quite surprised to see you here."

"Why is that?" ventured Emily.

"Well, you see, little goes on around this region that we don't know about. This is our part of Colombia. It's almost certain that you were on that plane that crashed over the border in Panama. And, you were spotted heading into Colombia this morning in the company of some acquaintances of ours."

Emily could not conceal her surprise.

"Yes, we know everything that happens in this part of Colombia. What I fail to see is how you are now here and not still with Ortiz and the other *narcotraficantes*." He walked back and forth in front of them and the women took the opportunity to drink the water they had been given.

"He let us go," said Duffy. "We persuaded him that we were of no value to him."

"Go on," prodded Morales.

"We work for the US embassy in La Paz," added Emily. "We were heading back to the plane wreck."

Morales stopped pacing and rubbed his bearded chin. "There is a problem with your story." He paused for effect and did another circuit around them. "One, you were both armed. The sergeant here tells me that you had a pistol and an assault rifle. I don't believe that Ortiz would have let you go with one of his M16s. The pistol, if it is yours, I could believe. But then, why would you have a pistol anyway? Secondly, you had two of his horses, a very valuable commodity here in our country."

He took a couple of paces forward so that he was within touching distance of the women and looked at each of their faces in turn. "Isn't it more likely that you escaped from his custody?"

Emily looked at Duffy and shrugged. "You are right. We were left unguarded and managed to escape on horseback."

Morales studied Emily as she spoke. Duffy added, "Why don't you take us across the border? The authorities will be looking for us and there could be a large reward for your help."

"Yes. I was thinking about a reward for your safe return." He looked at Cubrero and spoke to him in Spanish. The man called Cubrero led the women away.

63

Colombia

Jake followed the streambed downstream. He knew he'd taken more time than he'd anticipated, but he fully expected Duffy and Emily would be waiting for him. He missed the area where the women had exited the stream, mainly because he'd been expecting to see them. He traveled two hundred yards or so farther before he turned back.

He dismounted his horse and led it onto the bank, looking for tracks or signs. He quickly found tracks from the horses and, disturbingly, a lot of boot prints. *How could this happen?* Jake knew there were other groups in this part of Colombia, small guerrilla forces and parties carrying drugs up north, but the realization that the women were again missing, probably captive and after all his efforts, just crushed him. He sat down on the bank and took some of the dried fruit and nuts from the shoulder bag he was carrying.

Still determined to take the two women back to safety, he reflected on the investment already sunk into this rescue. He also thought of his father in hospital. Jake knew how serious a stroke could be and he now felt certain he would not make it back in time. He clearly had two options and knew he could be back at the crash site by morning. But that would mean leaving the two women to their fate.

He considered the possibility that they'd met people who were going to help them, but he doubted it. Westerners were routinely snatched from the tourist areas of Colombia and taken into the jungle to be held until families paid a ransom. Even then, the kidnapped were rarely released, more often killed once the payments stopped. He remembered a film with the Australian, Russell something or other, and Meg Ryan. No, he had to believe they remained in danger and time was important if he was to find them and head quickly back into Panama. The US authorities and the military, judging by the two Harriers he'd seen last night, would be all over the area to the north of the border. They might even be looking south. He needed to be ready.

He stood up, took the bridle and saddle cloth from the horse and gave it a smack on the rear. "Go," he said, and the horse headed off into the forest.

He checked the revolver—four rounds—and patted the knife at his belt. The M16 had a full magazine and he counted three more, roughly a hundred rounds in total. He looked at the tracks the group had made and he headed after them, conscious that there could be people watching him. He stopped every hundred yards or so to listen. His instincts were telling him that he walked alone. Only a couple of hours or so of light remained and, while darkness would help to hide him, it also made it more difficult to follow the others. He needed to find where they'd gone as soon as possible.

64

Colombia

The sergeant took the women toward the river and left them with two women soldiers. The women gave them food, a hot stew, and Duffy and Emily ate quickly, both very hungry. Afterwards, they washed in the river and took the opportunity to relieve their bladders.

It was their last taste of freedom. Back in the camp, a man arrived with handcuffs and some chain.

"Is this really necessary?" said Emily.

Whether the man heard or not, he cuffed one wrist on each and used the chain to tether them to a nearby tree, using a padlock to keep the two secure. About ten feet of chain provided some movement, but they weren't going anywhere in a hurry.

"At least we have our hands free," said Duffy.

The same man returned at last light and gave each of them a rough, gray blanket. The occupants of the camp were getting ready for the night.

"What a fucking mess we are in," said Emily, using a rare expletive.

"Yep," agreed Duffy. "Of all the places in the world to crash a plane."

"What do you think happened to Jake?"

"I hope he's still out there. He said he was going to create a diversion and meet up with us later by the stream. With the man I killed..."

"And the guy he shot before you arrived," added Emily.

"That left three against one," Duffy summed up.

"He'd be crazy to come after us here," said Emily.

"I know, but that doesn't mean I haven't been thinking of him. If anyone has a chance, it's him. He told me he was in the Special Forces and served in Iraq and Afghanistan. Shortly after Iraq was taken and they were still searching for Saddam, the helicopter he was in got shot down over Baghdad. It was near dusk and Jake said that the fighting throughout the city was so fierce that the survivors couldn't get an extraction until morning. Effectively, they were cut off."

"So what happened?"

"Well, to cut a long story short, he managed to get out alive, obviously, but several of his team and a female pilot never made it. He talked about the female chopper pilot and a young man, in particular, and how they were taken alive by insurgents as they sought to get back to their side. In due course, insurgents executed the woman and her execution video was uploaded to the internet. Jake felt he should have done more. It's why he left the army."

Emily put her arm around her friend's shoulder. "You've fallen for him, haven't you Karen?"

Duffy chuckled and Emily joined in. They were silent for a few minutes.

"I don't know what we are finding so funny," said Duffy. "In the morning, we are going to be taken farther into Colombia. It can take years for people to be released from a kidnap situation. Who's going to pay for me?"

"Hey, you are on duty for the government. They will do everything they can to get both of us out of here. My father will pay, if he has to."

Duffy put her head on Emily's shoulder. "Thanks. I'm just scared. That's all.

"And you're right; Mr. Walker has been on my mind for the last twenty-four hours. I don't want him to come, yet a part of me desperately wants him to try. What a hunk."

"I know. He has a certain way with those eyes of his," replied Emily.

They were both feeling the effects of their journey and a lack of sleep. They arranged the blankets and held each other. Within minutes Emily could tell that Duffy was asleep.

Boy, have I had an interesting life. She remembered the first day in the White House, a whirlwind of new people, new sounds, smells, and senses. There was an overwhelming feeling of history, of times past, and of all the famous people that had preceded them. Emily's father took everything in his stride, but for a young teenager it was an exciting experience to move from a semi-normal home life (her father had been the governor of Texas, after all) to one where everything had been done for her.

Emily remembered her first ride on Air Force One and the excitement of exploring all the different rooms and cabins aboard. It had been a magical time and an experience that would never be matched. Like all presidents before, the public had a natural fascination and interest in the president's children. At first, she'd found the media attention thrilling and remembered seeing her own face on the cover of *Marie Claire*. Later, the interest became obtrusive, particularly when the media would invent things, hurtful things, about her love life or people and friends that she knew.

As the youngest child, and a female as well, Emily was considered the baby of the family and treated quite differently than her sister, Belinda. However, this just hardened Emily's resolve to show people her maturity and toughness. She took up baseball at school and learned how to toss a decent fastball, even for a leftie. The girls were asked if they wanted to learn how to protect themselves and, while Belinda only went a couple of times, Emily went to the range at least once every year. Like everything she attempted, she wanted to do the best that she could and was able, in time, to shoot a ten-inch grouping at twenty-five yards with a man-sized pistol.

Back on the ground, Emily gazed up at the huge array of stars above. She no longer felt afraid. *I am Emily Parker, for God's sake!*

64

30,000 feet above Spain

The pilot's voice came over the intercom and a change in pressure brought Qadir out of a dreamless sleep. He'd adjusted his watch to the new time zone earlier in the flight and when he checked it now, it read 4:50 p.m. He watched their descent into Madrid and noted from the image on the overhead screen that they were passing through twenty-two thousand feet. He got to his feet, and the man on the aisle seat let him out. He stretched his legs and went forward to the nearest toilet. A small line of people had formed with the same idea and he waited until a cubicle became vacant and went inside.

He felt weary from the long flight, took off his jacket, and tried to wash away some of the tiredness. He looked in the mirror and saw a young man old before his time. He put on his jacket again and went back to his seat.

His fellow passenger turned to him and talked to him for the first time. "Long flight, huh? Where're you headed?"

"I have some business in Madrid," lied Qadir.

"That right?" Qadir realized he was American. "What sort of business are you in?"

The stranger continued to talk to him as they descended into the

Madrid airport. Eventually, the plane came to a stop at the terminal and Qadir and his new friend, John, stayed seated while the first and business class passengers exited the plane first. It took ten minutes, but their turn came and they got their hand luggage out of the overhead lockers. "Well, good luck selling carpet, Imran," said John.

"Yes. Thank you."

They made their way slowly forward, out of the left forward door and into the footbridge leading into the terminal. Qadir pretended to check his bag, as he didn't want further conversation, particularly with an American, and waited until the man had reached the top.

He walked to the top of the footbridge where a number of the cabin crew waited, all smiling. "We hope to see you again, sir," said one of the flight attendants.

He passed through. With a two-hour wait until his next connecting flight to Dubai, he went to find out information about where he needed to be and then planned to get some rest, wherever he could. He knew his suitcase was checked all the way to Karachi, so he didn't need to leave the terminal area.

As he wandered along the terminal, he noticed a group of men, including several uniformed police, heading toward him. Qadir tried to look around him and kept his pace steady. His ruse wasn't going to work as the men headed straight toward him. He stopped in front of them.

A young man came before him. He was clean-shaven and wearing a suit. "Mr. Imran Bajar?"

"Yes," replied Qadir. "Is something wrong?"

"We would like you to come with us, Mr. Bajar."

Qadir quickly assessed his situation, but could see no options. His home seemed very far away all of a sudden. "Okay," was all he said.

65

Darién Province, Colombia

Jake easily followed the obvious trail left by the group. *At least ten men in number*, he thought. He came to the fork in the logging trail where the group's tracks led down and to the left, and Jake realized more caution was required because the sun had gone down about an hour ago. He tried to think about whom he might be up against and, more importantly, he needed an escape strategy for all three of them.

Jake moved ten yards into the tree line and the ground started to slope downward. He stopped to rest, taking water and some of the remaining food. He felt a great tiredness come over him and reflected on his lack of sleep over the last twenty-four hours. He found a relatively clear area on the ground and lay down on his back. He looked at his Seamaster and saw it was almost eight and decided to rest a few hours before continuing after the group in the early morning.

His thoughts returned to his time with the 4th in the Middle East. He tended to internalize his thoughts, particularly before battle. *Cool hand Luke*. He wasn't feeling so cool right now. He had confused thoughts for Duffy, protective and more, much more, and he fully understood now that he would get the two women to safety or die in the attempt.

As he closed his eyes, his thoughts went back to the fight on the slopes of Takur Ghar ten years earlier.

◊

Luke watched as the machine gun engaged his team across the valley in front of him and saw that the rounds were only missing those standing by a matter of feet before expending their energy farther down the valley. Their extraction strategy would only work if he put the gun out of action. Otherwise, some of the team, his family, weren't going to make it, particularly Shocky, who would die if they didn't get him medical attention soon.

He peered around the rock protecting him. He could see the first signs of daylight to the east and he sighted along the scope of his M4 toward the gun, which continued to send bursts toward the ridge that concealed his team. He could see at least three men manning the gun about 120 yards away and above to his right. He also saw three men taking cover on the slopes above his team.

A few shots rang out above him. He estimated he had minutes before they got lucky or reinforcements arrived. The main operation had not yet commenced, but he knew the strike from the French Air Force would have attracted attention throughout the area. Jake clicked his throat mike. "Woody, give me cover when you see me move."

"Roger that."

Cap had been quiet throughout the contact, but his voice came through clearly in Luke's earpiece. "Go Luke."

Luke put a new HE round into the grenade launcher, checked his ammunition—about eighty rounds or so—and inserted a full magazine into his M4. Another burst from above. *Time to go.*

He rose to his feet and quickly assessed the best route up along the ridge toward the saddle above. Ignoring the small arms fire from above and to his left, Luke ran up the slope and across the top of the ridge line. *Keep going and I'll hit the summit itself,* he thought.

The light machine gun barked again and tracers came lazily toward him and passed over his head. Their own M60 started up and Luke saw his team pouring heavy fire onto the area of the gun emplacement. The enemy gun wavered and brought its fire to bear on the threat coming from Luke's team on the opposite ridge. As the rounds impacted the ridge line, he saw the team back down the slope and he knew they could no longer support him.

Luke reached the top of the ridge and looked to his right and saw he was about one hundred yards from the gun. Rounds were impacting around him and he quickly assessed the route across the saddle feature and then a steep climb up a slope that led up to the gun emplacement. He dropped to his knees and took aim along his grenade launcher sight. He pressed the trigger and watched as the HE projectile soared toward the gun, exploding into the embankment the enemy had created to protect it.

More small arms fire came from behind him. He took a direct hit in the back and he felt a sharp pain in the left shoulder blade as his vest took the force of the round. He spun around, assessed three figures engaging him from above and sighted along the scope atop the M4 firing three, two-round bursts. He hit at least one of them and quickly turned and headed down toward the saddle, pulling one of his last two HE rounds out of the belt on his webbing. As he ran along, watching his footing, he ejected the spent shell and inserted a new HE round.

The machine gun swung around but couldn't depress itself sufficiently, and Jake felt his luck change. His team recommenced pouring their collective firepower toward the gun and the enemy to his rear. As he sprinted across the saddle, more small arms fire came from his front as his opponents sought to put him down. At least four automatic rifles were firing at him, and Luke ran, firing from the hip. All his rounds missed, but his efforts put their heads down. He kept running and reached the slope leading up to the gun. He was now only thirty yards away and slowed to fire the HE round in the breach of his weapon. At this range, Luke knew he was good and the round impacted the ground only feet from where several figures were in a prone position attempting to get a shot at him.

Luke saw several men die from the explosion, and as he proceeded as fast as he could up the rocky rise, he pulled a M67 fragmentation grenade from a pouch on his webbing and pulled the pin. He stopped and lobbed the grenade up and into the gun emplacement and watched with satisfaction as it exploded exactly where he'd aimed it. He fired the M4 in short bursts to keep any remaining heads down and instinctively changed magazines when he felt the bolt fall on an empty chamber, then cocking the weapon. He breasted the final gap and on full automatic, shot all the bodies he could see. There were ten in all and he could see the damage done by his grenades.

He walked around emplacement quickly, checking that all were dead and headed into the cave system, which went back some twenty yards or so. He saw lots of stores, fire emplacements where they'd been eating and sleeping, and another dozen or so bodies, perhaps from the earlier jets. He looked specifically for another light machine gun before heading back outside. He clicked his throat mike. "Woody, this is Luke, call in the extraction."

"Roger that. Get back here ASAP," replied Woody.

Luke took a quick final look around and approached the gun. He wasn't sure, but he reckoned it looked like a variant of a Kalashnikov light machine gun. He considered getting it off the fixed tripod but took a grenade from his pouch instead, his last. He pulled the pin, placed it beneath the gun and quickly took cover within the cave. The grenade exploded and he went back and saw that the gun could no longer fire, most of the breach missing. He looked down over the emplacement and, from his elevated position, he could see the three men who were in prone positions on the ridge line, about fifty yards away down to his left. He sighted along his M4 and, with the benefit of his telescopic sight, hit two of the men before the third got to his feet and started running down the slope and away from the conflict.

Luke clicked on his mike again. "Coming now, Woody, wait for me."

◊

Jake opened his eyes and watched the sky above. It looked unfamiliar, and he understood that he normally looked at the northern sky. He checked his Seamaster and the luminous dial showed it was 1:15. The half-moon sat high in the sky and Jake felt glad of the light it would provide. The forest hummed with the sound of numerous insects and reptiles calling each other. Noise was good and would mask his movements.

He levered himself into a sitting position and uncapped his water bottle. It felt like it still contained almost a liter from his refill yesterday at the stream bank and he drank about half of it, feeling good as the cool liquid went down his throat.

He stood up, checked himself and his two weapons, and resumed a cautious passage down the hillside. The terrain was quite different from the time he'd pursued Ortiz and his men. Here, the trees were taller and the forest less dense. Looking at all the factors, Jake figured he was closer to the coast than he'd been since the plane crash the previous day. *Was it only a day ago?*

After descending the slope for about twenty minutes, Jake heard a stream or river ahead of him and commenced tracking along it in the direction he believed the women to be. The aroma of wood smoke drifted into his nostrils, and he stopped to listen and watch. He moved forward in a crouch and, after about thirty feet, he detected the glow from several fires. *This must be where they are.*

Jake stopped and went perfectly still, remaining so for about five minutes, looking for the sentries that surely must be posted in such an area as this. Sure enough, his wait was rewarded from a cough he judged from someone about fifty feet away, too far away to see. It suggested that sentries were about and awake, if not alert.

He move forward onto his stomach and, cradling the M16 in the crook of his elbows, slowly moved parallel to the river, which he now saw as being about twenty feet across. Eventually, he realized he'd crossed into the camp itself. He spent some time watching and listening. In his immediate vicinity, he could count about eight makeshift structures made from tarpaulins. The glow from fires remained, but only embers seemed to be burning.

He kept moving parallel to the river and presently came upon a proper tent, and from within he heard a cough and then sounds of someone getting off a cot or stretcher. Jake lowered himself as flat as possible to the ground and went absolutely still.

As he waited, the darkness took his thoughts once again to the instructor at basic teaching them about night vision during their first field exercise. He'd told them that at night the cones at the center of the retina, which are sensitive to color, are not particularly useful. They'd been taught to look to the right or left of an object so that the rods at the edges of the retina, which are more sensitive to light, could be used to see more effectively. The six Ss were also drummed into them—shape, shadow, shine, silhouette, sound, and scent—factors that could help you detect an enemy in the dark and that you needed to consider when you were trying to conceal your presence.

A figure emerged from the tent and walked toward where Jake lay. Jake tensed as the footfalls came closer and Jake could make out the outline of a stout man with short-cropped hair. Without warning, the man diverted from his path and approached a tree about three feet to Jake's rear. He heard the sound of buttons being undone and then the man urinating against the tree.

Jake exhaled and realized he had been holding his breath. The man did himself up and trod carefully back to his bed. Jake put up his head again and watched. If the women were under a tarpaulin or tent, how the hell was he going to find them? Should he wait until morning, when it was light and assess the options?

Jake resumed crawling and moved another fifty feet, coming to the edge of the other side of the encampment. Again, he stopped and listened. He checked his watch and found it was 3:30, the time of night when people were least alert. He crawled down to the river and filled his water bottle, taking a much-needed drink while he was there. If there was one thing he had appreciated about this place, it was the water. There were very few rivers in the States you could drink from. Up in the mountains, yes, but the closer you got to the coast, the more contaminated the water became.

Jake was sure there would be another sentry on the other side of the encampment and, keeping low, he crept another fifty feet along the river bank. He stopped and listened again before starting to make his way away from the river. After about thirty feet, the flash from a cigarette lighter revealed the location of another sentry, and he kept the person on his left as he continued moving toward the highest point on the camp. The lack of any real security suggested this group felt comfortable and safe.

As Jake moved forward he spotted some vehicles to his front. Again, he waited a full five minutes before he felt that the vehicles were not being guarded. Keeping low, he went forward to look at them. One was a Toyota Landcruiser, there was a covered troop carrier of some description, and there was also an armored personnel vehicle, or APV. Jake recognized the latter as a variant built in South Africa, which he'd seen in operation during one of his tours on the continent.

He opened the door to the Landcruiser. The interior light came on and Jake quickly hit the switch on the B-pillar to turn it off. He closed the door and waited to see if his action had alarmed anyone. He opened the door again. The keys were not in the ignition and he spent some time looking for them, without success. He checked underneath the car, feeling by hand and, on checking the tires, found keys on the driver's side front wheel.

Jake felt buoyed by this, but also knew that he still had to find the women and free them. He put one of the keys into the ignition and crawled underneath the adjacent truck. He found the main fuel tank and, using his knife, he severed the fuel line. Fuel spilled out onto the ground.

He moved onto the armored personnel vehicle. Sabotaging this would be more difficult as the underside was covered with armor plating, protection against mines.

He was about to look inside when he heard footsteps coming along the logging trail. *Two people*. He kept still and watched as the figures came alongside the area where the vehicles were parked and stopped. They conversed in Spanish and Jake discerned that one of them was a woman.

After a few minutes, they moved on up the track. Jake came out from under the vehicle and opened the driver's door. No light came on. He felt under the steering column and found the main wiring loom. Insulated wire can be difficult to cut with a knife, but Jake managed to cut through about a dozen wires in the loom using his knife. He knew that this would not stop them, but it would certainly delay them in pursuing him should he be able to find the women and get to the Landcruiser.

◊

Emily woke with a start, a hand clamped hard over her mouth. A voice said, "Shhh, it's me, Jake," and she went limp with relief. Jake released her.

Duffy was stirring awake and Emily leaned over her and whispered, "Karen, wake up. Jake is here."

Duffy opened her eyes. It was still dark, but she could clearly make out Jake, who was lying down above their heads. She reached out her arm, the one that was chained, and, realizing her error, brought her other arm from beneath the blanket and caressed Jake's face, feeling his stubble. He felt good.

"Time to move you two. Dawn is almost on us."

"There are about forty or fifty men and women here, Jake," whispered Duffy.

"All armed," added Emily. "We met the leader last night, a guy who calls himself Morales. This is the FARC, the People's Revolutionary Army. Part of it anyway. It's their territory."

"Whoever they are, they will be looking for us shortly. We can talk on the way. I have found a vehicle to get us out of here," said Jake.

"What about these?" said Duffy, holding up her handcuffed wrist.

"Hey, they're only handcuffs," replied Jake.

He pulled the shoulder bag he had been carrying from his body and pulled apart the buckle. With the sharp end of the buckle pin, he took Emily's cuffed wrist and inserted the pin. Jake twisted one way, then the other, and with an audible click, the cuff dropped open. "I would have thought this would be Secret Service 101," said Jake. "I learned this on Google."

Jake undid Duffy's cuff, put his bag back together, and motioned for them to follow him and keep low on their stomachs. Again, he headed back to the riverbank and followed the path he had taken earlier. It was now 4:40 and he knew they had to be quick as dawn was close.

After ten minutes, they were twenty feet from the position where he had last seen the sentry light a cigarette. Jake passed and then froze as he heard a woman exclaim, *"Quien está ahí?"*

Jake turned around slowly as he watched a figure emerge from near a tree and walk over toward where the women were lying. He slipped the M16 and bag from his shoulders and took hold of the knife.

The woman, or so he assumed, walked cautiously forward and repeated, *"Quien está ahí?"* She was armed with a rifle of some sort and was almost on top of Duffy, about ten feet from him.

Jake knew he would only get one chance at this and launched himself up and forward. In a second, he had a hand over her mouth and thrust the knife into her back, again and again. It was part of his training. The movie version of a sentry being taken down with a simple knife thrust was wrong. If you wanted to disable a person quickly, shock and awe was the only way. It looked ugly and frenzied, but Jake was taking no chances.

Nonetheless, the woman had a firm grip on her weapon and instinctively pulled on the trigger releasing a sustained burst of rounds high into the surrounding jungle.

Suddenly, Duffy was up too, and easily wrestled the rifle from the woman's grasp. The woman went limp and Jake dropped her. Looking down, he stooped to pick up something that was attached to her webbing. *Two grenades*. He went back to his bag, put them inside, and picked up his M16.

Already, there were some shouts from the camp. "Follow me, quickly," said Jake. The women needed no encouragement and shots rang out as they headed after him.

He was twenty yards from the Landcruiser when a flare suddenly illuminated the area. He noticed a figure, about thirty feet away and went to the ground as a burst of automatic fire swept the space where he had just been. Jake was on his knees in an instant and, as the figure moved to take aim at Duffy and Emily coming up on Jake's right, he fired a short burst from the M16 and the man went down.

Duffy came up and crouched beside him. The shots had drawn attention and a number of figures could be seen heading in their direction. Jake took aim and fired single shots at their pursuers. Some were obviously hit, others went to ground and, suddenly, a lot more rounds started to come in their direction.

Duffy had taken a Galil assault rifle from the sentry, and she returned fire, sending a burst into the area ahead of them. The rifle ran out of ammunition and she was about to ditch it when Jake intervened. "Don't throw it away; it takes the same round as the M16."

He crouched down with Duffy and took a fresh magazine out for the M16, popping out a dozen or so rounds. Duffy picked them up and refilled the magazine for the Galil. They received some protection from the undergrowth, but rounds still whizzed by, mostly very wide. Emily lay prone on the floor, but Jake could see the resolve in her eyes. There was fear also, but he felt happy to have both of them with him again. Duffy finished loading the magazine, inserted it into the rifle and cocked it.

"Here, take this," said Jake, passing her the M16. She took the weapon and gave the Galil rifle to Emily. He pulled Ortiz's revolver out and rechecked that there were four rounds remaining. He saw they were both looking at him. "Listen up. I am going to start the Landcruiser behind us. As soon as you hear it start, run for the doors. Try to keep your heads down."

Jake ran for the vehicle, and as he wrenched open the front door, another two flares whistled up into the air. He could hear Duffy and Emily provide covering fire and he jumped into the seat and inserted the keys. He turned the ignition and noted that they had a quarter or so of fuel in the tank. The engine fired the first time. He jumped up onto the side rail and, as the women sprinted for the vehicle, Jake spotted a number of figures moving in their direction.

He aimed the revolver and took two quick aimed shots that put down two more pursuers. Some rounds hit the vehicle and glass shattered. He sensed some movement and turned to his left, where a man appeared from behind the truck. Jake instinctively brought his firing arm around and fired off the last two rounds of the revolver and watched as the figure collapsed.

Jake jumped back into the vehicle just as the women dived into the back seat. With the doors still open, he put the vehicle into gear and floored the accelerator. The Landcruiser surged forward spinning its rear wheels and the doors shut from the acceleration. He left the lights off; he could see well enough from the flares. The trail loomed upwards to the right and he ignored the bumps and noises from the engine bay, concentrating on getting away. Shots were still coming in and he winced as two rounds shattered the rear screen and punched two holes in the glass in front of him.

Duffy leaned over the back seat and fired off another two, timed bursts from the M16. Within seconds they had gone a hundred yards up the trail and the rounds following them stopped.

66

Colombia

Sergeant Cubrero came to halt before Morales, breathless. Morales was lacing up his boots. "What do you have for me?" he said in Spanish.

"It was the women. They had help from one very experienced *hombre*. Vena was on the west watch. She has been killed, multiple stab wounds in the back. Seven others were shot dead in the firefight, another five are wounded, three seriously."

Morales stood up and picked up his assault rifle and strode off toward the vehicle pool. "When I catch them, they will die. I will not rest until we have them."

Cubrero struggled to catch up. "We cannot follow them, sir."

Morales didn't stop. "Why not?"

"Both vehicles have been sabotaged."

They reached the APV. Inside the cabin, a man was working to restore the cable loom.

Morales poked his head inside and saw it was the APV's normal driver, Perez. "How long to fix?"

"About another ten minutes, sir," came the reply.

"Make it five."

Morales turned to Cubrero. "Who is this man who has done this to us?"

"We can only assume that he was on the plane that crashed. He must have helped them get free of Ortiz's party as well."

"What about the truck?"

"The fuel line has been cut. We have no spare, so we are attempting to join it back up."

"How long?"

"I think the APV will be ready before the truck. We will also have to refuel it," Cubrero pointed to the pool of spilt fuel seeping into the soil around the truck.

"*Shit!*" Morales moved around the group of men and women who were watching the proceedings. "Munoz, Garza, Lopez, Torres, Ruiz, Vega, Romero. I want you all on the APV in three minutes, fully armed and ready to pursue the Americans."

Seven men headed off to make preparations.

"Sergeant, you are coming, too." Morales turned back to the man in the APV. He was joining wires by hand and taping them up. "Quickly, man!"

He turned back to the group. "Gonzales?"

A thin, bearded man stepped forward. "Sir!"

"We are heading after them. As soon as the truck is ready, I want ten soldiers in the back and three up front following us. Is that clear?"

271

"Sir!" He turned and went to see how the group under the truck was progressing with the repair.

Cubrero and the other seven came back and climbed into the APV. "Torres," he said. A man stopped in front of him. Morales pointed to the half inch fifty caliber machine gun mounted on top of the APV, operated from inside the vehicle with the top part of the gunner's body sticking out. "You take the gun."

Morales went around the other side of the APV and climbed into the passenger seat.

"That should do it," said the driver called Perez.

"Let's go then."

Perez climbed into his seat, said a silent prayer, and fired up the engine. He turned and grinned at Morales.

"There is nothing funny about this, Perez. Get moving after them."

67

Gulf of Panama

At 0500 precisely, Captain James entered the briefing room of the USS Peleliu. "Ten hut!" shouted the executive officer.

"At ease, gentlemen," said James.

He surveyed the room. Before him were Walt and Scott, Copperton and his gunner/co-pilot Forsyth, and four navy pilots of the Sea Knights. Beside him was the head of the marine flight team, Major Fred Lewis.

"Okay," said James, "as you would all know from yesterday, we have found no trace of the survivors from the plane crash other than the footprints that were found around the site and at the airstrip.

"We have left a platoon of marines onshore and two Sea Knights to support the ground search and the crash investigators that arrived on ground yesterday afternoon.

"The preliminary assessment by the crash guys is that the plane experienced an on-board explosion at altitude and, although this will require lab confirmation, explosives—C4, in fact—appear to be the cause, rather than any failure of the plane itself.

"The target appears to have been Emily Parker and, if our intel is correct, she is still alive, as is Special Agent Karen Duffy; the security guy, Jake Walker; and the co-pilot, Nigel Saunders." James turned to Major Lewis. "Fred?"

"Thanks, Captain," replied Lewis. "Our assumption right now is that the two women have been taken by six Colombian drug traffickers over the border and into Colombia. This view is partly based on an interview with the Cessna pilot, who was picked up by the air force and Customs yesterday morning as he tried to fly into Florida.

"We have no intelligence on the whereabouts of Saunders and Walker, so we are assuming they were either killed and we haven't found their bodies, or they have gone after the Colombians. Or they went to get help."

Scott put his hand up. "Davis?"

"Sir, I knew a Jake Walker in the Special Forces. Met him before I joined up. Found out he was awarded the Medal of Honor during his tour of Afghanistan in '02. Is this the same guy?"

"Yes, we believe it is the same man. He is no longer in the forces and took a discharge in 2004. Now works for a security firm, doing threat assessments, which was what he was doing for the US Embassy in La Paz."

"That kinda helps things, doesn't it, sir?" said Scott.

Copperton responded and looked Scott in the eye. "Look, the chances of this guy following the two women into Colombia are remote. My bet is the co-pilot and him went to get help and headed north. We just haven't found them yet."

"I disagree. Sir," said Scott, "I know this guy. He wouldn't have left the women. He knew the best option was to stay with the plane. Walker has gone after them, for sure."

"Thanks, Davis," said Lewis. "This part of Colombia and Panama is notorious for insurgents and drug traffickers, and there are numerous elements of the FARC, the communist-based, so-called People's Liberation Army. So little is known about the region; we know more about Mount Everest than we do about the land to our east."

James continued. "We have orders to remain here until the wreck has been examined and extracted, whereupon we will head back home. Border and Turner?" He looked at two of the navy pilots. "I want you and your crews to be on call to lift that wreck out. The crash guys reckon they will have finished the on-site by mid-afternoon."

"Copperton and Davis," said Lewis. "You guys are to get in the air as soon as possible. I want a final recon of the area to the south and east of the airstrip. Keep airborne until you need to refuel and then return. Any questions?"

"What if we see something in Colombia?" asked Scott.

James answered. "I have orders not to overfly Colombia. If you see anything, report it in."

68

Darién Province, Colombia

Emily said, "It looks like we've lost them. Any idea how much farther we need to go or where this is heading?

"We've only lost them for a while," said Jake. "The work I did to disable the other vehicles won't take them long to fix. I also don't know how many similar groups are in the area.

"As to where we are and where this will take us, I don't know. Following you two around has really stuffed up my bearings, but I figure we are within five to ten miles of the Panamanian border."

"What do you mean following us around?" teased Duffy. "We were going to get away; we were just waiting for an opportunity."

Jake and Emily looked at each other and grinned.

"Anyway," said Jake, "we are going to have to get into Panama and get someone from our side to notice us. You would have seen the Harriers overflying the airstrip and crash site the night before last. That tells me the navy will be around as well as crash investigators. So, if we can cross the border, I'll be feeling much safer."

Jake concentrated on driving for a while. The trail was rough and barely wide enough, but the Landcruiser was traveling well, considering. He was doing about thirty miles an hour, but sometimes had to slow for debris, rocks and pot holes. "For the moment," he said, "we will just have to keep following this track. It looks like it has been made for loggers to get in and out. At present, we are heading west and a bit north, but I can't rule out the possibility that we will need to get out and walk. Roads aren't that plentiful around here, in case you hadn't noticed."

"I am tired of walking, Mr. Walker," said Duffy. "If you were a gentleman—*look out!*"

The Landcruiser had just rounded a bend and, although Jake was only doing about thirty, he had nowhere to go when he saw the ditch that stretched right across the road. Even if he had been going faster, the vehicle wouldn't have been able to get across because the ditch was about five feet wide and several feet deep.

Jake slammed on the brakes, but the wheels locked on the loose surface, the front of the vehicle dropped into the ditch. Everyone was thrown forward.

The engine was still going, but it was evident from the way the nose was buried in the side of the ditch that they were stuck. Jake turned off the vehicle and turned to the women. Emily had hit the dash hard and the cut above her eye had reopened but was otherwise all right. Duffy appeared unharmed.

"Damn," said Jake. He got out and looked underneath the vehicle. The tail shaft was bent, and the front wheels were now about four inches closer to the rear. He popped his head up. "We're walking. Sorry, Duffy," he added.

Emily and Duffy got out and stood on the trail in front of the Landcruiser. Jake rummaged in his bag and took out the two grenades. "Here, take this," said Jake, handing the Galil assault rifle and his bag to Duffy. "There are some M16 magazines in there. Take some of the rounds out and fill up the magazine on the Galil."

"Is that what it is?" said Duffy, taking the proffered items.

"It's based on the Kalashnikov and made in Israel. Standard issue for a number of armies around the world, including Colombia, I do believe."

Jake went back inside the vehicle and, after a minute came back out and climbed underneath.

"What are you doing?" asked Emily.

"Leaving a couple of surprises," replied Jake. He got back up and climbed up and onto the trail.

"I figure we have, at most, a ten minute start. We made good time, but it won't be long before they are here. The cruiser takes up most of the road. Neither the truck nor the APV will be able to get past and they will need to manhandle or winch the vehicle out and push it into the trees in order to follow us. With luck, it will stall them and give us some time. Let's keep to the trail for the moment," he said, and headed along the trail, followed by the two women.

69

Darién Province, Colombia

Javier Perez felt nervous with the boss sitting next to him. He drove the APV as fast as he could, given the vehicle and the difficult track they were on, but Morales was clearly in a temper. "Come on, man, get some more speed going."

Speed, or rather a lack of it, saved the APV from the same fate as the Landcruiser. That and the fact that the APV was left, rather than right, hand drive, enabled Perez to see the vehicle and its fate sooner. As they reached the apex of the bend, Perez's foot was already on the brakes and they easily came to a stop some twenty feet from the other vehicle.

Morales turned and ordered the men out of the APV. "Torrez, stay on the gun and cover us."

"Yes, sir!"

The seven men in the back fanned out and Sergeant Cubrero and Private Ruiz approached the vehicle, rifles pointed forward ready to fire. Ruiz jumped down into the ditch and looked underneath, while Cubrero stayed at the rear, covering him and looking through the shattered hole of the back window.

"Broken tail shaft, Sarge," said Ruiz. He looked through the driver's window. "Keys are still in it."

Morales also exited the APV and stood back about ten feet from the Landcruiser, a chrome-plated Glock pistol in his hand. "Sergeant, we need to move it quickly and find a way around."

Cubrero turned around. "The truck has a winch, but let's see if we can't push it out. Ruiz?"

"Sir."

"See if you can get it started."

Ruiz opened the door and was about the climb in when he noticed the grenade sitting next to the seat and saw, detachedly, its striker flying off when the door was opened. He slammed the door shut. "Grenade!" he shouted and turned and dived into the tree line adjacent to him.

Cubrero was the nearest to the vehicle and just had time to throw himself down when an ear splitting *crunch* occurred. The driver's door flew off and landed close to Ruiz, who sprawled in the undergrowth as low as he could. The remaining windows of the vehicle were blown out and the surrounding men, including Morales, were peppered as glass and other bits of the vehicle rained down on top of them.

Cubrero lifted his head up. The vehicle was starting to burn. He got to his feet and noticed Ruiz emerging from the foliage to his right. He was about to say "That was close" when the second grenade, which Jake had lodged between the rear trailing arm and the chassis, went off. The first explosion had dislodged it, enabling it to arm.

The second explosion lifted the vehicle six feet into the air and both Ruiz and Cubrero were blown off their feet and suffered a number of shrapnel wounds from the grenade and pieces of the vehicle that formed part of the explosive mass that flew out in all directions.

Before the vehicle had fallen to the ground, the remaining fuel in the tank went off with a sonic boom and a huge fireball headed skyward. The Landcruiser lifted again and crashed down on its side, burning fiercely.

Morales lifted his head, which he'd tried to bury into the dirt. He found his tunic was burning in several places and immediately rolled to try and put the flames out. Two of his men came to his assistance and helped extinguish the flames.

He stood up unsteadily and registered that both Cubrero and Ruiz were dead, their corpses burning and belching smoke. He turned to the man next to him, Private Munoz, and said: "Don't just stand there, get the extinguisher and put those fires out."

Munoz disappeared into the APV and emerged with a fire extinguisher. He pulled the pin and doused Cubrero's body with carbon dioxide. His efforts were successful, leaving a blackened, bloody, smoldering mess on the ground. "The extinguisher is empty, sir," he said, holding his arms out.

"Fuck, fuck, fuck!" exclaimed Morales. He pointed to Ruiz's body, which continued to smolder. "Don't just stand there; put a coat or something over the other one."

With no winch and the Landcruiser burning fiercely on the side of the trail, they had no way forward. The fire was intense as the plastics and other components of the vehicle were consumed, and the fire hissed, spat, and crackled, spewing a huge plume of black smoke skyward.

Morales went over to the APV and Perez wound down the window. "Move back and as much over to the side as you can."

A minute later and the truck came cautiously up the trail, having seen and heard the explosion. It stopped behind the APV, but there was enough room to deploy the winch.

The truck's driver, a private by the name of Pena, jumped out of the cab and came over to Morales. "Pena," said Morales. "You see the problem. I want that vehicle shifted. The Americans are on foot, but we need to get after them before the trail gets cold."

Pena went forward and came back. "I think we can shift her," he said and went back to the truck and unlocked the winch. He pointed to one of the men. "Here, help me with this."

The two of them pulled out a large length of cable and went into the tree line to the left of the Landcruiser. Twenty feet past the vehicle, Pena found what he was looking for: a stout tree trunk. He called back to the group on the trail. "Give me some more cable."

Taking the cable around the tree, they approached the burning wreck but could only get within five feet before the heat pushed them backward. Pena took the cable and the large hook and tossed it into the cabin, but it took four tries before he the hook took hold of something solid. He held the tension and signaled for the tension to be taken up by the winch.

Five minutes later and the wreckage had been pulled into the forest adjacent to the trail, still burning, and there were a number of spot fires and trees also starting to go up.

Pena realized he couldn't get the hook back and one of the soldiers had to sever the winch cable using his assault rifle, even though it took a whole magazine to do it.

Meanwhile, Morales had inspected the ditch and found that it was impassable. "Everyone, over here," he ordered. The remaining men gathered around. "Trees, logs, rocks. Go and find some and fill that in," he said, pointing to the ditch in the road.

70

Darién Province, Colombia

Roughly a mile ahead of the Colombians, the threesome tired. They'd stuck to the track wanting to get as much distance between them and their pursuers. Jake was still setting the pace and Emily and Duffy did their best to keep up. The terrain cleared and they could smell, but not see, the ocean. Emily started to lag behind. She felt a terrible stitch in her side and her mouth felt very dry. Duffy stopped and waited for her and Jake came back assessing the situation.

Duffy was supporting her. "Hey, you're doing good, Em. Not much farther."

Emily had her head down and her legs started to give way. Jake darted in and grabbed her other arm. "Take her over to that tree so she can get some shade," he said.

In the limited shade offered by the tree, they sat Emily down. "She's dehydrated, Jake," said Duffy. "She can't keep this pace up for much longer." Jake unscrewed the water bottle he had. It was still full from his last visit to the river earlier in the morning. Duffy took it from him and helped Emily to drink. "Easy," she said.

Emily wiped her forehead. Jake looked at them both and realized how hard this had been, for everyone. They all had dirt encrusted on their faces, their clothes were torn and cuts and bruises were evident across their arms.

"I'll be okay," said Emily.

At that point, they all heard the first grenade explode and it gave them some bearing on how far they had come. Seconds later, the second grenade went off, followed by the fuel tank. The resulting blaze and smoke plume pinpointed the place.

"What was that?" said Duffy.

"Just a couple of grenades I left," replied Jake. "We've gone about a mile. Duffy, drink some water, too. With any luck, those explosions will have stuffed up one of the pursuing vehicles. But, we have to assume they will get past at some point and keep after us."

"I can smell the ocean," said Emily.

"Yes, you can tell also by the vegetation," said Duffy. "It can't be far away."

Jake stood up. "That's our destination, then up into Panama."

Duffy and Jake helped Emily upright. The rest and water seemed to have helped, but Jake supported her with his arm and the group continued on the trail, which was still heading up.

Duffy was up ahead and carried both the rifles. "She's a tough girl," said Jake to Emily.

"She sure is. Above and beyond the call of duty. Without her, I don't know where we both would be. Neither she nor I have experience with death, let alone being involved in killing someone. Yet, she did what needed to be done."

They trudged onward another few hundred yards. "You like her, don't you?" said Emily.

Jake thought. The answer was yes. Was it because of the situation they were in and the dangers they had come through? He had no experience in long-term relationships. Even in his current job, he kept to himself and was reluctant to make any steady friends, male or female.

"I guess that means yes," said Emily.

"What does?"

"Your silence."

"All right, I do like her, but it won't mean a thing if we don't get out of here."

They crested a rise and two hundred yards away was a stone structure. It appeared to have been a dwelling of some sort. Behind it was the Pacific Ocean. The dwelling, or ruin more precisely as it had no roof and most of the walls had collapsed, sat about thirty yards from a cliff.

"Wow," said Emily.

Duffy waited for them. "Plans?" she said.

"I was hoping for a different outcome, like a beach or something, mangroves, I don't know, but somewhere we could get some cover and hide," said Jake.

"I can hear vehicles," said Emily.

Jake listened and, sure enough, the sound of the APV and probably the truck could be heard. "Okay, head for the ruin."

They approached the structure and Jake noticed it had thick walls, probably two feet thick and waist high or higher, constructed of large stones. He was thinking fast. It was still only mid-morning and, if it were late afternoon, they might have a chance to get away under the cover of darkness. However, they had reached a headland and the ground was open. Their options were running out fast.

"Get inside and see what our ammunition situation is. I am going to check out if there is a way down the cliff face."

Duffy and Emily crouched down inside the ruin, which consisted of one large room, perhaps thirty feet by twenty, dominated by a chimney and fireplace at one end. Rubble lay everywhere, a little garbage, but it was old and no one had been here in a long time. The sounds of the vehicles got louder.

"This is it, isn't it?" said Emily.

"Jake will find a way out."

Duffy checked that each weapon had a full magazine. Sixty rounds, with one spare magazine for the M16 and a few additional scattered rounds.

"Where's my pistol?" asked Duffy.

"It was taken from you back at the stream, remember?"

"Oh well, I wonder if they will take it out of my pay. You okay if I take one of the rifles and Jake takes the other?"

"Sure, but if you need me, I have fired weapons before. I am the daughter of a president, remember?"

Jake reappeared and they could clearly hear the vehicles. "They are here now. The cliff face is impassable here. If we had more time, we could go north, but we are just going to have to make a stand. You take the M16," he said, looking at Duffy. "Keep to one- or two-shot bursts only. Make every bullet count."

He leaned over the wall. The APV was about a hundred and fifty yards away, with the truck coming behind. Jake aimed and put two rounds on the window of the APV. It stopped. He knew the armored glass wouldn't break, but he needed some distance between them. "Duffy?"

His next sentence was drowned out as the fifty caliber on the APV opened up. Rounds peppered the front wall as the gunner got his aim and then slammed into the wall on the far side of the ruin.

They all ducked down inside as large shards of stone and mortar sprayed everywhere, but the wall was solid. Jake got on his stomach and moved over to the edge of the wall and peered around it. Not being left-handed, he quickly squirmed across the gap so that he was behind the structure once more. He looked around and took up a firing position.

The truck was still coming and Jake took out the driver with one shot. It lurched forward and then went to their right. Jake took aim at the person in the passenger seat but missed, and somehow, the passenger pulled on the handbrake and it stopped. The engine died. Fortunately, it now blocked the APV.

Duffy saw figures emerging from the APV and spreading right and left. She focused on the figures on her right and took three aimed shots. She definitely hit one person but the others took to ground and she knew her other rounds missed.

Without the cover of the APV's gun, the truck was very exposed and Jake sent a burst of fire, about a dozen rounds, into the canvas. Figures hurled themselves out of the back, but he felt sure that he'd hit several.

The APV started up again and Jake took aimed shots at the men hiding behind the truck. The men that had debussed from the APV started to return fire. A few rounds came close and both he and Duffy had to duck down while the barrage continued. Then the APV's gun opened up and it was moving forward again.

"Duffy!" said Jake. She looked over. "Try and take out the gunner."

The noise and power of the fifty-caliber machine gun was frightening, but with no visible targets, the gunner simply sprayed the ruin all over. The walls continued to hold, for the time being.

Jake risked his head and took a number of aimed shots at the figures on the ground to his front. The APV was only fifty yards away. "Now, Duffy!" he yelled.

Suddenly, Jake felt a lancing pain in his right arm and knew that he'd been hit. He rolled to his right, past the gap in the wall, and saw Duffy fire two bursts from the M16. The gun went silent and Duffy ducked back down. They could hear the APV's engine, but the vehicle stopped, only forty yards from the wall that shielded them..

The firing stopped also, and Jake figured they must have been working out what to do. A frontal assault would succeed eventually; they only had about forty rounds left, but he believed they now understood that the three of them were not going to go calmly and they would be thinking about the further casualties they were going to bear.

"You're hit!" said Emily.

Duffy looked over in alarm. "Grab his belt and make a tourniquet." She reached over and took the Galil. It was nearly out of ammunition and she took the remaining magazine for the M16 and split the rounds between the two weapons.

Emily somehow ignored the volume of blood coming from Jake's bicep. His forearm was covered in it. Using his belt, she made a rough tourniquet. She realized that he would need his free hand to keep up the pressure. "Give me one of the rifles, Karen."

Firing from the ground forces resumed and Duffy risked a glance. A number of men had taken the lapse to move forward. She counted at least eight men within a hundred yards. She moved over to the corner of the structure, to her right. "Emily, stay down. Get up and shoot when I say."

Duffy took a firing stance again. Rounds were coming in and she fired a sustained six-shot burst to her right and then ducked back down. "One hundred yards, eleven o'clock. Okay?"

"Okay."

"Now," said Duffy and they both took up positions and laid down a sustained burst of fire at the men in front of them. One shot at a time. So focused were they on the task that they failed to see Morales pull the dead gunner down into the APV.

Morales got behind the gun, took aim, and pressed the trigger. A burst of fifty caliber rounds thudded into the wall behind Duffy and she threw herself onto the ground, as did Emily.

"Shit," shouted Duffy above the roar of the gun. "I felt them go past."

"Any ideas anyone?" said Emily.

71

Darién Province, Panama

With Copperton taking the lead, Scott and Walt followed him up and down the area around the plane crash.

Once over land, they headed over the crash site and Walt and Scott could see the two Sea Knights on the ground and a number of figures, including marines, all waiting for the investigators to call it a day, whereupon the largest parts (and a lot of the smaller pieces) of the wreck would be picked up and taken back to the ship.

Past the crash site, Copperton headed east and then started to quarter the area to the south. As he'd been instructed, Scott maintained station behind him, and he and Walt tried to focus on the ground to see if they could see any sight of the survivors.

"Do you believe this jerk?" said Walt off air. "Guy thinks he's king shit."

"Until the bullets start flying," said Scott. "You know, Walt. I don't think I have ever hated anyone, not even the enemy in Iraq, as much as I dislike this guy. What the fuck did I do to deserve this gig?"

"We embarrassed him and exposed his cowardice, that's what."

Copperton's voice came over their headsets. "Whisky Two, this is One. Over."

"Roger One, this is Two. Over."

"My fuel is getting low. We have seen nothing and I'm going to head down adjacent to the border. From there, we'll head back to the ship. Over."

"Roger One. Out."

"Can't even do this job right," said Scott off air. "I've still got half my fuel load."

The two Super Cobras headed west. The ocean loomed to their front when Scott noticed the flash as the Landcruiser's fuel tank went up to the south. Looking behind him, he clearly saw the flame and smoke from the explosion. "See that, Walt?"

"Sure did."

"Whisky One, this is Two. Over," said Scott on air.

"Yes, Whisky Two."

Scott slowed the helicopter and came around slowly so that he faced the border. "Whisky One, we've just witnessed an explosion across the border, no more than three or four miles away. Over."

"Whisky Two, we have our orders. Head back to the ship. Out."

"Boss, this could be related to the survivors. We have to go and look," replied Scott.

Copperton's voice came back. "Negative, Whisky Two. It could be anything. You are not authorized to go across the border. Please acknowledge."

Off air: "Walt?"

"Yep."

"You up for this?"

"Whisky Two. Please acknowledge and return to the ship. Over."

"Let's do it, Scott. That moron is never right."

Scott opened up the throttle and the Cobra surged forward, heading for the border.

"Whisky Two. You are going to cause a diplomatic incident…" Scott turned the volume down.

He was conscious of heading into Colombia, and within a couple of minutes the plume of smoke could be seen to their right.

"It's a vehicle, Scott," said Walt. "A four-wheel drive, and most of it is off the track down there."

"Logging trail?"

"Could be."

Scott spotted a dust trail about a mile away. "See that at one o'clock?"

"That has to be a vehicle of sorts. Let's keep it on our right and head to the southwest. I think we should be cautious at this stage," said Walt.

"Roger that."

Scott headed back toward the coast keeping the trail on their right. As they approached the coast, they both saw the ruin on the area east of the cliff face and could clearly see the APV and the truck behind it.

"Is that what I think it is?" said Scott.

"Its gun is firing at the dwelling. Looks like heavy machine gun."

Scott adopted a hover and they watched as the truck came around the APV and suddenly stopped. They could clearly make out muzzle flashes coming from the ruin.

"Couple of fighters in the structure," said Walt.

"Yes. I'm going to take us down and around. We'll come up from behind the ruin and see what's happening. Why don't you get the Hellfires and gun ready."

"Roger," said Walt.

The Cobra peeled away and went down over the cliff face. Scott brought her round, facing the cliff face. "You ready, buddy?"

"Yep, take her up."

Scott hit the throttle, and they rose quickly suddenly getting a view of inside the ruin and what lay in front of them.

"I see three," said Walt. "Can't quite tell, but looks like two women and someone on the ground."

"That could be Walker," said Scott.

The fifty-caliber gun was clearly operating and Scott could see a number of armed men approaching the ruin. "Good enough for me. Take the gun out, Walt."

"I have the aircraft," Walt took the controls and acquired the APV on his heads up display. The system told him it had a lock and he lifted the firing guard and depressed the firing switch. There was a slight jolt as the missile fell away and within half a second its solid fuel rocket propelled it to nine hundred miles an hour. They were only two hundred yards away and it was all over very quickly as the missile speared into the mass of the APV and simply blew it apart.

"Bit of overkill, Walt."

"I'll take us over the ruin."

"Roger."

Two figures were waving at them.

"That's Emily Parker," said Walt.

"Affirmative, buddy." Some rounds were coming their way from the ground troops. "How about you get those guns going and clear things up."

Walt let off another rocket toward the truck, watching as it struck the truck cabin and blew it apart, and then fired up the guns. The twin 20 mm cannon were electrically operated and devastating to those on the ground, capable of firing more than 100 rounds every second. As he swept the rounds toward the figures and then swept across their firing line, Scott watched and saw men being blown into pieces.

One sweep and they could clearly see several figures running away at high speed.

Scott turned up the radio. Presently, they heard: "Whisky Two, this is base, please respond. Over."

"Base, this is Whisky Two," replied Scott. "Survivors from the plane crash have been found. We are on the coast, approximately three miles south of the border. Send an extraction party. Over."

There was silence. Walt still had the controls and he headed around the area, checking for survivors that were still hiding.

"That's given them something to think about," said Walt.

"Yes. Give the area a bit of a blast with the minis, Walt. I don't want any nasty surprises."

Walt strafed the tree line, the remains of the truck, and any other areas where men could still be lying.

"Whisky Two, this is Captain James. Stay on station. Birds are heading your way. Out."

72

Darién Province, Colombia

Duffy and Emily watched as the Sea Knights headed towards them. Emily dropped her rifle and hugged her friend. "Yes! Yes!"

Below them, Jake struggled into a sitting position. "Hey, you two?"

Duffy let go of Emily and fell down beside Jake. "Hey, you." She kissed him gently on the cheek. "How's the arm?"

"Hurts like hell. Help me up."

Duffy took his good arm, which was still tightly clutching the belt around his right bicep, and they got him on his feet. Jake looked around. The APV was a smoking wreck, hardly recognizable. At least a dozen bodies were littered around them, some as close as thirty feet. The Super Cobra was still circling and they watched as a Sea Knight came over the horizon and landed in front of the ruin.

The women supported Jake and they went out. The closest door of the Sea Knight opened and several figures came out.

The first to reach them was Lieutenant Commander Valerie Booth. "You must be Jake," she said, recognizing him from the photo on his military records. "Welcome back. Your father has pulled through and is waiting for you."

Jake's emotions came bubbling up and his eyes went misty. Was it relief for his father or for other reasons? "Thank you. How soon can you get me there?"

Booth took his injured arm and had a quick look. "Well, Jake, first we are going to have to attend to your arm. We'll then fly you to Panama City where we have an aircraft waiting to take all of you back to the States."

Captain James joined her. "Hi, Jake, I'm Captain James. I don't know how you managed this, but a lot of my people have been hoping that you would make it. Getting you to L.A.? I think we can get you home by about midday tomorrow."

James motioned to a man and woman from the medical team and they came and assisted Jake onto the Sea Knight. He turned to the two women. "Miss Parker, Miss Duffy, hi, I'm Peter James, captain of the *USS Peleliu*. It looks like you have had a tough couple of days. We have now accounted for everyone except the co-pilot, Nigel Saunders. Can either of you fill me in?"

"Nigel died in the initial explosion," said Duffy. "Went out the hole in the fuselage when the plane decompressed."

"I see. I'm very sorry," replied James. "We're going to take you all back to the ship now. There'll be a number of people who will want to speak to you over the next few days or so. It's going to be an interesting tale. Come on, I guess you'll be hungry and in need of a bath and some clean clothes."

The two women grinned at him. White teeth shone through dirt. "That would be great," said Emily.

EPILOGUE

Emily

Two weeks after their "holiday" in Colombia, Emily was sitting with her parents on the terrace having afternoon tea outside their house near Houston. Again, the subject of her disappearance came up while they were talking about future plans for the Parker Foundation. Her absence had made her parents realize just how much they needed her.

"You have no idea," said her father, "the worry we were in while you were missing."

"Yes," agreed her mother, "but we are so glad you are home with us and safe once again."

Emily reflected on the events since the firefight in Colombia. She remembered clearly the helicopter ride back to the navy ship. It was exhilarating, but it also gave them time to think about what had happened, especially what had happened to her, Emily Parker.

She remembered that first visit to the officer's mess onboard the ship after she and Karen scrubbed away the forest in a long, long shower and dressed in clean marine uniforms. Jake was still getting the wound in his arm cleaned up. The smells, sights, and quantities of the food were just amazing and she wouldn't forget that moment. They piled their plates high and Emily reckoned it was the best meal she'd ever had.

They caught up with Jake the following morning and took another helicopter ride to the airport at Panama City where an air force transport was waiting. On the flight back to the States, they were all quiet, and Jake and Karen sat next to each other, happy to be together.

Since arriving back home, Emily had spent a long time resting, walking the dogs, and getting her strength back. Karen had been reassigned and there were new agents on her father's protective detail. Karen and Peter had been with her family for several years and she missed them both. Karen she'd see again she was sure, but at Peter's funeral, she realized just how quickly you could lose your life and she resolved to make the most of hers.

"I think you should stay here in Houston for a while, Emily," said her father. "Later this week, I have set up a meeting for you with my former campaign manager, George Bell."

"I'm sorry, Dad," said Emily. "I've made plans."

Both her parents looked at her.

"I've been accepted for officer training at Marshall Air Force base in Alabama. I am going to be a pilot."

Duffy

Upon returning to the States, Duffy said a tearful goodbye to Jake at the Houston airport. They'd promised to keep in touch. Duffy had fallen for him and hoped that he would call her when things settled down. But she was also realistic. Things happened for a reason and the events of the past few weeks had brought her strength and courage. If he called, then good, but if not, she was okay with that too.

Jake went on L.A. to see his father and Duffy went to the office in Houston for a debriefing, which lasted two days. At the end of the two days, she was taken into the director's office.

"Hello Karen," said Douglas Jackson, the local director. "Take a seat. We're glad to have you back. I am sorry that we've had to put you through the last two days. You must be anxious to get home to your family?"

"That's okay, sir," she replied. "It was important that we learn from what happened down there. The deaths of Pete, the pilots, and others was preventable and it's important that we be more vigilant in the future."

"We know who the person was that planted the device on the plane."

"Who?"

"He is known as Tariq Qadir and is a middle ranking operative in al-Qaeda. We received assistance from the Bolivians and were able to track his movements. He took a flight from La Paz to Lima on the day after the plane crash. He used a false name, but we were able to use facial recognition software to pick him out of security footage. A number of agencies—CIA, FBI and Military Intelligence—have been sharing intel on this guy for some time now and, once we had his movements, he was intercepted at the Madrid airport on his way back to Afghanistan.

"The president took an active role in this whole episode, obtaining permission for a rescue operation from the Panamanian president, getting our access to the security footage from the Bolivians. He even called the Spanish president and persuaded them to detain Qadir in Madrid. He is currently in a Spanish jail while we go through the process of extradition."

"That's good," said Duffy.

"Anyway, that's all background for you. You've been on protective detail since you left the Academy?"

"Yes, about seven years now."

"How would you like to go back there?" The director paused. "As an instructor."

Duffy smiled for what seemed like the first time in days. "Sir… that would be terrific."

"We think you've got what it takes to train our new agents who are entering the protective detail roles. We're also going to promote you, Karen. The courage you displayed down in Colombia will be talked about for years to come."

Duffy tuned him out. She had done her share of protective detail. An instructor role would provide her with stability. It was Washington, but heck, it was closer to home. Home…

"Agent Duffy?"

"Yes, sir. Sorry."

"I was saying thank you. You have a plane to Boston to catch. Your orders will come through while you are on leave, but I believe you won't start for another month."

Scott

Feelings had been mixed when Scott and Walt flew back onto the *Peleliu*. They'd just exited the Super Cobra when Copperton fronted them both on the flight deck.

"Davis and Kennedy! You two are grounded pending a full investigation. You disobeyed a direct and lawful order and have caused your country, the navy, and the president enormous embarrassment."

Scott and Walt took off their helmets and looked at each other.

"Shit. Sir," said Walt, "we didn't hear any orders. We used our initiative."

"Reminds me of that time you were too scared to support a colleague on the ground in Iraq," added Scott.

Copperton's face went a shade of beetroot and he looked like he was about to explode. "I am going to hang your fucking ass for this, Davis. You too, Kennedy. You are a disgrace to the corps."

Scott moved off and Walt followed. Scott turned around. "I think you know who has disgraced himself. And the corps. Sir," he added.

Walt and Scott were both shipped off the *Peleliu* the day after the incident and given leave to see their families. Three weeks passed and then Scott received a phone call to come into the base.

He waited outside the office of Colonel Pat Gregory for three quarters of an hour before the colonel's personal assistant told him to go on in.

Scott knocked on the door and entered the colonel's office. He walked in and snapped off a salute to the man who was seated behind his desk.

"Lieutenant Davis, thanks for coming in. At ease. Please meet Admiral Salzburg." He pointed to the older man in full dress navy uniform seated on his left.

"Pleased to meet you, Admiral."

"Have a seat, Scott. Have you enjoyed your leave?"

Scott sat in the empty chair opposite Gregory's desk. "Yes sir. I've been away for six months and my kids have really grown—you know how it is."

"Sure. You and Lieutenant Kennedy gave us a lot to think about. You realize that, don't you?"

"Yes, sir."

"Disobeying an order, illegally overflying Colombia, engaging an unknown force, and killing some of them without authority. Any one of these could have seen you court marshaled and in prison."

"I knew Jake Walker, sir. I had a hunch and it proved right."

Gregory looked to his superior.

"And that is the only reason you are still here, Lieutenant," said Salzburg.

"You have a good service record," said Gregory, "but this isn't the first time you and Captain Copperton have butted heads. It hasn't gone unnoticed. Now, I am not going to revisit the past. In many ways, your actions were seen as appropriate, even heroic. Even the Colombian president was pleased because the FARC has been weakened by your actions and those of Mr. Walker. Others take a dimmer view, but on balance, we are prepared to keep you on."

"In fact, *Captain* Davis," said Salzburg, "you have been viewed as deserving promotion."

Scott didn't know what to say.

"What's more, Scott," added Gregory, "you have been assigned here to instruct new pilots for the next few years."

"Any questions?" asked Salzburg.

"Er no, sir. I mean thank you, sir."

"Captain, you are dismissed," said Gregory.

Scott arose, snapped off a salute and turned to go. "One more thing, Captain," said Salzburg. Scott turned back. "Captain Copperton has decided to leave the marines. He is a great pilot, but he—shall we say—realized that his management of men was not the best that it could be. In a way, your actions brought this to a head, so thank you."

Scott looked at the admiral and smiled. "Thank you, sir."

Jake

As soon as the flight touched down in Houston, Jake was already thinking about his father. Sure, there were feelings for Duffy that went unsaid and their parting left him feeling empty and without closure. He pushed these feelings to the back of his mind and focused on his father.

In L.A., he went straight to the hospital and met his older brother, Dan, outside his father's room. Jake hadn't seen him for over ten years and they embraced.

"Hi, Jake," said Dan. "I'm so glad to see you." Dan held his shoulders and looked at him. "How's the arm?"

"It's fine. The bullet missed all the vital parts. How's Dad?"

"Come in and see him. He's good. Got some paralysis on his left side, but his faculties are fine. They managed to fix the blood clot and bleeding in time."

Dan held the door open for Jake and he went in. He sat down next to the bed. His father looked very old. His head was bandaged and there were lines and wires all over him. Jake hadn't seen him for four years; he'd been too busy.

His father opened his eyes. "Hello, Jake. Dan has told me what happened to you. Took the wrong plane, huh?"

Jake leaned over and kissed him on the forehead. "Hi, Dad. Yeah, you could say that. I didn't think I was going to get here either."

They chatted for a while and, when their father grew noticeably tired, Dan and Jake left.

Outside, the men embraced again. "Thanks again, Dan," said Jake. "I'm sorry I've been out of action. Since Iraq, I've been focused on work, too focused, and it's taken its toll."

"That's okay. I'm just glad you managed to get here."

"What's the prognosis?"

"The doc reckons he'll be fine. The paralysis is a worry, but I've been preparing to take him in for a few years now, and Maddy and I are okay with having him."

◊

Three weeks later, Jake's arm had healed well. He'd taken some leave to sort himself out, gone down to Laguna Beach, and rented a rundown place close to the water.

Every day he ran on the beach, and the sun and ocean rejuvenated him, inside and out. Bill Parker tracked him down and expressed deep thanks for the rescue of his daughter. He even offered him a job, but Jake had declined graciously.

He received a number of calls, sent through from Jerico, from the press seeking interviews. Even Ellen DeGeneres's people wanted to talk with him. As was Jake's way, he wanted no part of the publicity and spent his evenings reading and going to a nearby Italian restaurant, where he'd become a regular.

He also spoke with Duffy and shared her joy at being offered an instructor role in Washington. Their conversation had been somewhat formal and he blamed himself for not pursuing the relationship further. He realized he just wasn't ready.

His boss, Jared Taylor, called him one day. He was sitting on the veranda, just taking in the view, when his cell phone rang. Few people had the number, as it was new. "This is Jake."

"Hi, Jake, Jared here. How are things going?"

"Okay, thanks, Jared. I needed the break, and it's given me some time to rest and have a good think."

"We've got a lot of work on, Jake. A lot of it has arisen from the publicity generated by your exploits in Colombia."

"Yes, I know. A number of requests for interviews have been forwarded to me by Ann."

"As soon as you are ready, Jake, we want you back."

"How about I call you tomorrow?"

"Thanks, Jake. Talk to you then."

Jerico had been good to him, but the events of the past few weeks had given Jake a lot of time to think about his priorities. He owned an apartment in downtown L.A. and had money in the bank, all funded from his earnings from Jerico. He wasn't ungrateful. He'd needed the job and the security, but it failed to excite him like his years in the army had.

Jake went for a walk on the beach, and when he got back he had a voice message on his cell phone. It was from Ann at the office forwarding a message from a man called Iain Fisher and a number to call. Ann was usually good and took the trouble to let him know whom the callers represented. All he had that time were a name and a number. So it was probable that Mr. Fisher was not from the media.

He found some leftover pizza in the fridge and had something to eat. He then grabbed a beer and decided to call Fisher.

The man at the end of the phone spoke with an English accent: "Hello, this is Iain Fisher."

"Mr. Fisher, this is Jake Walker. I'm returning your call."

"Oh great, thanks Jake. I'm sorry to interrupt your leave."

"That's fine, Mr. Fisher. What can I do for you?"

"I have a proposition for you, Jake. You don't mind me calling you by your first name?"

"Not at all. Go on."

"To get to the point, I want a man found."

"I'm not a private detective, Mr. Fisher."

"It's not a matter for a private detective. I am a businessman, Jake. A very successful businessman. I need someone with a range of skills, someone resourceful, someone with courage.

"My home is north, in Washington State. I can have a plane meet you. Why don't you come up and I will explain."

"I'm supposed to be going back to work, Mr. Fisher. In any event, I'm not sure you are talking to the right man."

"I am sure you are the right person, Jake. As for your work, I am able to offer you five million dollars up front, to a bank of your choice, just for agreeing to take on the assignment."

Jake was silent, wondering who this man was and what he wanted.

"Please Jake, what have you got to lose? I don't want you to do anything wrong or unethical. I am sure that, when my story has been heard, you will want to help. And if not, I will fly you wherever you want to go."

What the hell... "Okay Mr. Fisher, let me know the details and I'll come up for a talk."

THE END

AUTHOR'S NOTE

Dear Reader,

The opening battle scenes in Afghanistan's Kunar province involve men from the 4th Special Forces Group, which does not exist, and to my knowledge was a number that was skipped for some reason between the 3rd and 5th Groups.[9] However, Operation Anaconda was a real battle in March 2002 involving forces from a number of countries that sought to weaken the Taliban and al-Qaeda forces that were believed to be regrouping in the Zhawar mountain region in eastern Afghanistan.

Jake Walker is a fictional character, but I hope that I have adequately described what it is like to be in a real theater of war. Special Forces ODAs have been involved across many operations in Afghanistan over the past decade, and Jake's team's mission—to set up observation posts so that they could direct air support—is just one of many roles they have undertaken over the decade-long conflict.

To all the people who are serving and those who have served in the US Special Forces, I salute you. The free world owes you and all the men and women that have sought to "liberate the oppressed" a huge debt of gratitude. I hope that I have described the experience of enemy contact

9   Grateful if someone who knows the real story would let me know.

successfully. Only those who have been there know what it's really like.

Darién province is one of the world's least explored wildernesses, a very dangerous place and the only area where the Pan American Highway has a break on its 29,800 mile journey from Prudhoe Bay, Alaska, to Ushuaia in Argentina (the southernmost city in the world). Bob Perry's comment that we know more about Everest than we know about Darién province, or the Darién Gap, is true.

As a result, and if you have been there, you will realize that many of my descriptions about the terrain, flora, and fauna came from either what little I could find on the internet or my imagination. I apologize for this. I was disinclined to visit and research the area first hand.

To the men and women of the *USS Peleliu*. All my intelligence about life on board, your capabilities, etcetera, were sourced from the net. I hope any errors can be forgiven and have not detracted from a good yarn.

With one or two exceptions, all of the characters within the book have been invented from my imagination.

As you will gather from the final chapter, Jake Walker will be back in *Rendition*. I trust you have enjoyed this book as much as I have enjoyed writing it.

My best wishes to you,

Christopher J Williams

January 2018

9 780648 143802